"What brings you to Denver?"

"It's not important."

She didn't believe him. Whatever his reason for being at Brick's, he'd made an effort to find her. She felt cheated by the lie, just as she'd felt cheated in Abilene. "If it wasn't important, you'd answer the question."

"I know what I'm doing."

When he smirked, she saw the man who'd left her pregnant, alone and ruined. "You haven't changed a bit, have you, J.T.?"

His eyes were even bluer than she recalled, and his cheekbones more chiseled. The sun, high and bright, lit up his unshaven jaw and turned his whiskers into gold spikes. The man was untouchable, unreachable.

"That's right," he finally said. "I haven't changed a bit."

"I have," she said quietly. "What happened in Abilene is in the past. I'd appreciate it if you'd respect my privacy."

His eyes clouded with something akin to regret. "I understand," he said quietly. "You won't see me again."

His surrender shocked her to the core.

Books by Victoria Bylin

Love Inspired Historical

The Bounty Hunter's Bride
The Maverick Preacher
Kansas Courtship
Wyoming Lawman
The Outlaw's Return

VICTORIA BYLIN

fell in love with God and her husband at the same time. It started with a ride on a big red motorcycle and a date to see a *Star Trek* movie. A recent graduate of UC Berkeley, Victoria had been seeking that elusive "something more" when Michael rode into her life. Neither knew it, but they were both reading the Bible.

Five months later they got married and the blessings began. They have two sons and have lived in California and Virginia. Michael's career allowed Victoria to be both a stay-at-home mom and a writer. She's living a dream that started when she read her first book and thought, "I want to tell stories." For that gift, she will be forever grateful.

Feel free to drop Victoria an email at VictoriaBylin@aol.com or visit her website at www.victoriabylin.com.

VICTORIA BYLIN

The OUTLAW'S RETURN

Steeple Hill®

Published by Steeple Hill Books™

STEEPLE HILL BOOKS

Steeple Hill®

Recycling programs
for this product may
not exist in your area.

ISBN-13: 978-0-373-82856-2

THE OUTLAW'S RETURN

www.SteepleHill.com

Printed in U.S.A.

The cowering prisoners will soon be set free;
they will not die in their dungeon,
nor will they lack bread.

For I am the Lord your God,
who churns up the sea so that its waves roar—
the Lord Almighty is his name.
—*Isaiah* 51: 14, 15

This book was the most challenging writing
experience I've ever had. For that reason,
it requires three dedications.

The first is to my editor, Emily Rodmell.
I'm beyond grateful for her insights into this story.

The second is to Sara Mitchell.
She's my dearest friend and a gifted writer.
I owe her more than I can say.

The third is to the people of CenterPointe
Christian Church in Lexington, Kentucky.
From the day Mike and I first stepped through
the doors, you made us feel welcome.
A special shout-out goes to the ladies
of the Flippin' Pages Book Club.
Let's hear it for Christian fiction!

Chapter One

Denver, Colorado
July 1876

When J. T. Quinn vowed to find Mary Larue, he never once imagined they'd meet on a perfect Sunday morning in Denver. On those long nights when he'd lain alone in his bedroll, he'd imagined seeing her on a stage in some high-class opera house. He'd pictured himself in a black suit and a white shirt leaning against the back wall with his arms crossed as he listened to her hit the high note only she could hit. Their eyes would meet and she'd recognize him. She'd miss a beat, but she'd pick up the song with even more power than before and he'd know…she still loved him.

That wasn't going to happen today.

It wasn't Saturday night, and J.T. wasn't wearing a suit.

It was Sunday morning, and he had trail dust in every pore. He also smelled like the inside of a saloon. He hadn't visited such an establishment for six months, but last night he'd walked past a gaming hall with a head full of memories. A drunken cowhand had stumbled out to the boardwalk with an open bottle of whiskey, and the contents had sloshed on J.T.'s trousers. The smell had sickened him in one breath and tempted him in the next. He'd have changed clothes, but the garments in his saddlebag were filthy. They stank, but not with whiskey. He'd resisted that temptation, and he'd done it because of his love for Mary Larue.

Heaving a sigh, he looked down at his dog. "What should we do, Fancy Girl?"

She whapped her tail against the boardwalk and looked up at him with her tongue lolling out the side of her mouth. J.T. didn't know what kind of dog she was, but they'd been best friends since he'd walked out on Griff Lassen at the Dudley place. They'd been running off Ambrose Dudley and his brother, squatters up in Wyoming, when the dog had charged at them and started barking. Griff had ordered J.T. to shoot her dead.

J.T. had done a lot of mean things in his life, but not even *he* could shoot a dog. On the other hand, he'd come close to shooting Griff. When the man aimed his Sharps at the mutt, J.T. had shoved the barrel downward. The bullet had ricocheted off a rock and creased Fancy Girl's head. J.T. had mopped her blood with his bandanna and fed her jerky from his pocket. When she'd followed him to his horse, he'd poured water from his canteen into a pot. She'd lapped every drop, and he'd filled it again.

He'd left the Dudley place with the job undone and Griff promising to get even, but the dog had followed him. That night he'd named her Fancy Girl because her fur reminded him of Mary's blond hair, and he'd made a decision. He didn't want to be the kind of man who hunted squatters and shot at dogs.

Over the past ten years, J.T. had sold his gun for money. He'd been nineteen when he'd first been paid to hunt down cattle rustlers, and next month he'd turn thirty. For a gunslinger, he had a lot of years on him. Today, standing outside a saloon and listening to Mary sing, he thought back on those years. He'd drunk oceans of whiskey and been with too many women. The whiskey had never failed to work its magic. The women, though, had lost that power, and it was because of Mary.

She'd been in his head for two years now, ever since Kansas, where they'd been a pair and she'd made him smile. Really smile. Not the sneer he usually wore. And not because she was generous with her affections. Mary made him smile because she believed he was a good man. He wasn't, but after the mess at the Dudley place, he wanted to try. Leaving that day with Fancy Girl, he'd decided to find Mary and make a new life. He had some money saved, enough to open a saloon, a place where she could sing and live the life she'd always wanted. He didn't plan to marry her. He'd changed, but not that much. Picking up where they'd left off seemed noble enough.

He and Fancy Girl had been searching for six months, and he'd finally caught a break. He hadn't touched a woman or a drop of whiskey since the mess in Wyoming, but he still had to eat. Last night he'd taken supper at the boardinghouse where he was staying with his dog. One of the boarders, an old man with bad eyes, had told him about a woman named Mary who sang like a nightingale.

You'll find her tomorrow morning at Brick's Saloon.

Not once had it occurred to J.T. that Mary would be singing a hymn in a makeshift church. His mind had gone in the opposite direction. He'd imagined her finishing up a night's work that involved more than singing. He'd been sick to think she'd fallen so low, but in the next breath he'd been relieved. No matter what Mary had done to survive, he still loved her. He wouldn't wish her the suffering of selling herself, but he rather enjoyed the thought of riding to her rescue. He didn't have much to offer a woman as beautiful and talented as Mary Larue, but he had plenty to give to a woman forced into prostitution. As a gunslinger, J.T. knew all about selling himself.

Mary's voice soared to a high note of a hymn. With that glorious sound, J.T.'s hopes crashed like a bird dying in flight. What did he have to give a woman who sang in church? Not a blessed thing. He didn't believe in God. The one time he'd cried out for mercy, the heavens had remained silent, and he had the scar to prove it.

Fancy Girl whined at his side.

"I know," he said. "We found her, but it's not going to work."

Inside the saloon, Mary's voice dipped and soared. As the hymn closed with a trembling "amen," Fancy Girl tilted her head. He could see where the bullet had left a lightning bolt between her ears. The dog had a keen intelligence and a way of reflecting J.T.'s thoughts. When she cocked her head, he saw the question he'd just asked himself.

"She doesn't need us, girl."

Fancy wagged her tail. *But you need her.*

"I know." He rubbed the dog's chin. "But she's happy now. She's got more than I can give her." He had a lot to offer a fallen woman, but a respectable one was beyond his reach. For all he knew, Mary could have found a husband. Did she have a baby of her own? Maybe a house with pretty curtains? J.T. didn't know, but he knew Mary had changed. The old Mary wouldn't have been caught dead singing a hymn. The new Mary sang the song with conviction.

If she'd been the woman he recalled, J.T. would have

fought for her affection, but how could a man like him compete with God? J.T. certainly couldn't, though he could have given the devil a run for his money. The thought offered an old and lonely consolation. If he couldn't have Mary, why not buy a bottle of whiskey, a big one with a fancy label? Why not get drunk and sink into oblivion? J.T. fought the urge to go down that road, but he felt his grip slipping. Without Mary, he'd cleaned up his life for nothing. Finding a place to buy liquor on a Sunday morning wouldn't be easy, but he'd seen a mercantile that probably had a stash behind the counter.

He stopped scratching Fancy Girl's ears. "Let's go," he said to the dog.

She barked.

"Shhh," J.T. cautioned. The last thing he wanted was a nosy minister poking his head over the batwing doors. He took a couple of steps down the boardwalk, but the dog didn't budge. Instead of following him like she always did, she whined.

"I know how you feel," he said. "But we're not good enough for her." A man couldn't turn a sow's ear into a silk purse, and J.T. was definitely closer to a pig than fine fabric.

When the hymn ended, the minister called out, "Amen!"

Chairs shuffled and a woman called to the crowd. "We've got pie and coffee. Help yourselves, folks."

J.T. had skipped breakfast, and he had a sweet tooth these days. Pie sounded good, but he had to go before the church folks started to leave. He aimed his chin across the street. "Come on, Fancy."

The dog perked her ears and tilted her head. J.T. considered the expression a smile, mostly because she got

that look when he told her stories by a campfire. He did
it to amuse himself, but mostly he liked the way Fancy
seemed to listen. She had that look now. She seemed
pleased, even eager to go inside the saloon, as if she
expected a big bowl of water, maybe even a meal of
scraps.

That's one thing J.T. could say for his dog. Fancy Girl
had hope. J.T. had no such optimism. Mary had found a
life better than anything he had to give. He had to leave
before someone noticed him. "Come on," he repeated
firmly to his dog.

The mutt looked at him as if he were an idiot, then she
walked under the batwing doors with her tail wagging.

"Traitor," J.T. muttered.

Thoroughly annoyed, he leaned against the wall of the
saloon, placing himself between the window where he'd
peeked inside and seen Mary and the door that would
put him directly in her line of sight. No way could he go
inside, but neither could he leave his dog.

Surely a high-and-mighty minister would throw the
mutt into the street. J.T. just had to wait for someone to
notice her. Squinting against the sun, he leaned on the
wall and crossed his arms. As soon as Fancy Girl learned
her lesson, he'd throw away six months of hope. He'd find
a place to buy whiskey, then he'd get his horses out of
the livery and he'd leave Denver fast and forever. He'd
find a tree by a stream, drink the whole bottle and push
Mary Larue out of his heart forever. First, though, he
had to get his dog back.

"A dog!" Mary declared. "It looks like she's coming
to church."

"Maybe she is." Reverend Joshua Blue crouched
down and scratched the dog's ears. The service had just

ended, and the congregation was headed to the refreshment table. Mary glanced to see if her sister and brother were behaving themselves. A month ago, their arrival had turned her life upside down, and she was still reeling from the shock. Her father had been gone for years, but her mother had died just a few months ago. Gertie and Augustus had come to live with her. She spotted them both in the back of the makeshift church.

Gertie met her gaze, then heaved a sigh worthy of the actress she wanted to be. At seventeen, the girl thought she knew everything. Mary had once had the same illusion, but she'd learned some hard lessons in her own acting days. She didn't want her sister to repeat her mistakes, but neither did she want to deny her dream.

As soon as Gertie turned eighteen, Mary planned to send her to New York to study with Maude Atkins, a theater friend who had moved back East. Mary wished *she'd* gone to New York, a city with classy theaters and modern stages. Instead she'd traveled west with a third-rate theater troupe. She'd made a name for herself, but she'd also been disgraced. Two years had passed since gunslinger J. T. Quinn had left her unmarried and pregnant, but she hadn't forgotten the miscarriage or the scandal that had erupted. People in Abilene had known she and J.T. had a special friendship, and some assumed the truth—that they were lovers. When she became pregnant, she was desperate to keep the news to herself, but she miscarried just before taking the stage. The gossip about her turned into a full-blown scandal and she lost her reputation completely. When a drunken bounty hunter assumed she'd welcome his attentions, she'd shot him in self-defense. After an ugly murder trial, she'd cut all ties to Abilene and the theater.

Her friends at Swan's Nest knew she'd killed a man,

but no one in Denver knew she'd been with child. Neither did the baby's father. She'd made her peace with God, but she had no illusions about people and gossip. She knew how it felt to endure stares and ugly talk. She cared deeply about her reputation, and she wanted to set a good example for Gertie. Her sister knew nothing about the scandal, and Mary intended to keep it that way. That's why she was sending Gertie to New York. If the girl pursued a stage career in Denver, she'd surely meet someone who knew about Mary's past. Someone would recognize Gertie's last name, the gossip would start and Mary would lose her reputation for the second time.

Her brother, Augustus, wouldn't understand the mistake she'd made, but he inspired other worries. He was twelve years old, thin as a bean and hadn't said more than "Yes, ma'am" and "No, ma'am" since he and Gertie had arrived from West Virginia. The boy was quiet because he stammered his words. As a singer, Mary had trained her voice. She'd tried to help Augustus control his breathing, but he'd only gotten more nervous with her attention. She didn't know what else to do, but she wouldn't stop trying to help him.

She loved her brother and sister, but her life had changed drastically the day they'd arrived. In some ways, it had changed for the better. In others, it had gotten so hard she wondered if God had stopped hearing her prayers.

Reaching down, she patted the dog. Its tongue fell to the side as it panted in the summer heat. "I think she's thirsty," Mary said to Josh.

"Hey, Brick!" the minister called to the saloon owner. "How about some water for our guest?"

Brick grinned. "Sure thing, preacher."

As the saloon keeper went to fetch a bowl, Mary

traced the ridge of the white scar between the dog's ears. "I wonder where she came from."

"There's no telling," Josh answered. "But she looks well fed." He fingered the red bandanna tied around her neck. "She's also wearing her Sunday best."

As Mary laughed, Adie Blue, Josh's wife and Mary's best friend, approached with Stephen, her one-year-old son, balanced on her hip. Mary ached a little at the sight of them. If she hadn't miscarried, her baby would have been about the same age.

Adie patted the dog's neck. "The poor thing! It looks like a bullet grazed the top of her head."

"It looks that way," Josh agreed.

Glad to be distracted, Mary touched the scar. "Who would shoot a dog?"

Even if the mutt had been raiding a chicken coop, she didn't deserve to be shot. Strays did what they had to do to survive. Bending slightly, Mary scratched the dog's long chin. She had a thick golden coat, big brown eyes and an expression Mary could only describe as a smile. Tinges of black feathered above her eyes to make brows, and she was brushed and clean.

She rubbed the dog's jaw. "Where's your home, sweetheart?"

The dog cocked her head as if to say, *Right here.*

Mary knew the feeling. When she'd come to Denver, she hadn't known a soul until she'd found Swan's Nest, a boardinghouse for women in need. There she'd met Adelaide Clarke, now Adie Blue, and made new friends. If someone had told her two years ago she'd be singing hymns in church, she'd have laughed at them. But that's where she was today and where she wanted to be. A bit of a stray herself, Mary appreciated having a home.

She rubbed the dog's ears until Brick arrived with the

water and set the bowl on the floor. As the dog lapped happily, Gertie sidled up to Mary. "Can we go now?"

"Not yet," she answered. "It's our turn to clean up."

"But—"

"Don't argue, Gertie." Mary sounded more commanding than she felt. She was ten years older than her sister, but they'd been close growing up. Disciplining Gertie didn't come easily, especially since Mary understood the girl's desire for excitement and fancy dresses. They'd grown up poor in a West Virginia town called Frog's Landing. Mary had been Gertie's age when she'd left in search of fame and fortune.

The fortune had been fleeting, and the fame had led to a broken heart. She'd never forget seeing Jonah Taylor Quinn for the first time. She'd finished her second encore at the Abilene Theater and had stepped backstage. He'd been leaning against a wall with his boots crossed at the ankle and a look in his eyes that could only be called scandalous. She'd blushed just looking at him, but then he'd greeted her with the utmost respect. He'd invited her to a midnight supper and she'd accepted. One meal had led to another, and they'd become friends. As spring arrived in Kansas, they'd traded stories and kisses, and she'd fallen in love with him.

Then he'd left.… She still felt the sting of that midnight parting. *It's been good, Mary. But it's time for me to go.*

But I have to tell you something. She'd paused to gather her courage. Instead of telling him she was expecting a baby, she'd revealed her feelings. *I love you, J.T.*

He'd smiled that wicked smile of his, then he'd shrugged. *Love doesn't mean a thing, sweetheart.*

She'd slapped him. Before she could say a word, he'd walked away. She couldn't bear to think about what happened next, so she glanced at the dog. It had finished the water and looked content. "I wonder if someone's looking for her," she remarked to Adie.

"I've never seen her before."

"Me neither," Josh added.

Adie gave Mary a knowing look. "You're going to take her home, aren't you?"

"Maybe."

Home for Mary was an apartment over the café she owned thanks to a mortgage from the Denver National Bank. She didn't have room for a dog, but neither could she leave the animal to fend for itself. Mary had always had a heart for strays. It didn't matter if they had two legs or four. That inclination had caused trouble in the past, but she'd learned her lesson. She loved children and dogs and wouldn't turn them away, but men couldn't be trusted.

She looked again at Gertie and Augustus. Her brother stood half-hidden in the corner, eating a piece of pie. Gertie was giving her the evil eye. In another minute, the girl would storm across the room and make a scene. Mary hated arguing with Gertie, so she turned to Adie. "I'm going to start cleaning up."

"I'll do it," Adie volunteered. "You work hard all week."

"So do you."

Adie shrugged. "I have to wait for Josh. Besides, I have a favor to ask."

"Sure," Mary answered.

"When you come to supper this afternoon, would you bring a couple of loaves of that good sourdough? If I know Josh, we're going to have a crowd."

Sunday supper at Swan's Nest had become a tradition, one that had grown from a simple meal shared by the women who lived there to a feast for anyone who showed up. Josh made a point of inviting everyone from church, and today Mary had noticed some new faces. "I'll be glad to bring all you need," she said to Adie.

Her friend smiled. "While you fetch the bread, I'll take Gertie and Augustus to Swan's Nest."

"If you're sure—"

"I am." Both women knew Gertie could be difficult.

"Thanks." If Mary left now, she could squeeze in a few chores. She had to plan next week's menus and inventory the pantry. Absently she patted the dog's head. When it sniffed her hand, she smiled. Stephen wiggled in his mother's arms and made a *D* sound.

"Dog," Adie prodded.

"Da!"

Mary felt a stab of longing for the child she'd lost. She loved children, but she had no desire to marry. After what J.T. had done, she'd never trust a man again.

Absently rocking the one-year-old, Adie turned to her. "Are you going to take the dog?"

Mary looked down at her. "What do you say, girl? Would you like to come home with me?" She didn't have a lot of space, but she had plenty of scraps.

The dog tipped its head.

"Let's go," Mary said to her.

As she crossed the room to speak to Gertie and Augustus, the dog followed her. Gertie fussed about going to Swan's Nest, but she didn't pitch a fit. Neither did Augustus, though Mary would have welcomed a tantrum in place of a nod. After waving goodbye to several members of the congregation, she left the saloon with the dog at her side.

She didn't immediately notice the man leaning against the saloon wall. It was the smell of whiskey that got her attention, then the rasp of a stifled curse. Expecting a cowboy with Saturday-night regrets, she turned to offer the man Christian charity and a slice of pie. Instead of a stranger, she saw J. T. Quinn. And instead of charity, she felt something else altogether.

Chapter Two

J.T. was thinner than she recalled and harder because of the leanness, a sign he'd been living on jerky and bad coffee. His brown hair had gold streaks from the summer sun, and his blue eyes still pierced whatever they saw. She felt the sharpness of his gaze and remembered.... She'd once loved this man, and she'd hated him when he'd left.

With the changes in her life, she couldn't give in to bitterness. She knew how it felt to be forgiven, and she had a duty to forgive others. She'd treat J.T. the way she'd treat a stranger, except he wasn't a stranger. She knew how he liked his coffee, and she'd seen the scars on his body from bullets and knives. None of those memories mattered. This man posed a risk to her reputation. If her friends saw him, they'd ask nosy questions.

She had to make him leave before someone else left the church. She gave him a curt nod. "Hello, J.T."

He tipped his hat. "Hello, Mary."

Unnerved by his husky drawl, she fought to steady her voice. "This is quite a surprise."

"Yeah." He eyed the batwing doors. "For me, too."

Was he surprised to see *her* or surprised to see her

leaving a church service? Mary didn't know what to think. Why would he seek her out after all this time? On the other hand, what were the odds he'd visit Brick's Saloon on a Sunday morning by chance? One in a million, she decided. Josh's little church was unusual and well-known. Any saloon keeper in Denver could have told him she sang here on Sunday morning.

That meant he'd come to see her, but why? No one stirred up memories—both good and bad—like this handsome, hard-edged man. Ten minutes ago Mary had been singing "Fairest Lord Jesus" from the depths of her heart. Looking at J.T., she couldn't remember a single word.

Help me, Lord.

With the dog at her feet, she spoke as if nothing were amiss. "The saloon's not open. I was here for—"

"Church," he said. "I know."

"How—"

"I heard you singing." He glanced at the mutt at her side. "So did my dog."

"*Your* dog?"

"Yeah." He looked sheepish, as if he'd admitted something embarrassing. She supposed he had. A man like J.T. traveled with the clothes on his back and his guns. He'd carry bullets before he'd pack an extra can of beans, yet here he stood looking at a dog as if it were his only friend.

When he held out his hand, the dog licked his fingers. "You crazy thing," he murmured.

At the sight of such tenderness, Mary's forgot to breathe. In Kansas she'd seen J.T. beat the daylights out of a man who'd disrespected her. He'd worked as a hired gun to ranchers wanting to chase off rustlers, and he didn't think twice about it. He was hard, tough and mean, except with her. Then he'd been as soft as butter, tender in the way of a man who knew a woman's need for love while denying his own.

But then he'd left her. She'd forgiven him for leaving, but that didn't mean she'd forgotten the coldness of the parting. J. T. Quinn couldn't be trusted, not with her heart and not with knowledge of the baby. He'd disrespected her. She refused to allow him to disrespect a child that had never been born. In Abilene he'd left her in the middle of a conversation. Today she wanted answers. *Why are you here? What do you want?* Any minute people would start leaving church. Since Gertie and Augustus were with Adie, the café would be empty. She thought of yesterday's stew in the icebox. J.T. looked hungry, and so did his dog. She'd never been good at turning away strays.

"I own a restaurant," she said. "You look like you could use a meal."

"No, thanks."

He sounded confident, but he had the air of a boy trying to be tough. Her heart softened more than she wanted to admit. "Are you sure?"

"No, thanks, Mary. I just…" He shook his head, but the gesture didn't answer her questions.

A terrible foreboding took root in her belly. Had he heard the talk in Abilene? Did he know about the baby but not the miscarriage? She couldn't stand the thought of the scandal finding her again, nor did she want to open old wounds. Trying to appear casual, she tipped her head. "What brings you to Denver?"

"It's not important."

She didn't believe him. Whatever his reason for being at Brick's, he'd made an effort to find her. She felt cheated by the lie, just as she'd felt cheated in Abilene. "If it wasn't important, you'd answer the question."

"I know what I'm doing."

When he smirked, she saw the man who'd left her pregnant and disgraced. "You haven't changed a bit, have you, J.T.?"

His eyes were even bluer than she recalled, and his cheekbones more chiseled. The sun, high and bright, lit up his unshaven jaw and turned his whiskers into gold spikes. The man was untouchable, unreachable.

"That's right," he finally said. "I haven't changed a bit."

"I have." She lowered her voice. "What happened between us in Abilene is in the past. I'd appreciate it if you'd respect my privacy."

"Don't worry," he said. "You won't see me again."

His surrender shocked her to the core. She wanted to know why he'd given in so easily, but she couldn't risk lingering outside the church and being seen. To protect her reputation, she'd have to live with yet another unanswered question. With her head high, she stepped off the boardwalk. To her consternation, the dog followed her. In the middle of the empty street, she stopped and turned back to J.T. "Call your dog."

His jaw tightened. "Come on, dog."

Mary scowled at him. "You named her *Dog?* No wonder she's not obeying you!"

"That's not her name," he muttered.

"Then what is it?"

He looked straight at her. "Her name is Fancy Girl."

Air rushed into Mary's lungs. Fancy Girl had been his name for her. He'd called her his Fancy Girl, because she'd liked to dress up for the stage. She'd enjoyed the makeup and the flamboyant dresses, particularly the costumes that had freed her from the dullness of Frog's Landing. "You named her after *me?*"

"Yeah."

She should have been insulted. The fool man had named a dog after her! Yet she knew it hadn't been an insult. He loved his dog. A long time ago, even though he hadn't said the words, Mary had thought he'd loved *her.* She'd been mistaken. J.T. didn't love anyone. "It's been nice seeing you," she said in a courteous tone. "But I have to get home."

"I understand."

She doubted it. He didn't know her at all anymore. Reaching down, she rubbed the scar between the dog's ears. "Goodbye, Fancy Girl."

After a final scratch, she continued across the street. When the dog tagged along, J.T.'s voice boomed behind her. "Fancy Girl! Get over here!"

Hearing her old name in J.T.'s baritone stopped Mary in her tracks, but Fancy Girl ignored him. Mary rather enjoyed the dog's rebellion. People usually did what J.T. ordered. Occasionally they did it with a gun aimed at them, but mostly they obeyed because he spoke with authority. He wasn't in charge now.

As he called the dog a second time, a man came out of the church, looked long and hard at J.T., and went on his way. Any minute the congregation would be in the street and he'd be a spectacle in his black clothing. Needing to persuade him, Mary flashed a smile. "I promised Fancy Girl a plate of scraps. It looks like she's holding me to it."

His eyes twinkled. "She's a smart dog."

"Would you like to come with us?"

He snorted. "For scraps?"

"Scraps for her. Pot roast for you." She tried to sound businesslike. "I really do own a restaurant."

"Oh, yeah?"

"The best in town. It's called Mary's Café." She raised her chin. "It's mine, and I'm proud of it."

"You should be." Still he didn't move.

"Come on." She aimed her chin down the street. "Your dog won't take no for an answer."

A smile tipped on the corners of his mouth. "Sounds like you won't, either." Looking pleased, he stepped off the boardwalk and strode to her side. With Fancy Girl between them, they headed to the café with Mary hoping they hadn't been seen.

J.T. smelled like dirt and mistakes, and he knew it. Apparently so did Mary. Her nose wrinkled as he stepped to her side, so he widened the gap between them. Fancy Girl smelled better than he did. He didn't understand why his dog had taken such a strong liking to Mary, but he felt the same urge to follow her home.

As they walked down the boardwalk, she made small talk about the weather. J.T. responded in kind, but his mind wasn't on the July heat. He couldn't think about anything except the changes in Mary. She still had a saucy attitude, but the lines around her mouth had softened into an easy smile and her brown eyes had a sheen of happiness. She wore her hair differently, too. The curls were still honey-blond, but she'd tamed them into a simple twist. Her dress, a demure lilac, could have belonged to a schoolmarm.

Six months ago, he'd have mocked her plain dress and the prim hairstyle. He'd have teased her into being his Fancy Girl again, maybe into his bed.

Not now.

Not today. He thought back to how he'd left her and he had to wonder… What would have happened if he'd stayed with her? Would they be running a saloon with Mary singing and J.T. pouring drinks? He could resist the temptation to drink if it meant proving himself to Mary. His other worry—being called out by an old enemy, someone like Griff Lassen—would never leave, but time would ease the threat. Today, though, everything had changed. Mary didn't need him at all. With no reason to stay, he decided to buy supplies and ride west. Whether or not those supplies would include whiskey, he couldn't say.

With Fancy Girl in front of them, he kept pace with Mary as she turned down a side street. In the distance he heard the blast of a train whistle. They were near the depot, a good spot for business from hungry travelers. She indicated a storefront between a tailor and a telegraphy office. It was painted butter-yellow and had green trim. A sign read Mary's Café.

"This is it." She unlocked the door and pushed it open.

Stepping inside, he saw cream-colored walls, tables set with red-checked linens and an assortment of chairs that didn't match but somehow went together. Every surface sparkled, even the floor. A man could relax in a place like this. Apparently so could a dog. Fancy Girl ambled to a corner near an unlit potbelly stove, circled three times and curled into a ball.

J.T. took off his hat and hung it on a hook by the door. "You've got a nice place."

"Thank you." She raised her chin. "I've worked hard to get it started."

In her eyes he saw the old Mary, the one who'd fight for what she wanted. He also saw bluish circles fanning down her cheeks. She was still beautiful, but he'd never seen her look so weary.

How hard did she have to work? Did anyone help her with the cooking and the washing up? The woman he'd known in Kansas hadn't been the least bit inclined to kitchen chores. Thanks to J.T.'s faro winnings, they'd ordered lavishly at the Abilene Hotel and he'd bought her pretty things for the fun of it. She'd grown up poor, and he'd liked surprising her. He wondered how she'd gotten the money to open a restaurant. Was she beholden to the bank? Or maybe she had a business partner, a man with money. The thought made him scowl.

She'd clam up if he quizzed her, so he beat around the bush. "How's business?"

"Good." She indicated a table by a wall decorated with paintings of mountains. "Have a seat. I need to light the stove."

Instead of sitting, he followed her into the kitchen. In the crowded space he saw two massive iron stoves, a row of high tables against the back wall, three baker's racks full of pies and bread, and cooking utensils hanging from rods suspended from the ceiling. Basins were leaning against the back wall, clean and ready for the next load of dirty dishes.

J.T. saw the pride Mary took in her business, but he also saw hours of drudgery. In Abilene she'd slept until noon, even later sometimes. Judging by the aroma, she'd baked the bread before church.

Maybe he *did* have something to offer her. He couldn't promise her a life of leisure, but running a saloon would be easier than serving full meals. He wanted to blurt the invitation to come with him to California, but first he had to rekindle the old sparks between them. Leaning against the doorframe, he crossed one boot over the other and watched her set a match to the banked coals. When they caught fire, he shook his head. "You must work day and night."

She shrugged. "There's nothing wrong with hard work."

"No," he replied. "It's just...tiresome."

She gave him a quelling look, then removed a jar from the ice box, poured the contents into a pot and carried it to the stove. Facing him, she said, "This will take a few minutes. Let's sit out front."

As she stepped through the doorway, her skirts brushed his boots. He followed her to the table, then moved ahead of her and held her chair. He didn't know what it would take to sweep Mary off her feet, but fancy manners had always impressed her. He slid in her chair, then moved to sit across from her.

The instant he hit the chair, Mary popped to her feet. "You must be thirsty. I've got sweet tea or cider. Coffee is—"

"Mary, sit," he said quietly. "I don't want you serving me."

She sat, but she looked uncomfortable.

At last, J.T. had the upper hand. Hoping to put her at ease, he used the crooked grin that had never failed to charm her. "What brought you to Denver?"

She shrugged as if she didn't have a care in the world. "Denver is famous for its opera houses. I wanted to see it for myself."

Her gaze stayed steady, but he saw a flash of pain. He survived as a gunslinger because he could feel danger coming. What he saw in Mary's eyes troubled him deeply. "I'm surprised you're not singing somewhere."

"It didn't work out."

J.T. knew this woman. Short answers weren't her style.

Unless he'd lost his instincts, she was hiding something. He kept his voice mild. "But you love to sing. You're good at it."

She moved the fork a quarter inch. "I sing in church now. That's all there is to it."

"I don't think so."

Suddenly wary, she turned to the window and stared out the shining glass. When she didn't speak, J.T. thought back to the early days of his search and his visit to the Abilene Theater. The new manager had heard of Mary but didn't know where she'd gone, and her acting friends had moved on. When she'd left the rowdy cow town, she'd done it fast and quietly. He'd assumed she'd run from a broken heart. Now he wondered if she'd had another reason. "Talk to me, Mary."

She took a breath, a deep one. "You're right. There's more to the story. After you left, I had a run-in with Sam O'Day."

J.T. knew all about Sam and his brother, Harvey. They were bounty hunters, and they behaved like animals. "What happened?"

"I shot him."

"You *what?*"

"I shot Sam O'Day," she repeated calmly. "Do you remember the pistol you gave me?"

"Of course." The two-shot Deringer had over-under barrels, pearl handles and a gleaming nickel finish. They'd taken a buggy ride to nowhere, and he'd discovered she didn't know how to shoot. He'd taken the pistol out of his boot, taught her to use it and told her to keep it handy. They'd kissed for an hour and he'd pushed for more. She'd said no, but a month later he'd convinced her to change her mind.

With her chin high, she described the encounter with

O'Day. He'd been drunk enough to get thrown out of a brothel. When he'd seen Mary leave the theater alone, he'd called her names and cornered her in the alley. "He grabbed me," she said calmly. "I told him to let go, but he wouldn't."

J.T. saw the fear on her face, the determination that had enabled her to fight for her life. He knew how she felt, because as a boy he'd been pinned down in an alley with a knife against his scrawny chest. His older brothers had been vicious. "It's a bad feeling."

"It is." She took a breath. "I had your gun in my pocket. When he tore at my dress, I shot him. He died."

"Mary, I—"

"Don't say anything. What's done is done."

If J.T. had been around, O'Day wouldn't have dared to touch her. He should have been with her.… He should never have left. What a fool he'd been to go off with Griff Lassen. He'd been looking for a fight to keep his own rep from slipping. Instead he'd made an enemy of Griff. He'd gotten Fancy Girl out of the deal, but he lost everything else and so had Mary.

Feeling bitter, he forced himself to meet her gaze. "What happened after you shot Sam?"

"I went to the sheriff. He believed me, but I had to stand trial for murder."

He held in a cringe. "Did they lock you up?"

"For a time."

Twice J.T. had spent time in a jail cell. No one knew it except Mary, but dark, closed-in places gave him nightmares. As a boy he'd been abused in an alley by his older brothers, often with a knife. More than once, Mary had comforted him when he'd been jarred awake by a nightmare. "I know what jail's like," he said. "It's like being buried alive."

"It was awful," she admitted. "The jury ruled it was self-defense, but Sam's brother didn't agree. When he threatened to kill me if I stuck around, I decided to leave."

J.T. let loose with a curse. "I'll hunt him down. I'll—"

"Don't."

"But, Mary—"

"It's over and done." She looked into his eyes. "I worried for a while that Sam's brother would find me in Denver, so I traveled a bit before settling here. Harvey O'Day never found me, so I figured he went back to bounty hunting."

"That's most likely," J.T. confirmed.

"As for Sam, I forgave him a long time ago. Frankly, coming to Denver was the best thing that's ever happened to me. I made friends at a boardinghouse called Swan's Nest. I have supper there every Sunday. That's where I'm going next."

J.T. realized she hadn't answered his first question. "Why not perform here in Denver?"

"Those last days in Abilene were awful," she said mildly. "The theater world is small. If I act here in Denver, the talk will start again. I can't stand the thought."

He'd have chosen a whipping over the guilt he felt for leaving her. Not once had he considered Mary's reputation when he'd set out to claim her. When she straightened her fork for the second time, he reached across the table and gripped her hand. His gaze dropped to their knuckles—hers red and rough, his scarred from brawling—and he felt the rightness of what he wanted to say. "I'm sorry I left. I should have—"

"Don't waste your breath."

When she tried to take back her hand, he held it tighter. "Leaving you was the biggest mistake of my life."

"I doubt that," she said, tugging again.

He had some convincing to do, and he had to do it with tenderness, not fighting. He let her go. "I don't expect you to believe me. Not yet. But I've missed you. That's why I'm here. Remember the dream we had about opening a saloon? Our own place in California?"

She bit her lip, but her eyes said she remembered.

"Come with me, Fancy Girl," he said in a hush. "We can pick up where we left off."

She didn't say yes to him, but neither did she slap his face. With his chest tight and his heart pounding, J.T. waited for her answer.

Chapter Three

Mary had pulled out of J.T.'s grasp, but the warmth of his touch lingered. Two years ago she'd yearned for what he'd just offered. That dream had shattered the night he'd left, and so had her hopes for marriage and a family of her own. Memories kicked in the place where the baby had nestled for three short months.

She couldn't let J.T. see the memory in her eyes, so she blinked hurriedly. "The answer is no."

"Why not?"

Because you hurt me, and I'll never trust a man again. Because you broke my heart and left me with child. "I'm different now," she said simply.

"So am I."

She doubted it. He hadn't mentioned marriage and he wouldn't. A man like J.T. wasn't the marrying kind. She'd known that all along, but she'd foolishly believed she could change his mind. She spoke with deliberate calm. "What we had in Abilene is gone. All of it."

Even the baby.

Memories assailed her…the blood, the pain. The guilt had been worst of all. She hadn't wanted the baby until she'd lost it. That morning she'd woken up with cramps.

Instead of staying in bed, she'd gone to the theater intending to perform as usual. She'd miscarried just minutes before she was supposed to take the stage, and the gossip had started instantly. Tears pressed into her eyes. If J.T. saw them, he'd know there was more to the incident with Sam O'Day.

Mumbling about the food, she hurried to the kitchen. Before she reached the door, he clasped her arms from behind. In Kansas he would have kissed her neck. She would have turned and gone into his arms. Today she felt trapped.

His voice came over her shoulder. "Come with me, Mary. It'll be good this time."

It had been good last time, but not good enough. Giving herself to this man had caused her nothing but grief. She'd lost her heart, her reputation and her career. She'd wept alone over their lost child, and that had hurt most of all.

As he tightened his grip, the smell of his unwashed skin reached her nose. She broke loose and faced him. "Leave me alone!"

He released her, but his eyes held her more tightly than his hands. "I need you, Mary."

"What you need is a bath!"

"I need more that," he murmured. "I need you."

"No, you don't."

"Mary, I—"

"Don't talk to me!" Turning, she clamped her hands over her mouth. The secret burned like fire in her belly. She wanted to punish him for what he'd done, but she couldn't. Not only did she have to keep the facts to herself, but she knew what it meant to need forgiveness. As much as she wanted to blame J.T. for wooing her into his bed, she'd gone willingly, even eagerly. God had forgiven her—she knew that. She thought she'd forgiven J.T., but the memories left no room for mercy. She couldn't stand the thought of the scandal coming back to life. She desperately wanted J.T. to leave, but her anger left a sour taste in her mouth. They'd both sinned. If she sent him way in anger, she'd be a hypocrite. She took a breath to calm herself, then faced him. "I'm sorry. I shouldn't have shouted at you."

Relief softened his mouth. "I had it coming."

He stood still, waiting for her to make the next move. She glanced at Fancy Girl. She'd promised them both a meal, so she indicated his chair. "I'll get the pot roast. Fancy can have a bone when you leave."

"Thanks."

She escaped into the kitchen, dished his food and brought a plate to the table. He smiled his thanks, lifted his spoon and ate. In Abilene they'd lingered over supper with quiet anticipation. Today she used silence like a stage curtain. It hid her memories the way velvet drapes hid the audience, but thoughts of a curtain reminded her of the career she'd lost. Yesterday Roy Desmond, the new manager of the Newcastle Theater, had asked her to star in *The Bohemian Girl*. Because of the scandal, she had decided to turn him down. If her name showed up on Roy's fancy theater posters, people might become curious about her past. At the time she'd thought briefly of J.T. and blamed him. She couldn't possibly sing on stage again, even though she'd been impressed with Roy. An actor himself, he had managed a theater troupe on a Mississippi riverboat. She hadn't heard of him, but he'd been in Abilene and had heard her sing. He'd mentioned the trial and the gossip, then assured her he'd keep the information to himself. She trusted him.

J.T. finished the pot roast, then broke the silence with

a contented sigh. "You sure can cook. I didn't know that."

"It's a family recipe." She reached idly to straighten the salt shaker.

His gaze dropped to her fingers, no doubt noticing the roughness. Her hands embarrassed her, but she refused to hide them. He arched one brow. "Are you sure I can't talk you into singing in that saloon in California? It's a long way from Abilene."

"I'm positive."

"Would you think about it?"

"There's no need." He'd push until he got what he wanted, and he wanted *her*. She had to give him another reason to move on. "My mother died a few months ago. I'm raising my sister and brother."

He didn't like children, so she figured he'd leave her alone. Instead he seemed interested. "How old are they?"

"Gertie just turned seventeen. Augustus is twelve."

He wrinkled his brow. "They're not that young. Gertie's practically grown. And Augustus—" He shook his head. "That's a dreadful name for a boy."

Mary didn't know what to make of his interest. "We've always called him Augustus."

"So give him a nickname."

"Like what?"

"I don't know." His eyes twinkled. "I bet we can think of something."

We? Mary had to set him straight. "Even if I wanted to go with you—*which I do not*—I have obligations. I own this restaurant. I have a mortgage to pay and women who work for me. They need the money. Frankly, so do I. I'm saving to send Gertie to New York."

He scowled, a reminder that he'd been left on those

crowded streets to fend for himself. "What's in New York?"

"Theaters. Gertie loves singing as much as I did."

"You still love it."

"Yes, but not the same way." She stood and lifted their plates. In Kansas she'd used his given name for only the most serious conversations. She used it now to make a point. "You're two years too late, Jonah. I wish you the best, but I don't want to see you again."

Dust motes hung in the light, swirling like ash from a burning bridge in a ray of sun coming through the window. The glare lit one side of his face and put the other in shadow until he pushed back the chair and stood. "I see."

When he looked at his dog, Mary remembered her promise to Fancy Girl. "I'll be right back."

She carried the plates to the kitchen, selected the meatiest soup bone she had, wrapped it in paper and carried it to the dining room. "Here." She handed it to J.T. "This is for Fancy."

He took it but hesitated before calling the dog. If the mutt refused to go with him, Mary didn't know what she'd do. With his brow tight, he spoke in a gentle tone Mary knew well. "Let's go, Fancy Girl."

When the dog ambled to his side, Mary breathed a sigh of relief. He took his hat off the peg and opened the door. With sunlight fanning into the room, he pulled the brim low and stepped outside, closing the door behind him. Mary blinked, and he was gone.

J.T. turned the corner, stopped and looked at his dog. "What now, girl?"

Fancy nudged the bone with her nose. J.T. wished his desires were as simple. He wanted a drink. The escape wouldn't last, but it would stop the ache in his chest. He'd wake up feeling even worse than he did now, but who cared? Without Mary, he had no reason to stay sober. As soon as he bought supplies, he'd leave town. Tonight Fancy could chew the bone in front of a lonely campfire.

"Come on," he said to her. "We're getting out of here."

He went to the livery for his horses, paid the owner and put the bone in a saddlebag. He secured the line to the pack horse, climbed on his buckskin and headed to the boardinghouse to fetch his gear. As the horses plodded down the street, he looked for a place to buy whiskey. He saw one closed door after another, then the gray wall of a large stone building. The granite gleamed white in the sun, and gargoyles jutted from the eaves. As he rounded the corner, he saw a sign that read Newcastle Theater.

"Hey, Quinn!"

He slipped his hand into his duster until it rested on the ivory grip of his Colt Navy, then he scanned the street for the person who'd called him. When he saw Roy Desmond, he wanted to spit. He knew Roy from the faro tables in Dodge City. The man cheated. Even worse, there was talk he'd killed a saloon girl. J.T. had no desire to speak with Roy, but he couldn't ignore him with Mary in Denver. The man had bragged about his life as an actor, and J.T. worried he'd seek out Mary. She'd sent J.T. away, but he wouldn't leave until he knew what Desmond wanted.

"Hello, Roy."

"This is a surprise." The man flashed a grin. "It's been what? Three years since Dodge?"

"More or less." J.T. had known Roy before Abilene, before he'd been with Mary. "What are you up to?"

Roy indicated the stone building behind him. "You're talking to the manager of the Newcastle Theater. I'm a legitimate businessman now."

Only a snake like Roy would need to announce he'd become legitimate. J.T. took in the man's sack suit and pleated shirt. A gold watch dangled from his pocket, and his shoes were newly blacked. His hair was still dark but thinner than J.T. recalled, and deep lines framed his mouth. Nothing about Roy could be trusted, not his appearance and not the words dancing off his tongue. If Roy had any dealings with Mary, J.T. would have to think again about leaving Denver. He needed information, so he feigned interest in the man's venture.

"Legitimate, huh?" He grinned. "Does that mean no faro?"

Roy chuckled. "I've got other cards to play. In fact, you're just the man to help me play them."

It was just like Roy to speak in riddles. "What do you have in mind?"

"It involves a mutual friend of ours."

"Who?"

"Mary Larue."

Live or die, J.T. would do anything to keep Roy away from Mary. "What about her?"

The man indicated the door. "Come inside and we'll talk."

J.T. swung off his horse and tied off the reins. With Fancy Girl at his side, he followed Roy into the opera house. Trying to look bored, he entered the cavernous foyer as if he walked around such places every day. He didn't, and the opulence stunned him. Thick carpet covered the floor, and the walls were crimson with gold stripes. Brass wall sconces caught the light from the open door and shimmered like flames. Even the air felt like velvet.

J.T. let out a low whistle. "Pretty nice."

"Nothing but the best." Roy led the way to a double door and opened it wide. "This is the stage."

With Fancy next to him, J.T. walked into the heart of the theater. At least fifty rows of upholstered seats fanned out from the stage, and a curtain the size of a barn hung from the ceiling. Five chandeliers formed the points of a star, and two balconies jutted from the wall. The last time J.T. had seen Roy, he'd been a two-bit gambler. How had he ended up among the Denver upper crust? And what did he want from Mary? He signaled Fancy Girl to sit, then surveyed the theater again. "This place is huge."

"It's the biggest opera house in town." Roy put his hands in his pockets. "Things are going well, but I've got a bit of a problem."

"Oh, yeah?"

"I manage this place for a group of investors." Roy's jaw twitched. J.T. had played cards with him and knew his mannerisms. The tic signaled a bluff. "Those men are expecting a solid return on what we've put into this place."

"Like sold-out shows?"

"Yes." His jaw twitched again. "There are two ways to make money in this business. Bawdy shows draw big crowds, but like I said, I've gone legitimate. Denver has money now. Big money, if you know what I mean."

"Yeah, I know." Denver was full of millionaires who'd made their fortunes from mining and the railroad. These folks wanted classy entertainment, not cheap burlesque.

Roy wiped his brow with a silk handkerchief. "My

investors have high expectations, so I'm putting on an opera. That's where you come in."

"Me?" J.T. pretended to misunderstand. "I can't sing a lick."

Roy chuckled. "No, but Mary Larue can. Rumor has it you two were quite a pair in Abilene."

How did Roy know about Kansas? Was Mary already involved with him? J.T. fought to sound casual. "Who told you that?"

"I was in Abilene during the O'Day trail." Roy shook his head. "What a shame. It ruined her career. That woman sings like a nightingale."

J.T. hadn't pressed Mary for details about the scandal, but he didn't mind quizzing Roy. "What happened?"

"You don't know?"

"I left on business."

The theater manager propped his hips on the back of a seat. "The whole town was buzzing about the two of you. After you left, O'Day figured she was up for grabs. He followed her out of the theater and tried to—" Roy let his implication stand. "She shot him."

J.T. knew all that. "What happened after the trial?"

"She left town." Roy shook his head. "That's when the gossip got really bad, if you know what I mean."

"Yeah, I know."

Roy laughed. "You dodged a bullet, Quinn. Be thankful."

The remark struck J.T. as odd, but Roy was known for talking in circles. Even so, J.T. wondered…what bullet? Thinking about it, he decided Roy meant marriage. For once J.T. had to agree with him. He felt bad about leaving Mary, but he wasn't the marrying kind.

Roy's eyes glinted. "Mary and I have gotten to be

friends. I asked her to star in my opera, but she turned me down. I'm hoping you'll help me change her mind."

J.T. looked around the theater with its chandeliers and velvet seats. The hall held the stuff of Mary's dreams, but she'd turned Roy down to keep the Abilene scandal a secret. He felt bad about the reason, but he liked her refusal. He looked Roy in the eye. "Mary said no. It's her choice. Not mine."

"I thought you might have some influence. From what I hear, you had her wrapped around your little finger."

No man wrapped Mary around his finger. She'd been good to him because she'd cared about him, and he'd taken advantage. The memory shamed him. "Mary's her own woman."

Roy's eyes gleamed like black stones. "So you don't have a claim on her?"

"What are you getting at?"

"If you're done with her, I'll take her for myself."

J.T. gripped Roy by the collar, squeezing until the man's jugular pressed against his knuckles. "You touch Mary and you're dead." Fancy stood silent at his feet, ready to attack if he gave the word.

Roy held up his hands. "Hold on, Quinn! I was thinking about Mary, what I could give her."

"No, you weren't."

"I swear it." Sweat beaded on Roy's brow. "I could make her famous. Rich, too. That's all. Okay?"

J.T. set Roy down, but he didn't believe a word the man said. Lust showed in his eyes. So did greed. J.T. forgot all about buying whiskey. He forgot about leaving Denver. He had to warn Mary about Roy. The man said he had investors, but J.T. sensed a lie. Had Roy's so-called investors given him money, or had he cheated them out of it? If he'd cheated them, what kind of payback did they want? J.T. saw a lot of self-proclaimed justice in his line of work. People paid him to administer it. Looking at Roy, he saw the familiar look of a man without shame. He matched the theater manager's stare. "Stay away from Mary Larue."

"Sure," he said too easily. "She's all yours."

She wasn't, but J.T. didn't mind Roy thinking along those lines. He paced out of the opera house with Fancy Girl at his heels and rode straight to Mary's café. There he slid out of the saddle and pounded on the door. When she didn't answer, he peered through the window and saw the table where he'd eaten pot roast. It was already re-laid with silverware and a clean plate. It looked as if he'd never been there, as if she'd erased him from her life. Maybe she had, but no way would he leave her a second time to deal alone with someone like Sam O'Day or Roy Desmond.

J.T. figured she'd left for the Sunday supper she'd mentioned at a place called Swan's Nest. Mary didn't want him around her friends, but he had to warn her about Roy. Annoyed, he looked at his reflection in a dark window. Mary was right about that bath. He'd clean up, then he'd track her down. He'd do his best not to embarrass her, but he couldn't leave until she promised to keep away from Roy Desmond.

Chapter Four

By the time Mary reached the iron gate marking Swan's Nest, she'd pushed J.T. out of her mind. At least that's what she told herself until the hinges creaked and she jumped. Walking up the manicured path, she looked at the stained-glass window above the covered porch. Pure and white, a swan glistened on a pond of turquoise glass. It didn't have a care in the world, but Mary did. She'd gone from nearly a soiled dove to a swan when she'd become a Christian, but she couldn't erase the past. If the scandal found her in Denver, gossip would start and men would hound her. Worst of all, she could lose Gertie's respect. Things could get ugly fast, and then where would she be? Silently she prayed that no one had seen J.T. leave.

As she climbed the porch steps, the door opened and she saw Adie. Her friend beckoned her inside. "We have to talk."

Mary worried about her sister. "Is it Gertie?"

"She's fine."

"Then what—"

"It's about you and that man I saw."

Mary's cheeks turned cherry-red. "You saw us?"

"I sure saw *him*." As Adie lifted the basket of bread, Mary wondered if she'd been impressed by J.T.'s good looks or his black duster and guns. She scolded herself for not being prepared for questions. She should have realized someone would look out the window. She wouldn't lie to Adie, but neither would she confide in her friend completely. Secrets were a burden, not a gift. "I knew him in Abilene." She tried to sound matter-of-fact. "It was a long time ago."

"You looked worried," Adie spoke in a hush. "That wasn't Sam O'Day's brother, was it?"

Mary had told Adie about the murder trial, but she'd never mentioned her relationship with J.T. "There's no connection."

"Then who was he?"

"No one special. He liked my singing."

Adie's brows rose. "The man I just saw—the one in black with guns on *both* hips—he tracked you down because he likes *music?*"

Mary felt chagrined. "Well, he liked me, too."

"Are you sure it wasn't more than *like?*"

"It wasn't." If he'd loved her, he would have stayed. He might even have married her.

Adie touched her arm. "Just so you're okay."

"I'm fine." She had no desire to have this conversation, not with a crowd in the garden, so she lifted the basket. "We better get supper ready."

"Sure."

Relieved that Adie didn't press, Mary carried the bread to the kitchen. Caroline, a brunette with a heart-shaped face, greeted her from the stove. Bessie, her sister and older by several years, was frying potatoes and teasing her sister about baking too many pies.

The routine of cooking helped Mary relax. As she

tied an apron, Adie told her Augustus and Gertie were in the garden with the other guests. Mary felt a familiar lump of worry. Her brother avoided people because of his stammering, and Gertie had taken to putting on airs. "I wish they'd make friends," she said as she sliced the bread.

Caroline stirred the gravy. "Gertie's with Bonnie Reynolds. Last I saw, they were looking at a *Godey's Lady's Book*."

Bonnie was a year older than Gertie and had a good head on her shoulders. Mary liked her. She didn't feel the same way about the other girl Gertie had met. Katrina Lowe was older by five years and had traveled alone from Chicago. She worked in a dress shop and dreamed of designing theater costumes. She'd been raised in a well-to-do family and had excellent manners, but she also had a defiant way about her.

Mary worried about Gertie because of her ambition. She worried about her brother because his shyness. "What about Augustus?"

Caroline kept stirring the gravy. "I haven't seen him."

Bessie chimed in. "I sent him outside with a bowl of apples."

"Maybe he's with the other boys," Adie said hopefully.

Doubting it, Mary untied her apron. "I'd better check on him."

As she headed for the door, Caroline spoke over her shoulder. "You might wander by the rose garden."

"Why?"

She grinned. "I saw a new man at church this morning. He's single *and* handsome."

Ever since she'd caught Pearl Oliver's wedding bouquet, Mary's friends had been conspiring to find her a husband. She wished Caroline had caught the bouquet. *She* wanted a husband. Mary didn't. All men weren't as untrustworthy as J.T., but she'd never take that chance. She tried to sound lighthearted. "I don't care about a husband. I've got Gertie and Augustus."

"You *did* catch the flowers," Bessie reminded her.

"And I wish I hadn't!" she laughed. "You're all impossible!"

Closing the door behind her, Mary stepped into the yard. Her friends didn't realize it, but the teasing stirred up memories of J.T. and the miscarriage. She needed to shake off the upset, so she put on a smile as she approached the visitors in the garden. She saw a group of boys playing tag, but Augustus hadn't joined them. Disappointed, she approached Gertie and Bonnie, who were seated on a bench under a crab apple tree. "Have you seen Augustus?"

"He left," Gertie replied.

Worry shivered up Mary's spine. "Where did he go?"

"I don't know." Gertie indicated the street. "The last I saw him, he had some apples and was walking that way."

Mary saw horses hitched to the fence. Maybe Augustus had gone to give them treats. "Thanks, Gertie."

As Mary headed for the street, Bonnie called to her. "Miss Larue?"

"Yes?"

"I saw some boys with him about twenty minutes ago. One of them was Todd Roman. He's older, and he's not very nice."

"You saw him talking to Augustus?"

"Sort of." Bonnie knew the boy stammered. "I don't know why, but Augustus went with them."

"Where did they go?"

"I didn't see."

"Thank you, Bonnie." Mary hurried to the gate and worked the latch. Her brother would never leave without telling her, nor would he have willingly gone with a group of boys he didn't know. Determined to find him, she stepped out to the street and called his name.

With his hat pulled low, J.T. guided his horse down the road that led to Swan's Nest. After leaving Roy, he'd returned his pack horse to the livery and gotten directions to the mansion, bought fresh clothes and gone to a bath house for a good scrubbing. Bay rum wafted off him, and he'd never had a closer shave. If he looked respectable, maybe Mary would believe him about Roy.

"What do you think, girl?" he said to the dog trotting at his side. "Is Mary in as much trouble as I think?"

Fancy Girl looked at him with a doggy grin, a reaction that gave J.T. comfort. For a while he'd been worried the mutt was going to trade him for Mary.

"S-s-stop it!"

The cry came from behind a wall. High-pitched and quavering, it sent J.T. back to a filthy alley in New York and his brother beating him for losing four pennies. Judging by the tone of the voice and the way it cracked, it belonged to a boy nearing adolescence…a terrified boy who needed help.

"Come on, Fancy."

J.T. turned the buckskin and dug in his heels. The horse wheeled and broke into a run. At the end of the wall, he reined the animal to a halt and leaped out of the saddle. Fancy Girl arrived at his side, growling and ready to attack if he gave the word. At the sight of a boy up against a brick wall, his nose bloody and tears staining his cheeks, J.T. wanted to rip into the attackers himself. The boy being beaten had blond hair and no muscle on his bones. The ones doing the hitting were older, heavier and mean enough to laugh at the boy's whimpering. Two of them were holding him spread-eagle against the wall, while a third threw a punch hard enough to crack a rib.

"Hey!" J.T. shouted.

The boys doing the attacking glared at him, but they didn't release the blond kid. The kid tried to pull away, but he didn't have the strength.

"L-l-l-let me go," he whimpered. "P-p-p-lease. I—I—I—"

The stuttering made J.T.'s throat hurt. The boy doing the hitting laughed. "Wh-wh-what d-d-did you say, Au-au—"

"I heard him just fine," J.T. dragged the words into a growl. "He said to leave him alone."

The boys holding the kid's arms watched him nervously but didn't budge. The third one—the leader, J.T. surmised—held his ground. With his small, dark eyes and lank hair the color of coffee, he had the look of a buzzard determined to pick the boy's bones—or his pockets—clean. He stared at J.T., then lowered his chin. "This ain't your fight, mister."

"It is now."

The boy's eyes gleamed with a compulsion to fight. J.T. would be glad to oblige, but not in the way the boy expected. He paced toward the two holding the blond kid spread-eagle, letting them see his knotted fists and cold stare. In unison they stepped back and raised their hands in surrender. The boy who'd been beaten groaned and slid into a heap.

"Get outta here!" J.T. shouted at them.

The two sprinted for their lives. J.T. turned to the third one. He looked closer to manhood than the others, maybe sixteen or so, and he'd stood his ground. He spat, then glared at J.T. "Get lost, mister."

With his duster loose and his gun belt tight on his hips, J.T. walked straight at him.

The boy didn't budge.

J.T. kept coming. When he got within a foot, he saw sweat on the boy's brow. "You want to fight?" he said in a singsong tone.

The kid said nothing.

He had no intention of using his fists, but this boy-man didn't know that. J.T. smirked, tempting the kid to take the first punch. It would be unwise and they both knew it. J.T. was faster, stronger and meaner. He didn't twitch, didn't blink. He simply waited.

The boy swallowed once, then again. When he blinked, fear showed in his gaze. The boy knew J.T. outmatched him, just as *he'd* outmatched the blond kid.

"How does it feel?" J.T. said in an oily voice.

"Wh-what do you mean?"

"N-now who's afraid?"

"Look, mister—"

"Shut your mouth." He grabbed the kid by the collar. "I could have you on the ground in two seconds and you'd be dead in three." He shoved him back and out of reach. "You leave my friend alone."

The boy answered by glaring.

J.T. strode toward him as if he were going to kick him. Instead he kicked up a cloud of empty dust. "Come on," he shouted. "Take a swing at me."

Just as he expected, the boy scrambled to his feet and ran. He got twenty feet away and turned. "I don't know who you are, mister! But you'll be sorry." He jerked a finger at the boy slumped against the wall. "So will you, Au-au-gustus!

The stutter mocked the boy who'd been beaten, but it was J.T. who felt punched in the gut. Mary's brother was called Augustus. How many boys in Denver would go by that awful name? Looking at the kid again, he saw Mary's wheat-colored hair and distinct cheek bones. He watched to be sure the boy who'd done the bullying kept running, then he turned back to Augustus. The resemblance couldn't be denied. "Do you know Mary Larue?"

"Sh-she's my s-s—" The kid sealed his lips.

J.T. took the stammering for yes. "I knew her in Kansas."

Augustus wiped the blood from his nose with the sleeve of his white shirt, probably his Sunday best. He sniffed, then looked at J.T. again. "Th-th—" *Thank you.*

"No problem, kid." The stammering hurt in ways J.T. had never experienced. He held out his hand to shake. "I'm J. T. Quinn."

The boy leveraged to his feet, then fell to the ground unconscious. Crouching at his side, J.T. rolled him to his back. The boy had probably fainted from shock, but he couldn't be sure. A blow to the head could cause bleeding in his brain. A busted rib could puncture a lung. He shook the boy's shoulder. "Hey, kid."

Augustus didn't move. He didn't twitch. Nothing but a shallow breath came from his parted lips. Fancy Girl put her cold nose on his cheek. No response. With fear pooling in his gut, J.T. lifted the boy's eyelid. The pupil shrank against the light, a good sign. "Come on, Augustus. Talk to me."

Nothing.

J.T. didn't know where to find a doctor, but he knew where to find Mary. He lifted her brother onto his horse, climbed up behind him and galloped to Swan's Nest.

Chapter Five

Mary walked to the end of the street and called her brother's name for the fifth time. When he didn't answer, she went back to Swan's Nest and looked for him again in the garden. Without a sign of him, she paced back to the street. A rider and a cloud of dust caught her eye and she stopped. The man's black duster billowed behind him, and he'd pulled his hat low against the wind. A dog ran at his side.

"Fancy Girl," she murmured. J.T. had tracked her down, and he was approaching at a gallop. What could he possibly want? She couldn't stand the thought of speaking with him in front of her friends. As he rode closer, the blankness of his silhouette took on color and shape. He was clutching something against his body. Not *something,* she realized. *Someone*…a boy with blond hair and a bloody white shirt.

"Augustus!" Hoisting her skirts, she ran to them.

J.T. reined the horse to a halt at the iron gate. With the boy limp in his arms, he slid from the saddle. "He needs a doctor."

"I'll fetch Bessie." A trained nurse, the older woman had served in the War Between the States. If she couldn't help Augustus, Mary would send Gertie for Doc Nichols. She flung the gate wide. "Take him to the parlor."

She waited until J.T. passed with the dog at his heels, then she raced by him and opened the front door. "Bessie!" she called down the hall to the kitchen. "Come quick!"

Wearing a white apron and drying her hands, the nurse hurried down the hall. "What is it?"

"It's Augustus. He's hurt."

J.T.'s boots thudded on the polished wood floor. "Where do you want him?"

"On the divan," Bessie ordered. "Who are you?"

"A friend of Mary's."

The nurse nodded, an indication Adie had shared her curiosity with Bessie before Mary arrived. It hadn't been gossip, just friends caring about each other, but Mary still felt uncomfortable.

With the boy cradled in his arms, J.T. strode across the room where only moments ago Mary had stood with Adie. He lowered Augustus with a gentleness she remembered from Abilene, then he stepped back to make room for Bessie. As he tossed his hat on a chair, Fancy Girl walked to his side and sat.

Bessie pulled up a chair and started her examination. Terrified, Mary hovered over her shoulder. Bruises on Augustus's cheek promised a black eye, and he had a bloody nose and split lip. Her gaze dropped to his shirt. Red smears in the shape of knuckles testified to what had happened. Her brother had been beaten.

She whirled to J.T. "Who did this?"

"We'll talk later," he said in a low tone.

She wanted answers now, but mostly she wanted her brother to wake up. She turned back to his limp body and saw Bessie taking his pulse. The nurse lowered his wrist, but her expression remained detached. "Get the smelling salts," she ordered. "And water and clean towels."

"Will he be all right?" Mary asked.

"I don't know yet."

Her eyes darted to J.T. Adie and Caroline were outside, and she needed help. "Come with me."

He followed her down the hall, his steps heavy on the wood while hers clicked. She wanted to know why he'd been near Swan's Nest, but she didn't dare ask. Augustus had urgent needs, and she didn't want to breathe a word of the past in front of anyone. In the kitchen she opened a cabinet with medical supplies and found the smelling salts. Next she filled a bowl with hot water and fetched clean towels from a shelf. J.T. lifted the bowl and carried it down the hall. Mary followed with the towels and smelling salts.

Bessie uncorked the bottle of ammonia carbonate and held it under Augustus's nose. She waved it once, twice. His nostrils flared, then his eyes popped open. Groaning, he rolled to the side and vomited. Bessie held a bowl under his chin and caught the mess. Mary saw streaks of blood and gasped. Was he bleeding inside? Were his ribs cracked? Bessie needed to know, so Mary turned again to J.T. "You've got to tell us what happened."

He shook his head.

How dare he withhold information! She raised her voice. "I want to know who did this."

He put one finger to his lips. It had been an old signal between them, a warning to guard her mouth around people he didn't trust. Considering the circumstances, it infuriated her. "Talk to me."

"I'll explain later." He looked disgusted with her. "The boy fought hard. Give him his pride."

Mary saw his point. Embarrassed by her outburst, she

dipped a towel in the hot water. While Bessie checked for broken bones, Mary wiped the blood from her brother's face and neck. When the nurse poked his ribs, he groaned.

"Do you think they're broken?" Mary asked.

"I'd say they're bruised."

Furious, Mary set the towel on the rim of the bowl and lifted a dry one. For her brother's sake, she had to stay calm. Augustus was twelve years old, but his stammering made him seem younger. In her heart, he'd always be the baby brother she'd rocked to sleep in Frog's Landing. Looking down, she smoothed his hair from his damp brow. "How are you feeling?"

"I—I hurt."

His lips quivered with the need to say more, but he sealed them in frustration. If she pressured him, the stammer would get worse. She had no choice but to wait for Augustus to calm down or for J.T. to enlighten her. With her lips sealed, she watched as her brother craned his head to look at the man in the corner. What she saw on his bruised face could only be described as awe. She didn't blame him a bit. It seemed that J.T. had come out of nowhere to help him. She didn't know who had attacked her brother, but Augustus's expression told her J.T. had stopped the beating. She owed the man her gratitude. She didn't want to owe him anything, but he'd been good to Augustus.

Bessie finished checking for broken bones then looked into Augustus's eyes. She held up three fingers. "How many do you see?"

The boy held up his hand to indicate three.

"Good," Bessie replied

Mary thought of the red-streaked vomit. "I'm worried." She indicated the bowl. "What about the blood?"

"It's from the nosebleed."

Fear drained from her muscles, leaving her limp. "So he's going to be all right?"

"I'd say so." Bessie looked at Augustus. "You took quite a beating, young man. I think you fainted from shock. Your ribs are badly bruised, and you're going to have a black eye. We'll get ice for that in a minute. I'm also going to bind up your ribs."

"Th-th-thank—" He bit his lip.

"You're welcome," Bessie replied. "You should stay in bed for a few days, then you can move around as much as you're able." The nurse patted his skinny shoulder, then left to fetch the wrapping for his ribs.

Mary took Bessie's place on the chair. "I'm so sorry this happened to you."

Her brother looked down at his feet. She'd never seen him look so defeated. Had he been bullied because of his speech? It seemed likely. He'd been teased about his stammering all his life, but people in Frog's Landing had known him. In Denver, a city populated by strangers, he'd become an outcast.

J.T. crossed the room. When he reached boy's side, he offered his hand. "Hello, Augustus. We met, but you might not remember. I'm J. T. Quinn."

"I—I remember."

Augustus took the man's hand and shook. Mary had never seen her brother do anything so grown up, or J.T. do anything so kind.

Augustus tried to sit up, but J.T. nudged him flat. "Don't torture those ribs. I've busted mine a couple of times. It hurts a lot."

The boy nodded vigorously.

J.T. pulled a side chair from the wall and positioned it next to hers at an angle where Augustus could see him.

He dropped down on the seat and hunkered forward. "We gotta talk, kid."

Figuring J.T. didn't know about the stutter, Mary cringed for her brother. "He has trouble speaking."

"I know that."

"You don't understand," she continued. "He—"

"He's fine." J.T. kept his eyes on Augustus. "All things considered, you handled yourself well."

In Mary's experience, her brother turned into jelly when kids bullied him. She looked at J.T., then wished she hadn't. They were side by side, so close she could smell the bay rum on his newly scraped jaw. When she'd seen him earlier, he'd been unshaven and reeking of whiskey and sweat. Now he looked presentable. More than presentable. Blinking, she recalled the man she'd met backstage in Abilene, the handsome stranger who'd pursued her with a look.

J.T. met her gaze and held it, signaling her with a mild glint to be quiet. She bristled, then realized he knew far more about the episode than she did. She didn't understand boys at all, and Augustus with his silence presented an even bigger challenge. She knew he needed a man in his life. She'd been asking God to send a grandfatherly sort of man from church, but the prayer had gone unanswered.

When she stayed silent, J.T. turned back to Augustus. His lips tipped into a smile. "There's nothing I like better than chasing off a bully. Thanks to you, I got to run off three of them."

When Augustus rolled his eyes, Mary realized J.T. was telling the story for her benefit.

"Yeah, they were big," he continued. "Mean, too. You're going to have a glory of a shiner."

Augustus made a face.

Instead of offering pity, J.T. laughed. "Welcome to the club, kid. You'll be fine in a few days, but I've been wondering… Has this happened before?"

Augustus looked down at his feet. "S-s-sort of."

Shivers ran down Mary's spine. "It has to stop. We'll go to the sheriff."

J.T. looked exasperated. "Don't waste your breath."

"We have to try," she insisted.

"Fine," he answered. "But there's not going to be a deputy in the alley next time Augustus gets waylaid. We need to solve this ourselves."

He'd said *we*. He didn't have that right. Her eyes snapped to his profile, but he was looking at her brother. She knew he could feel her gaze. He was dismissing her the way he'd walked out on her in Abilene. She wanted to tell him to leave Swan's Nest *now,* but the situation with Augustus complicated everything.

The boy kept his eyes on J.T. "They w-w-ant me to steal from…" he looked at Mary, pleading with her to understand.

She repeated for him. "They want you to steal from…?"

"Y-you!"

"Me?" Her brow wrinkled.

J.T. kept his focus on her brother. "Let me take a stab at this. Those guttersnipes know you're Mary's brother, right?"

"Yes," Augustus managed.

"They know she runs the café."

The boy nodded.

"They want you to take money out of that cash box she keeps just inside the kitchen."

Mary frowned at him. "How do *you* know about that box?"

"I saw it." His smirk reminded her that he'd ridden with the Carver gang before he'd become a hired gun. J.T. would never steal from her, but he knew how to do it. "You work hard, Mary. Put that box somewhere else."

"I will."

He turned back to her brother. "Do you know who these bullies are?"

In fits and starts, he described how they'd cornered him one day when he'd been running an errand. They'd threatened to beat him up unless he brought them five dollars. He refused, and for the past week he'd been afraid to leave the café. Today they'd followed him to Swan's Nest.

Mary's heart bled for him. "Sweetie, why didn't you tell me?"

He jerked his head to the side, but not before she saw hurt in his eyes. She smoothed his hair. "I'll fix it, Augustus. I promise. I'll talk to their parents. I'll—"

"Stay out of it," J.T. said quietly. "This is your brother's fight."

"But he's so young," she argued. "And he's small for his age. He can't protect himself."

"I say he can," J.T. replied. "He just needs to learn a few things."

She agreed, but he didn't need to learn them from an outlaw-turned-gunslinger. What could J.T. possibly teach the boy? How to beat someone into pudding? How to gamble and lie? How to charm a woman and break her heart? She didn't want him anywhere near her brother. Augustus was a gentle, tenderhearted boy who liked to whittle and play checkers. He didn't need J. T. Quinn in his life. He needed an older man who'd teach him to be respectful.

J.T. looked at her for five long seconds, then he sat

back in the chair and studied the boy. "Those lessons are starting right now."

She gasped. "Now wait just a minute—"

J.T. stayed focused on Augustus. "We'll start with your name. From now on you go by Gus."

"Gus?" The boy copied him.

"That's right." J.T. shifted his boot to his knee. "No more of this 'Augustus' stuff. It's a terrible name. Half the time even *I* can't say it."

The boy giggled. Mary refused to crack a smile, though her lips quivered. J.T. had a point. For a boy who stuttered, *Augustus* was a torture.

J.T. shook his head with mock drama. "How'd you get such an awful handle anyhow?"

The boy shrugged, but Mary knew. "He was born in August. Our mother loved the summer."

The man grimaced. "It's a good thing he wasn't born in a girly month like June."

"Or-or J-Januar-r-r-y!"

The three of them laughed until Gus hugged his ribs. "It h-h-hurts!"

But Mary knew it felt good, too. She hadn't heard her brother laugh in a long time.

Breathing light, the boy turned to the man. "Th-thank you, Mr. Quinn."

"Call me J.T." He sounded gruff.

Mary wanted to forbid the friendship, but she couldn't deny the excitement in her brother's eyes. For the first time since he'd arrived in Denver, confused and hurting after their mother's passing, he'd connected with someone.

J.T. pushed to his feet. "Get some rest, Gus. I need a word with your sister."

"S-sure."

Mary needed a word with him, too. If he thought he could weasel his way into her life by helping her brother, he'd be wise to think again. She had to keep this man as far from her family and friends as she could. Since he'd found Gus close to Swan's Nest, it was evident he'd been coming to see her. She wanted to know why.

"I'll be back," she said to Augustus—Gus now.

As she stood, J.T. offered his hand as if the boy were a grown man. "I'm proud to know you, Gus."

Her brother gripped J.T.'s fingers and shook hard. "I—I—uh—M-me, t-too."

J.T. let go and put his hands on his hips, pulling back the duster enough to show his guns. "Every man takes a beating now and then. Sometimes he wins, sometimes he doesn't. Those jerks today were bigger than you—older, too. You didn't steal the money like they wanted, so stand tall."

Instead of the man who'd hurt her, Mary saw Gus's hero. Her heart softened, but she steeled herself against any fondness. She had to remember J.T. had hurt her. The other feelings he inspired—the good ones—made her weak in the knees.

Bessie came through the door with a tray holding strips of cloth. "I'll bind his ribs now. Why don't you two get some supper?"

J.T. met her gaze. "Thank you, ma'am. But I need a word with Mary, then I'll be on my way."

"Whatever you'd like," Bessie replied.

Mary didn't know what to make of J.T.'s consideration. She'd have to answer questions when he left, but he'd saved her from being a spectacle in the garden. He picked up his hat and together they headed to the doorway. As he passed Fancy Girl, the dog pushed to her feet and followed. When they reached the hall, he clasped

Mary's arm and steered her to the door. "We need some privacy."

"Yes, we do."

With her heart pounding, she followed J.T. to the porch. As she expected, he paced to the railing and looked up and down the street. She saw the gunfighter who never let his guard down, but below the surface lived the boy who'd been brutalized by his own brothers. J.T. had hurt her, but life had hurt him first. It had hurt her, too. Not until she'd come to Swan's Nest had she found a measure of peace.

When she'd been brash, her friends had been kind.

When she'd been arrogant, they'd been patient.

She knew the value of that kind of love, and she tried to share it with others. She'd *thought* she'd been tested by Gertie and her haughty airs, but it seemed the Lord had sent someone else to try her patience…the man who'd hurt her more than anyone on earth. Even for Gus's sake, she couldn't risk J.T. staying in Denver. No matter the cost, she had to convince him to leave town tonight.

Chapter Six

J.T. didn't often get a chance to be kind. People paid
for his meanness, and they got their money's worth. He
counted saving Fancy Girl as his one act of goodness.
Befriending Gus would be the second. He genuinely liked
the boy, but he saw another benefit to helping the kid.
He'd hurt Mary when he'd left her in Abilene. Teaching
Gus to defend himself would help pay that debt.

If someone didn't teach the boy how to fight, he'd end
up dead or mean. J.T. couldn't let that happen. He had to
convince Mary to let him help her brother, so he dropped
his hat on a low table and propped his hips on the railing,
watching as she considered the porch swing but remained
on her feet. If things had gone as he'd hoped when he'd
arrived, he would have enjoyed sitting with her. He'd have
put his arm around her and nudged her head down to his
shoulder. They'd been a perfect fit in that way. Enjoying
the memory, he indicated the swing. "Have a seat."

"No, thank you."

She gave him the coldest look he'd ever gotten, and
that said a lot considering his occupation. If she wanted
to fight, so be it. He'd always enjoyed sparring with her.
Leaning back on the railing, he supported his weight with

his hands. The duster fell open, but he didn't think much about it. Mary knew he wore his guns all the time.

He got down to business. "I'm gonna stay in town as long as your brother needs help."

"That's not necessary."

"I say it is." He spoke so softly he barely heard himself. "Gus needs me."

"He'll be fine."

"Like I was *fine* in New York?"

She knew about the scar on his shoulder and how his brothers had beaten him. He'd told her the stories when they'd been alone in the dark, when his heart had been softened by her touch and she couldn't see his embarrassment. She'd held him after more bad dreams than he cared to recall.

Her eyes said she remembered, too. But her voice came out hard. "I understand the situation. Augustus is—"

"You mean Gus."

"All right," she said too amiably. "*Gus.* You're right about his name. You're also right about him being able to defend himself. I'll ask a man from church to talk to him."

"Talking isn't enough."

"It has to be."

"It's not." J.T. decided to take a chance. "Fighting is like kissing. You can talk all you want, but eventually you've got to do it."

She opened her mouth to argue, but nothing came out. Judging by the sudden blush, she remembered their kisses as well as he did. He wanted to go farther down that road, but first he had to prove that Gus needed him. "Your brother's a good kid, but he's puny and he stutters."

"I know that."

"If he doesn't learn to fight, he's going be bullied his whole life. Is that what you want for him?"

"Of course not."

Tense, she dropped down on the bench and pushed off. The chains began a steady, irksome squeak. "I know Gus needs help. I just don't think you're the one to teach him."

"Sure I am." He knew as much about fighting as anyone. "What are you worried about?"

Instead of the boldness he expected, he saw a guarded-ness that didn't fit Mary at all. In Abilene she'd spoken her mind freely. Today she looked nervous, even scared. He wondered why, but she wouldn't tell him even if he asked. He'd have to puzzle it out for himself. He lowered his arms, hiding the guns beneath the duster. "Do you think I'll teach Gus my bad habits?"

"Yes," she said. "Exactly."

"You don't have to worry, Mary." She truly didn't. J.T. wanted Gus to be a good man, not a hired gun like himself.

She lifted her chin. "Considering how you left me, why should I trust you with my brother?"

"Because I've changed. I haven't had a drink in six months, and it's been so long since I gambled, I don't remember how." Not exactly. He remembered, but he needed to make a point. "There's more. Do you want to hear it?"

"No." She pushed to her feet. "It doesn't matter, because I don't want you in Gus's life. He's fragile. You'll hurt him."

He touched her arm. "Are we talking about Gus or you?"

"Gus!"

"I don't think so." She was close enough to kiss, and

her lips were trembling. She wasn't just angry with him. He'd opened old wounds and they were bleeding. "I'm sorry, Mary. I'm sorry I left you, sorry I…" He shook his head. He'd used her like he used liquor, and he owed her amends. "You deserve to know something else. I haven't been with a woman since I quit drinking."

"J.T., don't—"

"Listen to me. Please." His voice dropped to a hush. "Just one more time, Fancy Girl. I need to say this to you."

A tremor passed from her arm to his hand. If she told him to leave, he'd do it. But he needed to make this confession. She closed her eyes and lowered her head. When she finally looked up, he saw a bleakness that troubled him, but she nodded yes. "All right. I'll listen."

He indicated the swing. She sat, but her face had lost its color. Leaning against the railing, he dragged his hand through his hair. "I don't know where to start, exactly. Back in Abilene—"

"I don't want to talk about Abilene." She sounded panicky and he wondered why. "Tell me about Fancy Girl. How did you find her?"

"It's more like she found me." He told Mary about the mess at the Dudley place and how he'd made an enemy of Griff Lassen. Feeling both silly and proud, he glanced at his dog, then looked at Mary with an apologetic smile. "Imagine that…J. T. Quinn going soft over a dog."

She said nothing, but her eyes said she could imagine it just fine.

The thought gave him hope. "That night I knew I had to find you. I went to Abilene, but no one knew where you'd gone."

Her cheeks flushed. "I left in a hurry."

"So I figured."

"It's been a long time."

The way she said it, he wondered if it would ever be long enough to forget the shame she'd endured. J.T. knew just how long—or short—a span of time could be. "It's been six months since I've tasted liquor." He paused, because his next words were personal for them both. "Getting drunk hurts the man doing it. Using a woman hurts *her.* I know how that feels, because I sold my gun as surely as a prostitute sells her body. You weren't that kind of woman to me, Mary. I cared about you, but I hurt you just the same. I'm sorry."

He wanted her forgiveness.

He needed it.

A bird twittered in a nearby tree. Laughter drifted from the crowd in the garden. Someone rang a dinner bell, startling them both. Silent as a lamb, he waited for her to speak. When she didn't say a word, he knew she'd send him away. She wouldn't let him near Gus, and neither would she believe him about Roy Desmond. If he told her about Roy now, he'd push her in the man's direction. Maybe he'd send her an unsigned letter from another town, or he could shove a note under her door. With everything lost and nothing else to give, he put on his hat, pulled it low and walked down the steps.

His boots thudded on the risers, then kicked up dust on the path. Fancy Girl followed him without being called, a consolation that eased the hurt but didn't erase it. As he lifted the latch on the gate, he heard the creak of the swing and Mary's footsteps hurrying down the path.

"Wait!" she called.

He turned and saw her running to him. She stopped a foot away, looking harried and confused and as beautiful as ever. Her eyes were shiny with tears, and her cheeks had turned from ashen to pink. Sunshine turned her hair into gold, while the brightness cast their shadows side by side.

"I forgive you," she said.

"You do?"

"Yes." She swallowed hard. "I forgave you a long time ago. It's just…" She bit her lip. "No one here knows everything that happened in Abilene. After you left, people called me a loose woman. The gossip was awful. If it started here, I'd—" she shook her head "—I'll deal with it if I have to, but I worry about Gus and Gertie."

He'd come to Denver to rescue her, not to make her life hard. "No one needs to know about our past. What's done is done."

"Yes."

Judging by her expression, she saw the flaw in his logic as plainly as he did. Their memories couldn't be erased. He knew how she felt in his arms. He'd laughed at her silly jokes and seen her wipe her nose when she had a cold. On the flipside of the coin, she knew him even better than he knew himself. He wanted that closeness again, though he knew he had to earn it. "I won't hurt you, Mary. I promise. I just want to help you."

"It doesn't matter what you promise." She clipped the words. "I don't trust you, J.T."

"I understand." And he did, perfectly. "I wouldn't trust me either just yet. But someday you will. It's up to me to change your mind."

She looked peeved.

"We'll start with Gus." He let his eyes twinkle as if they were in Abilene again. Though he had been ready to leave earlier, he couldn't bear the thought of never seeing Mary again. "Does he like to fish? I could take him—"

She frowned. "We need some rules."

"Sure." He usually looked at rules as things to break. For Mary, he'd obey them. "What do you have in mind?"

She stood as straight as a measuring stick. "No cussing."

"Agreed." He wouldn't be accountable if he stubbed his toe, but he'd try. He didn't cuss much anyway.

"And spitting." She wrinkled her nose. "I abhor spitting."

He put his hand over his heart. "My dear Miss Larue, have you *ever* seen me spit in front of a lady?"

She blushed. "No, but I want to be clear."

Feeling bold again, he clasped her arms to hold her in place. The gesture had come from the past and she stiffened, but he didn't regret it. He wanted her to feel his sincerity. "You can trust me, Mary."

To seal the promise, he kissed her on the forehead. She could make all the rules she wanted, but he'd gotten what he'd wanted for six months. He had a chance to win her back. He also had a good reason to stay in Denver, where he could keep an eye on Roy Desmond. *And* he'd be able to prove himself by helping her brother.

He released his grip and stepped back. "I'll visit Gus tomorrow."

"That's too soon."

"Then Tuesday." He didn't want to wait. He'd get bored, and boredom led to thoughts of liquor and cards.

Mary shook her head. "The café is busy that day. I close early on Wednesday. You can come for supper."

He'd have three days to endure, but he nodded. "Wednesday it is."

He stepped through the gate with Fancy Girl trotting at his heels and a smile playing on his lips. He liked the idea of taking a boy fishing, so he decided to ride out of town to find a good spot. The buckskin wanted to run, and J.T. needed to burn off the rush in his blood. He and Mary had a long way to go, but today had been a good start.

Mary watched as J.T. pivoted the buckskin, tipped his hat and took off at a gallop with Fancy Girl barking for the fun of it. When he turned the corner, she let out the breath she'd been holding. The kiss had been a vow of sorts, an apology for the past and a promise to mind his manners, but it stirred memories of other kisses, the ones she'd given to him freely. This time J.T. had done the giving, and she didn't know what to think.

She stared down the empty street, wondering where he'd go and realizing he hadn't told her why he'd been near Swan's Nest. She wanted to know, but she wouldn't go looking for him now. She hated the thought of him in Denver, but even worse had been the guilt she'd felt when he'd walked away thinking she hadn't forgiven him. Whether she trusted him or not, she couldn't hold a grudge. His offer to help her brother had stunned her. She had no doubt he'd be good for Gus. In spite of the threat to her reputation, Mary couldn't deny her brother's need for a man in his life.

She needed to think about what she'd tell her friends, so she headed back to the swing and sat. Adie would respect her reluctance to talk, but Caroline would ask a hundred questions. People who saw her with J.T. would speculate, and the gossip would begin even if Mary said or did nothing. She massaged her temples. *Please, Lord. I need help.*

"Mary?"

She looked up and saw Adie coming up the steps with two plates of food, one for Mary and the other presumably for J.T. Caroline stood behind her, looking both curious and kind. Mary managed a wry smile. "You found me."

"Is everything all right?" Caroline sat next to her on the swing.

"I think so."

Adie handed her a plate, set the other on the table and sat on the chair by the steps. "Where's Mr. Quinn?"

"He's gone."

"For good?" Caroline asked.

"No, he's staying in Denver." Mary trusted her friends, but secrets had a way of leaking into everyday conversation. She wouldn't dodge their questions, but neither would she tell the whole story. Uncovering the plate of chicken, she feigned a wry smile. "My past just caught up with me, I'm afraid."

Caroline, an uncontrollable matchmaker, had a sparkle in her eyes. "Bessie said he's good-looking."

"Oh, he is," Mary said casually. "A woman knows J.T.'s in a room, but he's not likely to stay there." She wanted to bite into the chicken to feign normalcy, but her stomach knotted. She set the plate on the table, looked at Adie and then Caroline. "I've never told anyone about J.T."

Caroline touched her arm. "Did you love him?"

Yes! With everything in me. I was carrying his child. I wanted to marry him. How foolish she'd been. How naive about men. Lowering her gaze, she whispered, "I thought I did."

Caroline gripped her hand. The brunette had lost a husband after the War Between the States. He'd been a man of color, and she'd kept the marriage a secret from everyone except Bessie. She'd understand if Mary blurted the truth about J.T., but Mary couldn't take the risk.

Adie offered a hankie. Mary took it and wiped her eyes. "I expected too much from him."

"No, you didn't," Adie said gently. "You wanted what most women want. A husband. A family of her own."

Mary thought of the baby she'd lost and the hole it had left in her life. Adie didn't know about the miscarriage, but she would have understood the pain of an empty womb. She and Josh had Stephen, their adopted son, but they'd been married a year and Adie hadn't conceived. Mary wished she could share her story. Instead she focused on the obvious. "J.T. hurt me terribly, but I should have known better than to fall in love with him."

Caroline squeezed her hand. "We can't choose whom we love."

"No," Mary agreed. "But I should have been careful. I should never have…" She shook her head. "I don't want to talk about it."

"It might help," Adie prodded.

The more Mary talked, the more her friends would want to know. But if she said nothing, they'd wonder. "He's a gunfighter," she finally said. "And he gambles, or he used to."

Caroline sat back in the swing, causing it to rock. "He came looking for you. You must matter to him."

"A little," she admitted. "But not enough."

Adie watched her. "You said he's staying."

"He is, but only to help Augustus." She grimaced. "He had the nerve to tell my brother to change his name to Gus."

"It's about time!" Adie declared.

Caroline laughed softly. "Didn't you say you were praying for a man to help your brother grow up?"

"Yes, but—"

Adie chuckled. It wasn't rude, just annoying. "I don't know why God does what He does, but I'd say He answered your prayer in a *very* interesting way."

"Me, too." Caroline smiled.

Interesting wasn't what Mary wanted her life to be. Dull and ordinary suited her fine. So did running the café and forgetting the past. She had no desire to dance on the edge of the truth, but that's what she'd be doing until J.T. left Denver.

As he neared the stream where he planned to take Gus, J.T. slowed his horse to a walk. Fancy Girl came up to him running and barking at the same time. He knew how the dog felt. Mary had forgiven him, and he wanted to shout to the world.

High and bright, clouds skittered past the sun in a way that sent shadows running from him. Raising his eyes to the sky, he wondered what a good woman like Mary saw in a mongrel like himself. Forgiving him had cost her something. She didn't want him in Denver, yet she'd honored his request. She'd always been generous to him, but today she'd been merciful.

How could she be so kind when he'd hurt her so badly? J.T. thought of his brothers beating him in that New York alley. A few years ago he'd learned that all three of them had died from cholera. Old feelings had come back, and he'd cheerfully spat on their graves. He'd wounded Mary as surely as his brothers had hurt him, yet she'd forgiven him. He had to admire her kindness.

He looked down at his dog, panting and happy from the run. "You look thirsty, girl. Let's find water."

He nudged the buckskin onto the stream where he'd camped a couple of nights ago. He'd eaten his fill of trout and so had Fancy Girl. The spot was perfect for what he had in mind for Gus.

The way J.T. saw things, the boy needed confidence more than he needed to know how to fight. If Gus didn't know how to handle a gun, they'd do some target practice. He'd teach the boy how to throw a punch, but mostly he wanted Gus to carry himself with pride. Bullies were like wolves. They cut the weakest animal from the pack and took it down. If Gus stopped being a weakling, the bullies would find other prey.

As J.T. approached the stream, Fancy trotted on ahead of him. He followed more slowly, checking out the terrain for signs of drifters and men like himself. Near an old fire pit he saw a pile of cigarette butts. He didn't want Gus to consider tobacco a good habit, so he climbed down from his horse and ground them into the dirt. Looking around, he saw broken branches where horses had been tied. He checked out the hoofprints and decided the spot had been used by a lone man with two horses, someone much like himself. J.T. worried all the time about old enemies, but the rider had moved on. The spot would be fine for camping with Gus.

"Come on, Fancy," he called to his dog.

When she barked, he rested his hand on his gun. When she barked a second time, he worried she'd gotten stuck in the willows lining the stream. Approaching cautiously, he saw her in the middle of the water, looking down with her ears pricked and her tail wagging. When she pawed at something, a trout escaped her grasp with a small leap. J.T. laughed out loud. How many dogs knew how to fish? He called her again and she came bounding to him, her chest wet and her eyes full of triumph. He dropped down to his knees and hugged her hard. He hoped that someday Mary would come as willingly into his arms.

Chapter Seven

On Monday morning, Mary saw Roy Desmond walk into the café for breakfast. He took his usual table in the corner, greeted Gertie with a debonair smile and ordered ham and eggs. She wondered if he'd made his selection for Arline, the lead character in *The Bohemian Girl*. Gertie had been nagging her to accept the part, and she wouldn't let up until Roy picked someone else. There was a lull in the crowd, so Mary dried her hands on her apron and went to say hello.

Roy saw her coming and stood. "Good morning, Mary."

"Hello, Roy."

He indicated the chair. "Would you care to join me?"

"Yes, but just for a minute." She sat before he could hold her chair, making small talk so that she didn't look anxious. When the moment seemed right, she brought up the new opera. "How's the casting going?" she asked.

"Just fine," he said. "Except for Arline. I'm still hoping you'll change your mind."

The role of Arline, a gypsy princess, appealed to Mary in every way. The music soared, and she liked the girl's bravery. Until Roy filled the part, she'd yearn to take it. "I hope you find someone soon."

He held her gaze. "The role's yours. Just say the word."

"No. But thank you."

"At least look at the audition poster." He put his elbows on the table, laced his fingers and leaned slightly forward. "Do you recall the advertisement for your show in Abilene?"

"Of course." Chill bumps erupted on her arms. She had no desire to remember those days, especially not with Roy.

"The same artist did the drawing." He lowered his voice to a murmur. "Of course, that was before the trouble you had with O'Day."

Had Roy meant to assure her that he'd keep her secret, or was he using the old scandal to blackmail her into playing Arline? Mary didn't know, but she didn't take kindly to threats. The thought of the scandal erupting made her tremble, but threats made her fighting mad. Which had Roy intended? She needed to find out, so she looked him in the eye with deliberate poise. "I'm sure the poster is lovely."

"It is."

"I appreciate your interest," she said. "But my singing career is over.

He lowered his chin. "That's a tragedy."

"It's my choice." It had been, sort of. If she hadn't lost her reputation, she would have never left the stage. "I have a good life now. I'm happy."

He teased her with a smile. "You'd be even happier singing for me."

Laughing, she stood to leave. "No one will be happy if I don't get back to the stove. Have a good day, Roy."

"One more thing." He stopped her with a hand on her forearm. "I ran into a mutual friend of ours."

She thought of the dozens of people she'd met in her acting days. Even a distant acquaintance could stir up gossip about the scandal. Her stomach churned. "Who?"

"J. T. Quinn."

She felt relieved. J.T. wouldn't talk. "I saw him on Sunday."

"Just thought I'd mention it," Roy added.

Mary excused herself and headed to the kitchen. Whatever worries she had about Roy disappeared. Considering his knowledge of her past, warning her about J.T. had been considerate. If she could have taken the role of Arline, she would have done it. Instead she grabbed the three new orders Gertie had left on the counter and went back to the hot stove.

It was Tuesday, almost night, and J.T. had slept away the afternoon. He'd woken up five minutes ago, sweating and tense. He didn't like small places, and this room could have been a closet. He'd taken it because it was close to a side door. He wanted a private exit for himself, and Fancy needed to go out at night to do her business. Irritable, he looked out the tiny window high on the wall. Night was coming fast. He had to light a lamp or get out before the darkness grabbed him.

He couldn't stand the thought of another evening with nothing to do. Feeling twitchy, he stood and reached for his hat. "Come on, Fancy. Let's take a walk."

The dog ignored him in favor of the bone Mary had given her. She'd gnawed it clean and was still enjoying it. J.T. had no such comfort. What did a man do with himself when he didn't drink, smoke or gamble?

He slept.

He ate.

He thought too much. "Come on, girl," he said with more excitement than he felt.

Fancy looked over her shoulder. With her tail wagging and the bone between her paws, she tipped her head at him, then went back to chewing with an intensity J.T. saw in himself.

"You've got a one-track mind," he said to her.

The dog's thoughts were on the bone. His were on places he couldn't go and things he didn't do anymore. He needed to get out of the tiny room, and he needed air that didn't smell like the sauerkraut cooking in the kitchen. The smell reminded him of the food he'd scavenged from garbage cans in New York when he was a child. He hated cabbage and always would. He'd eat somewhere else tonight.

"Okay, Fancy. You can stay." He put on his gun belt and duster, scratched the dog's head and left the boardinghouse.

The day had cooled with the setting sun, and he welcomed the fresh air. He *didn't* welcome the temptation nipping at his heels. *Just one drink…just an hour of faro.* He walked faster, but his thoughts kept pace. He wished he'd taken Fancy Girl with him. Most saloons didn't appreciate four-legged customers, and having her at his side made it easy to walk by the open doors.

One street led to another until he found himself on the corner of Market and Colfax Avenue. A whisper of conscience told him to stay on Colfax, but his feet turned down Market. A block later he was surrounded by saloons and dance halls. Pianos filled the air with tinny music, and girls in skimpy dresses were giving him easy smiles. He looked away, but his toe caught on a warped board and he stumbled. Off balance, he found himself staring through the open door of a saloon. Two men were standing at a counter. Between them a bottle glistened amber in the lamplight. One had an empty glass, the other a full one he was raising to his lips. J.T. could taste the poison, feel it running down his throat. A faro dealer sat at a table shuffling cards. The rasp called to him like the morning crow of a rooster.

As much as he missed the oblivion of liquor, he missed faro even more. Beating the odds gave him a thrill. So did winning big. If he made a bet or two, he could double the money in his saddlebag and secretly give it to Mary. If he gambled tonight, it would be for a good cause. He put his hand on the half door and pushed. As it moved, a fight broke out in the street. He turned and saw a cowboy sprawled on his back. Two men were going after him, shouting and kicking and cussing. The cowboy had blond hair, and in his drunken state he couldn't put words together.

J.T. came to his senses in a rush. As much as he liked faro, he cared more about helping Gus fight off bullies. Needing to get away from temptation, he walked away from the saloon at a rapid pace. In the distance he saw the Newcastle Theater and decided to walk by it. It wouldn't hurt to remind Roy that he had his eye on Mary.

When he reached the theater, the doors opened and the crowd began to go inside. Among the wealthy couples, he spotted Roy speaking to a girl in her late teens. Dressed in pink, she had cinnamon hair and a sparkle that reminded him of Mary. Next to her stood a brunette wearing a crimson gown with gold trim. He guessed her to be in her twenties and far more sophisticated than the girl. He was sure of it when Roy made the younger girl blush with just a look.

J.T. didn't know the girl at all, but he wanted to drag her home to her family. What was she doing at the theater without a chaperone? The thought surprised him, because he didn't like chaperones. The ones he'd encountered had been nosy old women who'd gotten in his way. Watching Roy with this girl changed his mind about the custom. She was smiling too brightly, encouraging him without knowing the nature of his thoughts.

J.T. recognized that innocence. He'd been seventeen when Zeke Carver recruited him to be the lookout on a bank job. He'd done well and had ridden off with them. That night he'd gotten drunk for the first time. He didn't remember much, but it had been the start of his worst years. With regret thick in his throat, he watched the girl and her friend enter the theater. Roy watched them with too much intensity. J.T. stared hard at the man, willing him to look at him instead. It took a long minute, but the man finally turned and their eyes locked. Roy smiled.

J.T. didn't.

Smirking, Roy followed the last of his guests into the theater and closed the door.

More distrustful of the man than ever, J.T. walked past the building. Near the doors he saw a poster in a glass case. Below a drawing of a gypsy woman, it read:

Coming Soon!
The Bohemian Girl
Auditions for the role of Arline
Saturday, August 3rd at 2 p.m.

Did the sign mean Roy had given up on Mary? J.T. didn't think so. Knowing how much she loved to perform, he saw the poster as bait. Tomorrow after supper she'd get an earful about Roy.

As he entered a quieter part of the city, he slowed his pace. To his surprise, he ended up in front of the saloon where he'd found Mary a few days ago. Instead of the shuffle of cards, he heard fiddle music. And in the place of whiskey, he smelled chili so hot it stung his eyes. Mary used to tease that he didn't know good food when he had it, because he'd burned off his taste buds. Maybe he had. He'd burned a lot of things in his life—bridges, women, even friends. His life was one big pile of ash, but a man still had to eat.

With his stomach rumbling, he pushed through the door. He glanced at the fiddler, an old man playing "Buffalo Gals," and headed for the counter. The barkeep, a large fellow with red hair, greeted him with a nod. "What can I get you, friend?"

"A bowl of chili."

The man indicated a stool. "Have a seat."

J.T. ambled to the far side of the counter and sat where he could see the door. The place wasn't busy, and he wondered why. Maybe the owner served cheap whiskey, or maybe he didn't serve whiskey at all. He looked behind the bar. Instead of bottles, he saw a hodgepodge of canned goods, tin plates and a row of glasses. A mirror hung on the wall, reflecting both the room and J.T. himself. Six months ago, he'd had deep crevices at the corners of his mouth, and his eyes had been bloodshot. The man staring at him now looked almost young, though J.T. felt as burdened as ever.

The barkeep put the chili in front of him. "That stuff's hot. Want something to put out the fire?"

Beer. "Just water."

"Got some sweet tea," he offered.

"Sure."

After the barkeep left, a man with the look of a

gunfighter walked into the saloon. He was wearing dark clothing and he was surveying the room as J.T. had done. J.T. glanced at the man's waist. When he didn't see a gun, he guessed him to be a preacher, maybe the one who'd spoken here on Sunday. He'd expected the man to be older, maybe with a paunch and gray hair. The fellow who pulled up a stool was his age or younger. If life had marked him, it didn't show.

The barkeep returned with the sweet tea and a plate of jalapeños. He put the items in front of J.T., then poured coffee for the reverend. J.T. ate his meal, half listening as the men discussed the progress on a church they were building. The sides were going up fast, and they needed to get the roof in place. J.T. didn't think much about the talk until the minister mentioned a familiar name.

"You know how Roy Desmond is," he said to the barkeep. "He's not happy about having a church next to his theater."

"What did he say?" the barkeep asked.

"He wants to buy the property." The minister sipped his coffee. "He offered us a lot of money, too."

"What's he want it for?"

"A hotel."

J.T. nearly choked on a chili bean. If Roy opened a hotel, it wouldn't be reputable.

The barkeep dried a glass on his apron. "Maybe we should sell to him and build somewhere else."

The minister shook his head. "I want to be in the heart of the city."

"So do I, but—"

"We aren't selling." Judging by the minister's tone, he'd build that church or die trying. J.T. understood the feeling, because he felt that way about protecting Mary. J.T. had no interest in churches, but he and the minister had a common enemy in Roy Desmond. They also had needs that fit like a handshake. The minister needed someone to put a roof on the church, and J.T. needed to keep an eye on Roy. Working on the roof would give him a bird's-eye view of the theater manager's activities.

J.T. set down his spoon and spoke to the minister. "I heard you say you needed a roofer."

"That I do."

"I can swing a hammer, and I don't mind heights." Small dark places were another matter. "I'd be interested in the job."

The man named a wage that struck J.T. as pitiful, but he didn't care about the salary. If he could keep an eye on Roy, he'd have the pay he wanted. Neither did he balk at the man's description of the steep roof and bell tower. The minister gave him a steady look. "That's the job. It's yours if you want it."

"I'll take it."

He walked up to J.T. and offered his hand. "I'm Reverend Joshua Blue. Call me Josh."

J.T had a hunch the man would recognize his name because of Mary. He gave him a look that dared him to judge, then held out his hand. "I'm J. T. Quinn."

"You're Mary's friend."

"The same."

The minister's grip tightened with a warning. *Hurt Mary, and you'll answer to me.* "She's a good woman."

"The best," J.T. replied, squeezing even harder. It was easy to imagine the reverend staring down the devil himself, a fact that gave J.T. comfort. He was glad Mary had people who cared about her.

The man's lips tipped upward. "I'm glad we understand each other, Mr. Quinn."

"Yes we do," he answered. "Call me J.T. When do I start?"

"How about tomorrow?"

"Sounds good."

"Do you know where the church is?" Josh asked.

"You said next to the Newcastle."

"That's right." The reverend indicated the barkeep. "This is Brick."

The man studied J.T.'s face as if he were matching it to a Wanted poster. "I know about you, Quinn. You rode with the Carver gang."

J.T. had no desire to recall those days. "It was a long time ago."

The man's eyes narrowed. "How long?"

"Years." *A lifetime.*

"So you weren't there for that silver heist in Leadville?" His tone accused J.T. of more than stealing silver, a sign he'd been harmed by the Carvers.

J.T. had heard such accusations before. He'd spent three years with the gang before he'd gone off on his own, but he still carried the stench of that time. Not only had the Carvers robbed banks and stagecoaches, they'd been cruel about it. J.T. would never forget Zeke tormenting a scrawny old man while his daughter watched. He'd left the gang soon after that job. If he was going to stay in Denver without getting shot, and without embarrassing Mary, he needed to stop Brick from digging up the past.

"I rode with the Carvers before Leadville," he admitted. "Those were ugly times and I want to forget them." He also wanted to forget his time with Griff Lassen. J.T. didn't think Lassen cared enough to hunt him down, but the man might take a shot if he had the chance.

The reverend spoke with a Boston accent. "We all have things we want to forget."

"Some of us can't." Brick spat the words.

J.T. knew the feeling. Confident, he looked the barkeep in the eye. "I don't want trouble, Brick." He used the man's given name to take control, but he said it kindly. "I owe Mary Larue a favor. I'm going to be in Denver until that debt is paid. That's all."

The man scowled. "You better mean it."

"Yes, sir. I do."

Brick heard the "sir" and relaxed. "All right, then."

Josh interrupted. "We'll leave the past buried. But to be clear, gentlemen, I don't mind a little trouble for a good cause."

J.T. wondered what cause the reverend would call "good." The ministers he'd known had all been gutless. The worst had been the old man in New York. He'd given J.T. and his brothers food when their mother died, but he'd done nothing when the landlord threw them into the street. Looking at Reverend Joshua Blue, J.T. had a hunch he'd fight for orphans, even ornery ones.

The minister said goodbye and left, leaving J.T. to finish his supper. He chewed a jalapeño, swallowed and then sat, rather amazed that he'd just taken an ordinary job. Not only had he become a working man, he'd be helping to build a church. J.T. finished his supper and headed back to the boardinghouse. He didn't know what tomorrow held, but he felt a pleasant mix of possibilities.

Chapter Eight

"**Y**ou're late!" Mary cried as Gertie came through the back door to the café.

It was nine o'clock, and her sister had promised to be home in time to help serve breakfast to the crowd that arrived on the morning train. In the dining area, travelers filled every seat, and a dozen were standing outside the door. Enid, the other waitress for the morning, had threatened to quit unless Mary hired more help. Older and fighting rheumatism, she didn't hesitate to complain. In the chaos, Mary had nearly set fire to a pound of bacon.

Gertie grabbed an apron hanging on the back wall. "I'm so sorry, Mary. I—uh—I...I overslept."

When Gus dragged out his words, Mary ignored it. When Gertie hesitated, she suspected her sister of twisting the truth. Turning from a bowl of half-scrambled eggs, she took in Gertie's appearance. She'd pulled her cinnamon-colored hair into a hasty coif, but Mary could see remnants of elaborate curls. She also smelled traces of expensive perfume, something a woman would wear on a special occasion.

Gertie had spent the night with Katrina supposedly

to help finish a dress. It seemed they'd had time to do other things. Exactly what, Mary didn't know. But whatever those things were, they'd put a determined gleam in Gertie's eyes.

Mary beat the eggs harder but she kept her voice casual. "What did you and Katrina do last night?"

"We…" Gertie fumbled with the apron strings. "It's a long story. Could we talk later?"

Mary would be taking lunch to the workers at the church, and J.T. was coming for supper. The thought made her nervous enough without having to contend with Gertie. Neither did she want to give her sister time to scheme. "Now is fine."

Gertie pulled the apron strings tight. "You're going to be mad, but I'm not sorry. Katrina and I went to the Newcastle last night."

"You *what?*" Mary stopped beating the eggs.

"I knew you'd be upset," Gertie said. "But I *had* to go! Oh, Mary. It was wonderful. The music—"

"I know about the music." She dumped the eggs in a pan. "Gertie, we've talked about this. You're too young. You promised—"

"I know, but—"

Enid steamed through the doorway with an armload of dirty dishes. "There you are!" she said to Gertie. "Get movin', girl! We've got a trainload of hungry people out there. They're going to eat *me* if we don't get 'em fed."

"I'm sorry, Enid." Gertie gave Mary a defiant look, then lifted a notepad and pencil from a standing desk. "I'll get busy right now."

Mary watched as her sister paced into the dining room. They had a plan, the best one Mary could imagine. But Gertie had no patience. Mary needed to know what had happened last night, but first she had to finish serving breakfast.

Sighing, she added a rasher of bacon to the frying pan. Gertie had as much sense as Mary had had at that age, but she also had an older sister who'd protect her. That meant keeping Gertie at home until she was eighteen, then sending her to study acting with Maude. They'd had this argument before. This morning they'd have it again.

When the breakfast crowd thinned, Mary told Enid to write *Closed* on the chalkboard in the window. As the last customer paid Gertie, Mary took off her apron and looked at Enid carrying an armload of dirty dishes. Gus usually helped with the washing, but Mary had kept him in bed. He'd improved and wanted to get up, but she figured he needed the rest.

"I hate to ask," she said to the waitress. "But could you finish the dishes? I'll pay you extra, or course." She needed to hire a dishwasher, but she was reluctant to pay another salary when she needed money for Gertie.

Enid looked peeved. "I'll do it for you, Mary. But that sister of yours—"

"I know."

"One waitress can't handle the train crowd." Enid rubbed her back. "Especially *this* waitress. If it happens again, you'll have to find *two* new waitresses, because I'll quit."

"I'll speak to Gertie," Mary promised.

"It's not just my achin' back." Enid made no effort to lower her voice. "I don't like getting the evil eye from people we've kept waitin'. Word'll get out that you're slow, and folks will go somewhere else."

"I understand."

"That sister of yours—"

"Yes, Enid." Mary had heard enough. She respected Enid for her age and her hard work, but she didn't need a lecture about Gertie. Nor did she want Enid listening when she spoke to her sister. "Why don't you go on home? I'll do the dishes myself." She'd do them after she'd made sandwiches for the men at the church.

"Don't mind if I do, miss."

The older woman took off her apron and waddled out of the restaurant. When the door clicked shut, Mary went into the dining room where Gertie was placing fresh napkins on a table she'd wiped clean. The girl usually balked at helping in the café, but today she'd done a good job.

"We need to talk," Mary said.

Gertie straightened the last napkin, then looked up with rebellion burning in her eyes. "I know I should have asked for permission to go to the show at the Newcastle, but you'd have said no."

"That's right."

"I don't understand." Gertie's voice trembled. "We live in a city with a dozen theaters. I could—"

"You're too young," Mary answered. "Maude Atkins can teach you things."

Gertie put her hands on her hips. "*I* know someone who can help me right now."

"Who?"

"You know him, too."

Mary hated it when her sister played coy. Instead of seeming sophisticated, she sounded like a brat. "And just who is this man?"

"Roy Desmond."

She should have guessed. Gertie usually waited on his table, and he enjoyed telling her stories about his acting days. Mary liked Roy and didn't mind the distraction, but she'd begun to worry about Gertie thinking too highly of the man. She needed to choose her words carefully to keep her sister from defending him. "I like Roy, too. But New York has far more opportunity."

"But I don't want to wait," Gertie protested. "I know what you've done for me, Mary. I love you for it, but I don't want to wait *a whole year!*"

"It's not forever…just until your birthday.'

"That's eleven months!"

Gertie marched into the kitchen with the empty napkin tray. Mary heard the clang of the wash basin, then the splash of water from the pump. Enamel plates slammed together as Gertie scraped the remnants into a slop bucket.

Mary didn't blame Gertie for being upset. Who wouldn't choose singing on stage over running a restaurant? If she could have taken the role of Arline for herself, she'd have done it. But performing in Denver was out of the question, both for herself and Gertie. She went into the kitchen where the girl was scrubbing dishes with a vengeance. Mary stepped to her side, lifted a towel and dried a plate. "I know how much you want to audition. Really, I do."

The dish in Gertie's hand sank to the bottom of the murky water. She wiped her teary eyes with her sleeve, then looked at Mary. "Have you seen the Newcastle on the inside?"

"No." She avoided the building.

Gertie stepped back from the basin. "It's beautiful. The chandeliers are like diamonds floating in the sky, and the seats are so velvety it's like sitting on a throne. I've never seen anything like it."

Neither had Mary. She'd performed in theaters all over the West, but nothing could compare to the opera houses in Colorado. Denver didn't even wear the crowning jewel. Some of the best theaters were in Crescent City and Leadville, mining towns with gold and silver pouring out of the ground. Mary didn't want to think about the luxury right now, not with a dish towel in her calloused hands.

"I'm sure the theater's lovely," she replied

"It is." Gertie bit her lip. She'd had that habit since she was small, and Mary knew what it meant. Her sister wanted something she shouldn't have. The girl looked at her with owlish eyes. "I have a favor to ask."

"What is it?"

"Katrina and I spoke with Mr. Desmond last night. We talked about *Bohemian Girl*."

Mary imagined herself as Arline and swatted the picture away. "What did he say?"

"You know he wants you to play the lead." Gertie let the temptation tangle. "He'd give me a part, too."

Mary wiped the plate more vigorously. "Gertie, no."

"He just wants to *talk* to you."

"Didn't you hear me?" Mary stopped wiping the plate. "I said *no*."

"I don't understand!" Gertie flung the dishrag into the water. "I know you think I'm too young, but you'd be with me."

"Gertie—"

"Do you know what I think?" The girl turned from the basin. "I think you're afraid of something!"

"That's not it!"

"Then what is it?"

You don't know the risk. Mary sealed her lips, but she couldn't stop a sudden grimace.

Her sister's eyes widened. "You're hiding something, aren't you?"

Mary shook her head. "My concern is for *you*, Gertie.
I know what theater life is like."

"What does *that* mean?"

Gertie had hit a nerve, and she knew it. She'd push
until she got an answer. Mary had to confide in her sister
or make a concession. The thought of Gertie at the Newcastle filled her with dread. The theater world was small.
Someone was sure to know about Abilene. They might
connect her and Gertie. They might think Gertie was like
Mary had been. The men might try to take advantage. As
long as Gertie's last name was Larue…but Gertie didn't
have to be Gertrude Larue. She could take a stage name.
She could be Gertrude Jones or Penelope Smith.

Mary didn't want Gertie acting at such a young age,
but neither did she want her sister asking questions. Mary
had to guard her secret, and that meant giving in—just a
little—to Gertie. She'd have to convince the girl to use
a stage name, but she suspected Gertie would agree to
anything.

Even with her sister using a different name, Mary had
to be cautious. She'd agree to meet with Roy to pacify
Gertie, but she wanted to see the posters outside the
Newcastle. If she recognized the names of the actors,
she'd have to back out of the meeting no matter how hard
Gertie pushed. Until now, Mary had avoided the theater
as much as possible. Today, when she took the lunches to
the church with Gus, she'd scan the posters for familiar
names.

Pulling herself together, she faced Gertie. "I'm not
saying I've changed my mind, but we can meet with Mr.
Desmond."

Gertie bounced on her toes. "What are you doing this
afternoon?"

"Why?"

"I told him we'd meet him at two o'clock."

"Gertie!" Mary didn't like being pushed. "I bring lunch to the church today. Besides that, Mr. Quinn's coming to supper." And Gus had been nagging her for two days to bake a chocolate cake.

"I know," Gertie said quickly. "I'll help with everything. I'll clean the apartment, whatever you need. Just name it."

Mary raised one brow. "How about being on time for work in the morning?"

"I will," she promised. "I'll do anything. Roy said—"

"Roy?" Mary's brows snapped together. Since when did her seventeen-year-old sister get to use the man's given name?

Gertie blushed. "He said all the actresses call him Roy, and that I should, too."

Mary didn't like Roy's familiarity at all. Not only had he overstepped a polite boundary, but he'd put a wedge between Gertie and herself. She felt manipulated and didn't like it. "What time will he be here?"

"He won't." She grinned. "We're going to the Newcastle. Isn't that grand?"

Mary's stomach flipped. While looking at the posters put her at risk, going inside the theater meant entering a lion's den. "He should come here."

"But it's all arranged."

Mary thought for a minute. If she protested going to the theater, Gertie would ask why. It was the middle of the week and the middle of the day. The theater was dark on Wednesday, so the chances were good the actors wouldn't be around. She also saw a chance to bargain with Gertie.

"All right," she agreed. "I'll meet you at two o'clock, but there's something I want from *you.*"

"What is it?"

"Until I say so, you'll address Roy as Mr. Desmond. Do you understand?"

"No," she said with a saucy look. "But I'll do it."

Gertie would have agreed to anything at the moment. She needed to understand why Mary had to insist on proper conduct. "It's more than manners, Gertie. Roy is older. He's experienced in ways you're not."

The girl huffed. "I know that."

Mary held in a sigh. "I don't think you do."

"You worry too much."

When it came to Gertie, Mary didn't think she could worry enough. Wanting to keep peace between them, she faked a scowl. Gertie laughed and they hugged. With her eyes closed, Mary remembered being seventeen and unafraid. She'd never have that innocence again, but she could protect Gertie. Mary knew all about the temptations of theater life. If her sister was as ambitious as Mary had been, Gertie would do anything to win the best roles. She'd flirt with theater managers and flatter them. She'd taste her first drops of liquor, and she'd wear clothing that revealed too much. More than anything, Mary wanted to protect her sister from going down that empty road. She thought of J.T. coming for supper and shuddered. Looking at him, she'd remember the compromises she'd made, then she'd think of the baby and wonder.… Would the child have been a boy or a girl? Would it have had his eyes or hers?

J.T. had promised to mind his manners, but the sparks between them had always been obvious. If Gertie sensed more than an old friendship, Mary would have some explaining to do. She hoped J.T. would be on his best behavior. As for herself, she'd play the role of "old friend" perfectly. It would be the performance of her life, but she had to protect her brother and sister from any threat of the old scandal, and that meant protecting her reputation.

Four hours later, Mary and Gus were walking down Sixteenth Street with a handcart full of sandwiches and cobbler for the workers at the church. The sun couldn't have been brighter, but she couldn't stop worrying about what she'd see on the posters. To build her confidence, she'd worn the blue suit and lace jabot she saved for special occasions. Her best hat was pinned at a fashionable angle, but she felt none of its boldness.

When she and Gus reached the front of the theater, she indicated a spot of shade. "Wait here," she said to him. "I'll be right back."

"S-sure."

She walked alone to a glass case displaying the poster for the current show. Five performers were listed, and she didn't recognize a single name. Allowing Gertie to take a small part, if Roy agreed and she used a stage name, seemed like a reasonable compromise. Turning, she spotted the poster for *The Bohemian Girl*. The drawing of Arline shot her back to the day she'd left Frog's Landing with a satchel full of dreams.

In St. Louis she'd met Maude and joined a traveling theater troupe. While touring the West by train, Mary had done everything from selling tickets to mending costumes. The shows ranged from burlesque to Shakespeare, and she'd loved every minute. Her big break had come on a humid night in Dodge City. When the star of the show fell ill, she'd filled in. In a theater full of cowhands and ruffians, she'd closed the show with "Home Sweet Home." There had been no applause, not even the squeak of a chair, and she'd thought she had flopped.

Then a man sniffed.

Someone murmured, "Amen."

A cowpoke jumped to his feet and broke into applause. The crowd rose in a wave, clapping and stamping their feet until she thought the walls would tumble to the ground.

She'd loved every minute of the applause.

She'd basked in the compliments.

When a reviewer called her a sensation, she'd read the newspaper story a hundred times. She'd gained a name for herself that day, and later she'd signed a contract to star at the Abilene Theater. There she'd met J.T., and there her career had ended.

Feeling melancholy, she walked back to Gus. The boy was standing by the cart, nervously looking up and down the street. After speaking with him, she was certain Todd Roman was among the boys who'd bullied him. Yesterday she'd visited Deputy Beau Morgan. He'd promised to keep an eye on the streets near the café, but as J.T. had predicted, the law couldn't do much else. She walked to Gus's side. "How are you doing?"

"G-good."

"I'm glad." She tousled his head. "You should lie down after lunch."

"I d-don't *want* to l-l-lie down."

Mary liked her brother's spunk, but she worried about his tone. He needed to be strong, but she didn't want to lose the sweet boy he'd always been. "Just don't overdo it," she said mildly.

Frowning, he shoved the handcart down the boardwalk. As they passed the corner of the theater, he pointed to the top of the unfinished church. "L-l-look!"

Near the peak of the roof she saw a man darkened by shadow, balanced on scaffolding as he hammered wooden planks onto the rafters. He had long legs, broad shoulders and a fringe of brown hair sticking out from his hat. Lean and muscular, he looked as comfortable as a mountain lion lazing on a tree branch. When he reached into the nail bucket, the light shifted and she recognized J.T.

She forgot about the sandwiches in the cart.

She forgot about the jugs of tea and the cobbler she'd brought.

She forgot everything except the man on the scaffolding thirty feet above the ground, out of reach but in the middle of her life. How had someone like J.T. ended up on the roof of a church with a hammer in his hand? It made no sense…none at all. What had he told Josh? If he'd revealed any of the details from the past, she'd be furious.

She turned to Gus. "Set up the cart. I have to speak with Pastor Josh."

As her brother headed for a patch of shade, Mary went into the unfinished building. She spotted Josh standing at a table, making notes on the building plans with a stubby pencil. Sunlight filtered through the rafters, then turned to full shadow as she stepped under the planking. Aware of J.T. working above them, she walked quietly to Josh's side. He looked up and smiled. "Must be time for lunch."

"It is."

"Good, I'm starved."

She wanted to ask him about J.T., but the hammering would force her to shout. Frustrated, she glanced up. J.T. had moved a few steps, giving her a view of his legs through the rafters as he pounded nails in a steady rhythm. Before she could look away, he shifted his feet to the right where the boards had yet to be placed. His upper body came fully into her view. So did the gun belt hanging from his trim waist.

Look away, she told herself.

But she couldn't do it. Seeing J.T. on the roof of a church left her stunned and gaping. Instead of his usual dark clothing, he was dressed in dungarees and a blue shirt that matched the sky. He didn't look anything like the gunslinger who'd left her in Abilene, nor did he appear to have gambled all night while indulging in liquor. He looked rested, healthy and sober.

He glanced down, maybe to speak to Josh, and saw her startled expression. Even with the height of the church between them, she saw a twinkle in his eyes. He'd surprised her, and he'd enjoyed doing it. Mary didn't know what to make of the feelings rushing through her. J. T. Quinn was a handsome man, and she'd once loved him. Her feelings had died, but she couldn't deny the leap in her belly at the sight of him. She quickly squelched her feelings. This man had broken her trust. She didn't want to feel anything for him. Not anger. Not love. She wanted to feel…nothing.

She gave a courteous nod. "Good afternoon, Mr. Quinn."

"Good afternoon, Miss Larue."

When a smile lifted his lips, she felt as if they were meeting for the first time. *Nothing* suddenly turned into *everything.* She recalled seeing him for the first time in Abilene and how he'd looked at her. He had that same recklessness now, and it took her back to their first kiss… their first everything.

Josh shouted up to J.T. "Come on down. Mary makes the best cobbler in town."

"I know."

And he did. In Kansas they'd taken a buggy ride to

nowhere. She'd brought a picnic lunch with cobbler made from the recipe she'd used this morning. They'd traded stories, and he'd kissed her for the first time. She hoped the memory didn't show in her eyes, but she saw it plainly in his. In the past they'd traded secrets with just a look, and she'd enjoyed the closeness. Today she feared it.

She lowered her eyes as if she hadn't seen him at all, but she heard every creak as he climbed down the scaffolding. When the noise stopped, she turned to Josh. "You hired J.T.?"

"I met him at Brick's last night." He told her about offering J.T. the job and how he'd been willing to work on the roof. "I was glad to hire him. Is there a problem?"

"No," she said. "I'm just surprised."

"Surprised I hired him, or surprised he said yes?"

"Both, I guess." She wanted to know what J.T. had said to Josh, but she couldn't pry without looking anxious. She settled for the obvious. "He's not exactly a church-goer."

"Maybe that'll change."

"There's more." Did Josh realize he'd hired a gun-fighter? J.T. had killed fourteen men. "He's done things, bad things. As far as I know, he's not sorry."

Josh considered her words, then spoke in a hush. "I don't know what's in J.T.'s heart, Mary. I *do* know God brought him here. I also know J.T. carries a gun, and I'm sure he's used it."

"He has."

He swatted a fly away from the drawings. "Every man has regrets. It's how he deals with them that matters. It seems to me J.T.'s in the right place."

"He is. It's just—" she shrugged. "I don't know."

"You're afraid," Josh said simply.

Mary's cheeks burned. No one knew exactly what had

happened with J.T., but she wondered if Josh and Adie suspected. Their adopted son had been conceived out of wedlock by Josh's sister. Josh had judged the woman harshly, and he'd paid a terrible price for his lack of compassion. He and Adie wouldn't hold Mary's mistake against her, but other people would. She didn't know what to say to Josh, so she said nothing.

He lowered his voice. "Stay strong, Mary. If you're confused about J.T., talk to Adie."

"I'll think about it." But she already knew her decision. If she told her secret to anyone at all, she'd lose control over it.

Josh indicated the doorway. "Let's get lunch before it's all gone."

They left the building with Mary leading the way. The workers had helped themselves to the meal, so she searched for J.T. and Gus. She found them leaning against the wall of the opera house, holding sandwiches and grinning as Fancy Girl did tricks at J.T.'s command. She'd never seen her brother so happy, and she couldn't help but be touched when J.T. gave the dog half his sandwich. The man she'd known in Abilene wouldn't even pet a dog. She could have been indifferent to the old J.T., but the new one inspired other feelings altogether. If she'd met him today for the first time, she would have welcomed him to Denver. She'd have smiled and even flirted a little.

No way would she go down that road. She'd forgiven J.T., but she'd never forget the pain of his betrayal. She knew how Josh had met him, but she still didn't know why J.T. had taken the job. Was he trying to impress her? Did he need the money? She didn't know, but the facts couldn't be denied. Instead of gambling and drinking, he was sharing his lunch with a hungry dog.

The changes in J.T. counted as the second biggest

surprise of her life, the first being the changes she'd experienced for herself. Who'd have thought an actress with a scandalous past would sing in church and love it? If she could change, so could J.T. If he'd changed as much as it seemed, where did that leave the rebellious leap of her heart? Mary didn't know, and she didn't want to find out. J.T. had ruined her life once and he could do it again.

She couldn't love this man because he'd betrayed her, and she couldn't hate him because of her faith. That left being his friend. She fetched another sandwich from the cart and headed in his direction. The gesture didn't mean a thing. Neither did the blush on her cheeks or the eager thrum of her pulse.

Chapter Nine

J.T. saw Mary and nudged Gus. "Looks like your sister found us."

"Yeah."

The boy didn't sound happy about it, but J.T. was. He'd been looking forward to seeing her from the moment Josh mentioned she'd be bringing lunch. Watching her now, he saw a sparkle in her pretty brown eyes and the tilt of a smile. He'd also seen her hesitate at the hand-cart. He'd have to watch carefully to read her feelings, but he didn't mind. She looked beautiful in a blue suit that nipped in at her waist, and her golden hair was up in fancy twist.

He wanted to think she'd dressed up for him, but of course she hadn't. Earlier he'd surprised her and he'd enjoyed doing it. Looking at her now, he wondered why she'd dressed so formally to serve lunch to a work crew. He considered quizzing Gus, but the boy couldn't answer fast. By the time he managed the words, Mary would be at their side.

She approached with a smile and a paper-wrapped sandwich. "If I'd known Fancy was going to be here, I'd have brought her a bone." She offered J.T. the sandwich. "This is for you."

"I had one."

"You gave the entire thing to Fancy," she said, scolding him but not really.

"Thanks," he said as he took the food. "I'm half-starved."

Mary shifted her weight. "I have to admit I'm surprised to see you. How did you end up working on the roof?"

He'd just taken a bite. Chewing, he decided to tell her the bald truth. "I'm so bored I can't stand myself. Pounding nails gives me something to do."

"Is that all?" She looked baffled.

"More or less." He decided against mentioning Roy. Explaining his concern required a lengthy conversation, and he didn't want to talk in front of Gus. He planned to speak to Mary tonight.

She looked at him thoughtfully. "Are you enjoying the work?"

"Yeah, I am." He indicated the peak of the roof. "I like being high up."

Not only could he keep an eye on Roy, also he enjoyed being away from danger and temptation. Watching the clouds wander across the sky, changing shape and moving at the whim of an invisible wind, he felt a yearning to put down his guns. What would it be like to live without that burden? J.T. didn't know, and he'd never find out. A man had to protect himself, because no one else would. He also intended to protect Mary and her family.

Standing in the sun, Mary reached into her drawstring bag, took out a hankie and dabbed at her forehead. "It's warm today, isn't it?"

J.T. agreed, but it wasn't the heat that had his attention.

He recognized Mary's bag from Abilene. She'd used it for special occasions—like auditions. His gaze went to the fluttering hankie, then to the white lace gloves covering her hands, and the delicate ribbons tied at her wrists. The pieces of the puzzle slammed together. They were standing in the shadow of Roy's opera house, and he'd seen her studying the poster for *Bohemian Girl*. Did Mary have plans to meet with the theater manager? It seemed likely.

Gus smiled at his sister. "F-F-Fancy does tricks. W-w-ant to see?"

"Sure," she answered.

J.T. wanted to question her, but not with Gus there. Showing off Fancy Girl would give the boy what he needed, then J.T. could speak with Mary. "We'll start off easy." He focused on Fancy. "Okay, girl. Sit."

The dog sat.

"Roll over."

The dog rolled in a full circle and popped to her feet. Gus laughed and so did Mary. J.T. had never heard such a lovely sound. He wanted to hear it again, and Fancy had plenty of tricks. With nothing to do at night, he'd spent hours teaching her, both to amuse himself and to keep her safe. If someone came after him, he wanted the dog to take orders. Not only did she respond to his voice, she followed hand commands.

"Sh-she's smart," Gus said.

"There's more." At J.T.'s command, Fancy sat up, shook hands, played dead and woofed. Last, he dropped to a crouch and said, "Kiss goodnight." The dog enthusiastically licked his face.

Both Mary and Gus applauded, but Mary spoke for them both. "She's wonderful, J.T. You're a good teacher."

He'd never thought of himself in that light. "She's a smart dog."

Gus sighed. "I—I—I wish I c-could m-make her s-s-sit."

"You can," J.T. replied. "Watch this."

He pointed to the ground and Fancy sat. He flattened his hand and made a cutting sign. She dropped down and played dead. Last, he gave the dog a thumbs-up. She jumped to her feet, watching diligently for his next command. Gus's eyes were as wide as saucers.

"You try," J.T. said. "Start with pointing to the ground."

When Gus pointed, Fancy hesitated, but only slightly, then she sat. Gus's face lit up. He still had a whopper of a black eye, but his grin was even bigger. For the next few minutes, J.T. taught Gus the hand signals, with Fancy Girl obeying perfectly. J.T. felt proud, and the boy and dog looked even happier.

He clapped the kid on the back. "You did a good job."

"It—it worked!"

"Sure it did," J.T. replied. "You gave Fancy the right signs, and you did it like you meant it."

Gus beamed at his sister. "I—I want a dog!"

"We'll see," she said, smiling.

For the first time in years, J.T. felt genuinely good. The feeling was on the inside, not because of whiskey or winning at cards, and he didn't want it to leave. How did a man hold on to such goodness? He didn't know, but he wanted to try.

He broke off a bite of the second sandwich for Fancy Girl. As she licked his fingers, Mary gave him a stern look. "I brought that for you."

"I figured I'd fill up on cobbler."

Her cheeks turned pink, a sign she remembered that picnic in Kansas as plainly as he did. Their eyes stayed locked—his daring her to remember, and hers filled with something akin to fear—until she turned to Gus. "Would you get cobbler for J.T.?"

"Sure."

As the boy left, Mary turned to him. "Thank you for helping Gus."

He considered mentioning the camping trip he had in mind, but he wanted to speak to her out of Gus's earshot. "I haven't done much."

"You've done more than you know." She patted his dog. "So has Fancy Girl. She's amazing."

They chatted about the dog, an easy subject for them both, until Gus came back with two bowls of cobbler. He gave one to J.T. and offered the second to Mary. She refused it, so he happily claimed it for himself. She touched the boy's shoulder. "Collect all the dishes when you're done eating, then wait with Pastor Josh until I get back, okay?"

Gus's brow wrinkled. "I—I—I don't want to wait with P-P-Pastor Josh. I—I'm not a baby!"

"I know, sweetie."

J.T. would have given his left thumb to hear Mary call him sweetie, but he wasn't a twelve-year-old boy with something to prove. He punched Gus playfully on the shoulder. "Hey, kid. How about you get the dishes and then work with me?"

"Really?"

"Sure." He indicated the scaffolding. "Do you mind heights?"

Gus's eyes lit up, but Mary frowned. "It's too dangerous."

J.T. understood her concern, but Gus needed to do

something manly. Climbing high would give him a reason to brag. "I'll keep an eye out for him. It's high, but the scaffolding's wide."

Gus looked at his sister with a silent plea. She must have felt the urgency, because she smiled at him. "Are you sure you want to climb that high?"

"Y-yes."

"All right. But do what J.T. says."

"I will."

He had to speak with Mary alone about Roy, so he gave Gus a job. "See that bucket over there?" He pointed to the bottom of the scaffolding. "It's for nails and it's empty. Ask Josh where you can fill it."

As Gus ran off, J.T. turned to Mary. "You look pretty," he said, meaning it and hoping to disarm her at the same time.

"Thank you."

"Are you going somewhere?" He tried to sound matter-of-fact, but worry sharpened his tone.

She arched her brows. "I don't think that's any of your concern."

Oh, yes, it was! She'd dressed up for something— or someone. He pushed back a surge of jealousy, but it leaked into his voice. "It sounds like you're visiting a secret admirer."

She glared at him.

Eye to eye, they each waited for the other to crack. J.T. vowed it wouldn't be him, but looking at Mary and standing close, seeing the curve of her lips and the tilt of her chin, he felt the hammer of the past. This woman made him feel tender inside. He had to work to sound tough. "You're not going to tell me, are you?"

"No, I'm not." She took the longest breath he'd ever

seen her take, then she lifted her chin. "My life is *none* of your business."

"It used to be," he said quietly.

The look she gave him was scathing. No matter what she wanted to believe, or what she wanted *him* to believe, J.T. knew she wasn't indifferent to him. She cared far more than she wanted to admit to herself or to him.

"Mary!" Someone shouted from the street.

He turned and saw the girl with cinnamon hair. Flushed and nervous, she was wearing a fancy getup and walking in their direction.

Mary sighed. "That's my sister."

The girl called out again. "Hurry! We're going to be late."

Not bothering to hide his upset, J.T. squared off with Mary. "Are you meeting with Roy Desmond?"

"What if I am?"

He wished he'd told her about Roy sooner. "You have to trust me. He's not who you think he is."

Before she could react, Gertie reached her side. "It's two o'clock. We have to go *now.*"

Mary turned to her sister. "Mr. Desmond won't mind if we're a bit late."

"*I* mind!" Gertie declared. "I'm so nervous I can hardly think!"

"Take a deep breath," Mary instructed. "It'll calm you."

J.T. needed calming, too. But breathing wouldn't do the trick. Nothing short of throwing Mary over his shoulder and carrying her away from Roy and his opera house would take away the burning in his gut. He gave her a hard look. "I know Roy. He's dangerous."

She arched a brow. "I don't believe you."

He deserved the jab, but he cared about her and Roy didn't. "Mary, you have to listen—"

"This is none of your business," she insisted.

Gertie studied him, pulling back as if he were a toad. "Who are you?"

He looked her dead in the eye. "I'm J. T. Quinn, and you're too young to be going to the theater without your sister."

"I beg your pardon!"

"I saw you last night." He didn't want Mary siding with Gertie, so he calmed his voice. "Mr. Desmond spoke to you for quite some time."

"Yes, but—"

"Don't trust him, Miss Larue." He was old enough to call her Gertie, but he wanted her to feel the weight of being a grown woman. "I know Mr. Desmond better than you do."

"You have no business—"

Mary broke in. "Gertie, don't be rude. I'll handle Mr. Quinn."

The girl didn't argue, but she shot him a look of pure contempt. J.T. turned to Mary. "What's this meeting about?"

She hesitated. "He wants me to star in *Bohemian Girl*. There's a part for Gertie, too."

J.T. smelled twice the trouble he'd sensed earlier. Roy had upped the ante by involving Mary's sister. Unless J.T. found a way to influence Mary, he'd lose her to Roy and the theater. He needed more time. "Have that meeting, Mary. But I want you to promise me something."

"What?"

"Don't give him an answer today. We were friends once. Give me a chance to prove I'm right."

"I don't owe you anything."

"I know," he said quietly. "I'm asking a favor." J.T. rarely asked for anything. He usually took what he wanted, but Mary's trust had to be given freely.

"All right," she finally said. "We'll talk tonight."

"That's all I'm asking."

She said goodbye to Gus, took Gertie by the arm and headed for the theater. No harm would come to them today. The danger lay in Roy convincing Mary to trust him and then taking advantage. J.T. worried about her, but he worried about Gertie even more. The girl had all the sense of a child playing dress-up. Tonight he'd speak his mind, and he wouldn't give up until Mary cut all ties with Desmond.

As Mary and Gertie approached the theater, Roy opened the door with a sweep of his arm. "Good afternoon, ladies! Welcome to the Newcastle."

"Hello, Roy," Mary replied.

Gertie nodded a bit too graciously. "Good afternoon, Mr. Desmond."

Mary stepped into the foyer with seeming calm, but the quarrel with J.T. had unnerved her. She'd seen honest worry in his eyes, but she also knew J.T. to be overly cautious. She felt certain he was overreacting to Roy's interest in Gertie, but she'd agreed to his request because she'd once respected his judgment. For all his faults, J.T. was a good judge of character. Today she'd gauge Roy's conduct for herself. Tonight she'd weigh the risks and make a decision.

Roy gave her a warm smile. "This is your first time in the Newcastle, isn't it, Mary?"

"Yes."

"Let's start with a tour." He raised his arm to indicate

the foyer. "As you can see, my investors have spared no expense."

Mary had been in dozens of theaters, but none of them had been draped in velvet and gilded with gold. The burgundy carpet squished beneath her best shoes, and she smelled traces of the expensive perfume worn by the women at last night's show. On the sides of the foyer, staircases swept up to the balcony that held a mix of plush boxes and less expensive stalls.

She felt Roy's eyes on her face and instantly schooled her features. "It's lovely."

"I'm glad you like it." He looked at Gertie and made a hook with his elbow. "Shall we show your sister the stage, Miss Larue?"

"Oh, yes!" Blushing, Gertie took his arm.

Mary didn't like her sister's reaction, but she couldn't find fault with Roy's manners. Mildly uncomfortable, she followed them through a set of doors that led into the main part the theater. A few steps behind them, she stifled the shock of seeing hundreds of seats waiting to be filled. She turned to the balcony and saw even more seating. She'd sung in front of large crowds but never in a building of this size. Overhead, chandeliers reflected sunlight pouring in through windows framed by open drapes. The high walls were covered in the newest flocked wallpaper, and the window frames were painted gold. The stage boasted even more grandeur. A red velvet curtain hung in secretive folds. Behind it lay music, a story. She'd always loved the moment just before the curtain opened, when she could feel herself sliding into being someone else, into a world of make-believe and adventure.

"Mary?" Roy's voice broke into her thoughts.

"Yes?" She couldn't take her eyes off the curtain.

"You seem impressed."

"I am," she admitted. From the time she could talk, she'd imagined herself in faraway places. Performing had brought those dreams to life a few hours at a time. Looking at the stage, she felt that call with a yearning she'd forgotten.

Gertie touched her arm. "It's even more amazing with an audience."

"I'm sure it is," she murmured.

"There's more," Roy said. "Follow me."

As he led them down the center aisle, she felt as if she were in a trance, caught between a brilliant dream and a drab reality. She knew where Roy was taking them. In a moment they'd walk past the stage. He'd lead them through a hidden door and they'd be in a hallway that led to the place of dreams and make-believe. Just as she expected, Roy opened a concealed door and they emerged into a backstage area full of scenery. Mary smelled paint for the backdrops, sawdust, powder and face paint.

Gertie scampered to a rack holding costumes in an array of colors. "They're beautiful!"

"They're for *Bohemian Girl*." Roy lifted one and offered it to her. "This is for a peasant girl. I believe it's your size, Miss Larue."

Holding the dress to her shoulders, Gertie spun to face a full-length mirror. "Mary, look!"

She blinked and saw herself ten years ago. "You look beautiful."

Roy startled her with a polite hand on her back. "This way," he said, turning her to the stage.

Mary let him guide her across the wooden platform. The curtain blocked her view of the seats, but she could imagine the music and the applause.

"Stay here," he instructed. "And look straight ahead."

He left her alone center-front on the stage. She heard the glide of ropes and the whoosh of velvet as the curtains parted. The air stirred, and she saw seats stretching into the darkness under the balcony, and then up in the balcony almost to the ceiling. She'd never seen any place so glorious.

Roy crossed the stage and stood slightly behind her. "Is it as wonderful as you imagined?"

She couldn't lie. "Yes."

He motioned to Gertie. "Miss Larue, come and join your sister."

Gertie set down the gown and came to stand next to Mary. Excitement rippled off the girl's skin as she took in the velvet seats and the beams of light from the windows.

Roy stayed behind them. "The role of Aline is yours, Mary. There's a role for Gertie, too." He sounded sublime, even generous.

Her sister clutched her arm. "Say yes. It's the answer to everything."

She yearned to accept Roy's offer, but the risk of reigniting the scandal was too great, especially with J.T. in Denver. In order to provide a good life for Gertie and Gus, she had to protect her reputation.

Roy spoke over her shoulder. "Shall we discuss the terms of the contract in my office?"

"Not today." She'd made a promise to J.T., and she'd keep her word. "I'd like an evening to think things over."

Gertie huffed. "But Mary—"

"Shhh." She hated treating her sister like a child, but she was acting like one.

Roy smiled at Gertie like a father. "Your sister needs time, Miss Larue. It's perfectly understandable."

Gertie calmed down instantly. "Yes. Of course."

Mary appreciated Roy's intervention. "Thank you. You've been very understanding."

He smiled. "Whatever you want, Mary. It's yours."

What Mary wanted, Roy couldn't give. She wanted to be free of secrets and scandals. She wanted her brother to speak normally and for Gertie to be patient.

Her sister turned to Roy. "Excuse me, Mr. Desmond. But what time should we come tomorrow?"

"I'll come to the café. We can finalize the arrangements when you're done serving breakfast."

Mary appreciated his thoughtfulness. "I'll give you my answer then."

After exchanging goodbyes, the women left the theater. As they passed the church, Mary looked up at the scaffolding. J.T. must have been looking for her, because he stopped hammering as soon as she came into sight. He tipped his hat, then said something to Gus. Her brother set down the nail bucket and waved, smilingly so wide that his teeth glistened in the sun.

She'd never seen Gus so pleased. Neither had she seen J.T. so determined. Tonight they'd talk about Roy's offer, but Mary knew what she had to do. She couldn't say yes for herself, but she could make Gertie's dream come true. She acknowledged Gus and J.T. with a wave, then turned to her sister. "We might be able to work something out with Mr. Desmond."

Gertie gasped. "Do you mean it?"

"I do, but Roy might not agree with what I have in mind." She prayed silently that Gertie wouldn't press her for details. "I'm done performing. With the café and

Gus, I have no desire to go back to the stage. But you're younger. You're just getting started."

Gertie nodded furiously. "That's right."

"*If* Mr. Desmond agrees to give you a role without me as Arline, I think you should choose a stage name. Gertrude is old-fashioned."

The girl grabbed Mary had hugged her. "I *hate* 'Gertrude'! And 'Gertie' is for a little girl. I want to be Emmeline. That's my middle name…Emmeline Larue!"

Mary shook her head. "Larue confuses people. They'll think you speak French. How about Emmeline Duncan?" Duncan was their mother's maiden name.

Gertie thought for a minute. "I like it, and it would honor mama."

Mary liked it, too. "Then it's settled. I'll speak with Roy tomorrow. If he agrees, you can take a *small* part."

Gertie hugged her hard. "Thank you, Mary. You're the *best!*"

With her secret buried, though not as deeply as she would have liked, Mary walked arm in arm with Gertie to the apartment, where she'd bake a chocolate cake. She'd promised Gus, and she owed J.T. for his concern. She wouldn't let him sway her about Roy, but she'd do him the courtesy of listening.

Chapter Ten

Seated in front of a nearly empty checkerboard, Gus raised his arms in triumph. "King me!"

J.T. had to hand it to the boy. They'd played five cut-throat games of checkers, and Gus had won four of them. With each win, the kid had signaled to Fancy Girl and she'd given a victory bark. J.T. had enjoyed every minute. Grinning, he offered a handshake. "Congratulations. You're good at this."

Gus gripped his fingers hard. "Thanks."

"He's the best," Mary said proudly.

She was standing behind him, drying her hands on a towel that fanned the air with the lingering aroma of chocolate cake. Earlier she'd served fried chicken and potatoes, corn and biscuits as light as the clouds he'd watched all afternoon. High on the scaffolding, he'd enjoyed pounding nails with Gus. They hadn't spoken at all, not because Gus stammered but because they didn't need to talk.

J.T. had enjoyed the quiet, but he'd also liked the chatter at supper. After his run-in with Gertie, he'd expected her to give him a cold shoulder. Instead she'd been friendly. While he played checkers with Gus, Mary and her sister had done the dishes, quietly conspiring in female tones he rarely heard and greatly enjoyed. He hoped the cheerfulness meant that Mary had no intention of arguing with him about Roy. With a little luck, she'd seen the man's true character for herself.

"All right," she said to Gus. "It's bedtime."

"B-but—"

J.T. stood. "Your sister's right, kid."

Satisfied, Gus swept the checkers into a box, said good-night and went down the hall with Fancy at his heels. Gertie had excused herself earlier, leaving J.T. and Mary alone in the front room. When she sat on the divan, he positioned himself next to her but not too close. Once they were done talking about Roy, he hoped to stay awhile longer. While working with Gus, all sorts of thoughts had filled J.T.'s head. He'd had his fill of drifting and killing, and he'd started to wonder.… What would it be like to start a new life?

If anyone could understand, it was Mary. In Kansas she'd been as wild as he'd been, yet now she had a home and a business…and faith, he reminded himself. Of the three changes, the last one surprised him the most. Earlier today he'd considered the odds of a man like himself putting a roof on a church. A year ago, he'd have said they were a million to one. J.T. hadn't thought much about God except to dislike Him, but Mary felt otherwise, and he wanted to understand her.

He leaned back on the divan. "Thanks again for supper. I had a good time."

"I did, too."

He felt at home tonight, something he'd never experienced before, though he'd often visited her hotel suite in Abilene. There she'd had two rooms, a sitting area and her bedroom. The bed had been soft. The divan in the sitting room had been short and stuffed to the point of being uncomfortable. He wasn't uncomfortable now. The divan felt as familiar as his saddle, and the room was pleasantly cluttered with Mary's treasures. He recognized a vase he'd given her in Abilene. She'd filled it with dried sunflowers like the ones they'd seen on that buggy ride to nowhere.

He wished now that the ride had gone somewhere, anywhere, as long as he'd gone there with Mary. He wanted to rekindle that closeness, but first he had to finish with Roy. He draped a boot over his knee. "How did it go this afternoon?"

"Good."

When she took a breath, he got a bad feeling. "You took the role, didn't you?"

"No," she said firmly. "My career's over, but there's a part for Gertie. I'm keeping my promise to hear what you have to say, but I'm inclined to let her give acting a try."

"Mary, no." The evening had been nice…too nice, he realized. Gertie had been on her best behavior, because she wanted something from her sister. Mary had kept the evening light, because she wanted him to accept her decision.

J.T. figured he had double the trouble. He still had to worry about Roy's interest in Mary, and now Roy was using Gertie to manipulate them all. Mentally he kicked himself for not telling her about Roy sooner, but she didn't trust him enough to take his word. He couldn't stand the thought of Mary dealing with Roy. He wanted to block the door with his body, keeping her in this land of checkers, fried chicken and sunflowers dried into a memory.

In a burst of clarity, one like the moment on the roof,

he realized he wanted to be locked in this room with her. The admission startled him in one breath and infuriated him in the next. What did a fool like him have to offer a woman like Mary? She was smart not to trust him, but he knew Roy's intent. He needed to convince her to keep Gertie away from the Newcastle, so he stood and offered his hand. "Let's take a walk."

Her brows lifted. "A walk?"

"Yeah."

"Where to?"

"I don't know," he replied. "But I don't want to have this talk with Gertie's ear pressed to the door."

He'd caught Mary by surprise, and she laughed. "That's exactly where she is."

He kept his hand steady, waiting and hoping, until she clasped his fingers and allowed him to guide her up and off the divan. The touch connected them, not in the past but in the present. J.T. put on his gun belt, then he led Mary to the door, lifted her shawl from a hook and draped it over her shoulders. Other nights came back in a rush of memory, the times he'd walked her to the hotel after the show and they'd kissed…the times he'd followed her upstairs to her suite of rooms.

He couldn't fix the past, but he could protect her from Roy Desmond. Maybe someday she'd trust him again.… Maybe someday she'd let him back into her life.

Mary followed J.T. down the outside stairs, saying nothing because she didn't know what to say. She'd expected a quarrel. Instead he'd swept her into the night for a walk. She needed the air to clear her head, and he'd been right about Gertie eavesdropping. Mary had no intention of going back on her word to Gertie. Roy might say no, but she'd try to get Gertie a role. If she broke her promise to her sister now, the girl would ask too many questions. She loved Gertie and wanted her to be happy.

She doubted strongly that J.T. could say anything that would change her mind. She wasn't completely comfortable with Roy, but she trusted the theater manager more than she trusted J.T., though tonight he'd been wonderful with Gus. He'd boosted her brother's confidence in a dozen small ways.

You carved these animals? They're really good.

You've got a lot of books. You've read 'em all? I wish I'd done that.

By the end of the meal, Gus had been sitting tall and eating enough for two boys his size. J.T. had been just as respectful of Gertie, calling her Miss Larue as he showed Gus how to pull out his sister's chair. The old J.T. had been as approachable as barbed wire. The new one had grinned when a boy beat him at checkers. She wondered if he let Gus win, then decided he hadn't. Gus played a good game, and she'd seen the competitive glint in J.T.'s eyes. He had wanted to win, and he wanted to win now. What the prize was, she didn't know.

When they reached the bottom of the stairs, he pointed to the center of town. "Let's go this way."

She didn't ask him where they were going. She doubted he knew, and she was content to listen to the matching rhythm of their steps. Her problems seemed insignificant beneath a sky full of stars. Unconsciously, she started to hum.

"Is that from Roy's show?" he asked.

"No, it's a hymn."

As she tipped her face in his direction, his lips curled but not into a sneer. Neither was he smiling. He looked befuddled. Turning slightly, he met her gaze. "I guess that's one I haven't heard."

Come to church and I'll sing it for you. The words danced on her tongue, but she bit them back. She didn't want J.T. to be a part of her life, yet how could she not invite him to church? Not only would the refusal be self-serving, but she'd be a hypocrite. Not that it mattered.... He'd surely refuse the invitation. Feeling safe, she looked up at him. "Come to church on Sunday, and I'll sing it for you."

"Let's go right now."

Mary laughed. "You're kidding."

"No, I'm not." He reached for her hand. "I'll show you what Gus and I did today. Besides, the building's a good place to talk about Roy."

His fingers felt warm on hers, strong and tender in the way she remembered. It was also dark, and the boardwalk had as many warped boards as it did flat ones. The silence between them felt gentle, the way it did between old friends who'd talked themselves out, but Mary felt nothing akin to friendship for this man. Her feelings—both sweet and painful—ran too deep. She'd vowed to never trust him again, but she hadn't expected to be having a conversation in a church. As they neared the unfinished building, moonlight turned the raw pine into silver beams. Behind the framework, she saw the stone wall of the Newcastle.

J.T. guided her through the opening left for the door, then indicated the table at the far end of the building. The two chairs had been tucked in place, and a lantern stood waiting to be lit. She didn't know what to think as they walked across the diagonal floor planks. God didn't need walls and a roof to be present, nor did He turn His nose up at men with bad habits and blood on their hands. Mary felt that same compassion for J.T., but she couldn't trust his judgment. At the same time, she trusted God, and somehow He'd brought J.T. to Denver. For what purpose, she didn't know. Nervous, she walked with him through the bar-like shadows formed by the open rafters.

When they stepped beneath the solid portion of the roof—the portion J.T. had hammered into place—he pulled back a chair. "Have a seat."

She dropped down on the chair, watching as he struck a match and lit the lantern. With the light casting his shadow against the wall, he pulled the second chair out from the table and sat facing her. "You're not going to like what I have to say about Roy, but you've got to believe me."

"I said I'd listen." She indicated the empty church. "Here we are."

He sat straight with his hands on his knees, his spine rigid and his eyes as hard as gunmetal. "You know I saw Roy talking to Gertie. She's too young to read a man's signs, but I know what he was up to."

Mary sighed. "I don't think—"

He dug his fingers into his knees. "I'm telling you, Mary, Roy ogled Gertie like a wolf stalking a lamb. If you let her take that role, Roy will pressure you both in all the wrong ways."

Roy had always been polite to her. She knew him. "That's a bit extreme."

"It's not."

"I know you mean well." She spoke quietly to calm him. "But why should I believe you? Roy's a customer—a good one. He's been a friend." She didn't mention that he knew about the miscarriage and the murder trial and that he hadn't shared the information with anyone in Denver.

J.T. looked her in the eye. "I know what I saw. I also know what I heard."

"What?"

"Do you mind if I speak plainly?"

J.T. never asked permission for anything. The respect startled her. "Go ahead."

"After I left you on Sunday I ran into Roy." He told her about going inside the theater and how Roy had asked him to influence her to take the role of Arline. She didn't like Roy's attempt to manipulate her, but she could understand his need to pay off his investors. Unlike J.T., she believed Roy to be a real businessman.

She interrupted him. "I haven't heard anything that makes me worry. He manages a theater. He wanted me to sing—"

"He wants more than that." The words came out in a growl. "He said he *wants* you, and he didn't mean just for the stage."

She'd stopped trusting J.T. two years ago. She saw no reason to start now, especially with such an unseemly observation. "I don't believe you."

"You've *got* to."

"Why should I?"

"Because he told me straight out." He took both her hands in his and held them like he'd never let go. "He looked me in the eye and said, 'If you're done with her, I'll take her for myself.'"

Sam O'Day had made a similar remark when he'd trapped her in the alley. In the days before she'd left Abilene, even men she knew to be honorable had given her disturbing looks. Roy knew the gossip about her, what she'd done. She wanted to deny J.T.'s claim, but she couldn't. How well did she really know Roy? Not as well as she knew J.T. He was suspicious by nature, smelling smoke where there wasn't fire, but he was also a shrewd judge of character. Shaking inside, she pulled out of his grasp and paced to the side of the church closest to the theater. Looking up at the dark windows, she prayed. *Help me, Lord. Should I trust J.T. or not?*

Her heart cried no.

Her common sense said otherwise. He had no reason to lie to her, and deep down she'd been troubled by Roy's attention to Gertie. If there was even a remote chance Roy would use Gertie for improper purposes, Mary couldn't allow it. But the cost… She stared up at the dark theater. If she went back on her word to Gertie, her sister would demand to know why. Just as threatening, Roy could destroy her good name with a single rumor. What would Gus do when other boys called his sister ugly names? A lump pressed into her throat.

"Mary?"

J.T.'s voice came over her shoulder. He was standing behind her, close enough that she could again smell the bay rum that had tickled her nose all evening. She needed to tell him what she'd decided, even thank him for protecting her, but she didn't trust her voice.

Stepping closer, he put his hand on her arm. "There's more."

She shook her head. "I've heard enough."

"Roy killed a saloon girl in Dodge." His fingers tightened. "If he gets near you or Gertie, I'll—"

"Stop!" She couldn't stand another word. "I'll tell Gertie no. I'll never speak to Roy again."

How many times did she have to pay for what she'd done in Abilene? And why did Gertie have to suffer with her? She pressed her hands against her cheeks to hold back a flood of tears, but a sob broke from her throat.

J.T. clasped her elbow. Turning her slowly, he drew

her fully into his arms until she nestled her head in the familiar crook of his neck. Her lips were an inch from tender skin she'd once kissed. She could hear the whisper of his breath, his baritone as he crooned to her. She wanted to hate this man for hurting her, but he knew her in ways no one else did. She'd shared her dreams with him, the shame of growing up poor. He knew how much her career had meant to her. What he hadn't understood was that *he'd* meant more to her than anything.

He bent his neck so that his cheek brushed the top of her head. "It's just not right," he murmured. "I wish…I wish all sorts of things."

For two years she'd lived silently with her shame. Tonight the tears refused to stop. J.T. was smoothing her hair and murmuring about wishes and regrets. When his lips brushed her temple, she felt the tenderness to her toes. She hadn't been held in a very long time. She felt protected, and that made her cry all the more.

"It'll be all right," he murmured. "I won't let anyone hurt you."

The next thing she knew, his mouth was an inch from hers. She expected him to kiss her, but instead he shifted his lips to the shell of her ear. "I've missed you, Mary… so much."

"J.T. I—"

"When I'm with you, I can believe there's good in the world, maybe even some good in me."

Stroking her hair, he tilted his head to match the angle of hers. She knew the look in his eyes, knew the purpose of it and what he wanted. It wasn't just a kiss. He wanted things she had no power to give. He wanted peace. He wanted hope. Only God could meet those needs. She had to stop him from kissing her, but she couldn't find the words, couldn't move her limbs.

In Abilene he'd have taken the kiss without asking. Tonight he stopped an inch from her mouth, waiting for her to signal her willingness. Regardless of her feelings. She had to be wise for them both.

Cupping his jaw, she whispered, "No, J.T. Not again."

Releasing her abruptly, he turned and walked into the shadows. In the dark, he put his hands on his hips, raised his face to the half-finished roof and muttered something not meant for her ears.

With J.T., defeat always turned to anger. She braced herself for it now.

Standing in the dark, beyond the glare of the lamp and Mary's reach, J.T. figured he had a choice. He could let her push him away, or he could fight to win her back. He knew she cared about him. She'd been gentle when she'd cupped his jaw, and even more tender when she'd held him back. She wanted to kiss him, and she didn't kiss a man casually, so what stood between them? Who did he need to fight?

A year ago he'd have waged the battle with Mary. He'd have tempted her until she gave in. Tonight that scheme struck him as wrong, even evil. It was the kind of thing Roy would do. J.T. didn't see the theater manager as a rival. An enemy, yes. But Roy wasn't standing between them in this half-finished church. What stood between them, he realized, was the past. *Who* stood between them was her God. The faith she'd once had in J.T., she now had in someone he couldn't see. A dry laugh scraped his throat. He'd fought a lot of hard men in his time, but he'd never taken on someone invisible.

How did he do battle with this kind of enemy? J.T. didn't know, but for Mary he was willing to find out.

With his jaw tight, he glared at the sky above the unfinished roof and muttered in his head. *If You're hiding up there, show Yourself!*

Nothing happened.

Lightning didn't flash.

No one dropped dead.

But deep in his chest, J.T. felt a pounding he couldn't explain. He'd called out enemies before. Not once had he felt the trembling that plagued him now. He wasn't afraid. He couldn't be, because fear killed men like himself. If a shootist hesitated, he died. Mentally J.T. pulled the quiver into a tautness of mind. To win Mary, he had to learn a whole new game. If he tempted her with kisses, she'd dig in her heels. If he treated her right, she just might trust him again.

He liked the idea, but it came at a cost. Considering her beliefs, treating her right meant marrying her, and marriage meant giving her children. J.T. liked Gus, but squalling babies were another matter. He'd never pictured himself as a father, and he still didn't. When it came to marriage, he had nothing to offer. Mary had been wise to remember his failings before he'd kissed her the way he wanted.

Like the scoundrel he'd been in Abilene, he leaned against a post, crossed his arms and faced her. "Was that, 'No, I'll never kiss you again,' or 'No, but I'll think about it'?"

Instead of getting riled, she looked at him as if he were Gus's age and acting tough. "It wasn't either."

"Then what was it?"

"It was, 'No, but I wish I could.'"

"Oh, yeah?" He'd wanted to sound wicked, but his voice came out hopeful. Embarrassed, he turned his head to the doorway, an opening that provided a way in *and* a way out. He had that choice now with Mary. He could play tough, or he could talk to her like he'd imagined when he was on the roof looking at clouds. When he finally spoke, he was still looking at the door. "I did some thinking today."

"About what?"

"Clouds, mostly." He finally looked at her. "And us. I know I hurt you, Mary. What would it take to earn back your trust?"

"You can't."

He didn't want to believe her. "I've got a long way to go, but I'm hoping you'll give me a chance. I'd like to do something for Gus."

She hesitated. "Like what?"

"A camping trip. We wouldn't be gone long, just four or five days."

She didn't say no right away, but neither did she look eager. "Where would you go?"

"The stream a mile or so past the Slewfoot Mine. It's loaded with trout." If he proved himself with Gus, she would have to admit he'd changed. He still had worries about marriage, but the thought wasn't as awful as it had been two minutes ago. He had to convince her. "Gus is a good kid. Did you see him working today?"

"A little bit."

J.T. smiled at the memory. "He filled the nail bucket so full he needed two hands to carry it. The boy's determined to grow up."

"I know, but he's so young."

"Not that young." J.T. had spent his twelfth birthday stealing food for his brothers. He'd spent his thirteenth hiding on a train bound for St. Louis. He hadn't celebrated since then, though he privately marked each year with amazement that he'd lived so long.

Mary bit her lip. "If I say yes, will you tell me something?"

"Sure."

She gave him a long look that pinned him in place. Whatever she asked, he'd have to be truthful, and she knew how to get to him. She waved her hand to indicate the church. "Why are you here?"

"In Denver?"

"No, *here*." She meant the building. "You don't need the job, and you don't like to work. You don't belong—" she bit her lip, then said, "You've never been to church in your life."

"You were going to say I don't belong here."

She looked at him with sad, guilty eyes, a sign of the chasm between them. Earning her trust would take more than being nice to Gus or warning her about Roy. He needed to understand the woman she'd become.

She looked pained. "You belong here as much as I do. Anyone who comes through that door is welcome."

He smirked. "Not me, apparently."

"No," she said. "You, especially."

She hadn't meant to sound so earnest, but J.T.'s denial had hit a chord. When she'd first come to Swan's Nest, she'd felt unworthy of singing in church. Josh had set her straight, and she wanted to show others the same goodwill. She didn't doubt J.T. belonged under this roof. Whether he belonged back in her life was another matter. She'd realized how much he'd changed when he hadn't kissed her. It seemed that the old J.T. had died. The new one had been conceived six months ago but was yet to be born. She couldn't trust him fully, but neither could she send him away.

He needs You, Lord. What do I do? What do I say?

She didn't have a perfect command of Scripture, but she had a story of her own and she could tell it. They were facing each other in the circle of light. Blinking, she turned down the wick to hide her churned-up feelings. Instead of putting distance between them, the circle tightened like a lasso drawing them together. She felt the rightness of the moment and it made her bold. "I think I know how you feel."

His lips curved into a sneer, but his eyes were bleak. "I doubt it. You've never killed anyone."

"Yes, I have," she reminded him. "I shot Sam O'Day."

The bleakness drained from J.T.'s eyes, making way for annoyance. She'd bested him, and he didn't like it. "Sam doesn't count."

"Why not?"

"It was self-defense."

"That's true," she acknowledged. "But I still watched him die, and I was the cause."

She understood guilt far better than J.T. realized, but not because of Sam O'Day. She'd always wonder if she'd caused the miscarriage by going to the theater instead staying in bed. She considered telling him about the child she'd lost, but she doubted he'd console her. His reaction would likely be relief. She'd never tell J.T. about the baby. It would hurt too much to see his disdain, but he needed to know she understood him. She thought back to shooting Sam and how it had changed her. The baby had changed her more, but remembering Sam served her purpose. "I won't ever forget that night in the alley. I couldn't get away from the talk, so I left."

He said nothing, but she knew he understood. He'd walked away from the Dudley place as surely as she'd left Kansas.

"Leaving Abilene was like jumping off a cliff," she

continued. "I didn't know what would happen. I just knew I couldn't do what I'd always done."

"That's it," he murmured

"I hit the ground at Swan's Nest." She'd been weak and broken, but with time she'd healed. "You jumped off a similar cliff. You're still falling, and you're looking for a branch to grab."

He looked at her a long time. "When did you get so wise?"

"I'm not wise at all." She waved off the compliment. "I'm just someone who jumped off a cliff and found a branch."

She hoped J.T. would grab the same one she had. Her faith sometimes faltered, but the branch wouldn't break. Was he reaching out the way she had? It seemed possible, even likely. They were standing in a half-finished church. He owned a dog, and he'd been generous to Gus. She wanted to encourage him, so she smiled. "I'd be glad for you to take Gus camping."

"He's a good kid."

"The best."

"I'll be careful around him," he said. "He can't talk right, but someday he'll be a good man."

Mary's throat tightened. "There's good in you, too."

"I don't think so."

"I mean it."

She recalled the scar she'd seen on his shoulder, a reminder of the time his brother had cut him because he'd refused to steal. He hadn't had an aversion to stealing, he'd said. He'd been as hungry as they were, but he'd been terrified of getting caught and being separated from them. The confusion of it, the desperation, still put tears in her eyes.

She blinked them back. "I see the good in you, J.T., because God loves people, everyone, even you."

She ambled to the side of building, leaving him in the light while she stood in the shadows. As she expected, his expression turned wry. "Considering my bad habits, that's hard to believe."

She wished she had Josh's command of the Scriptures. She wished she was like the apostle Paul with his education, or Peter, who'd been renamed "The Rock." She supposed she was closest to John in temperament, the apostle who wrote about love. Her good intentions would have to suffice. "This is what I know," she said simply. "God knows about every mistake I've made and every ugly thought I've had. He still loves me."

J.T. huffed. "It can't be that simple."

"It's not," she acknowledged. "I could talk about sin and mercy, but the branch I grabbed was love. He loves you, too. J.T. You've done terrible things. You know it, and you want to make things right. That's the good I see in you."

He shook his head. "You're a fool, Mary. A blessed fool...."

"No, I'm not."

His eyes locked with hers in a dance she recognized from Abilene. He wanted something from her. In Kansas, it had signaled physical desire. Tonight she saw a longing for more than pleasure. He wanted hope. Six months ago he'd started a desperate search. If he looked long enough, he'd find answers...eventually. She couldn't trust him yet, maybe not ever, but she could pray for him. She crossed back to the table and held out her hand. "Let's go. If Gus is awake, you can tell him about the camping trip."

J.T. took her hand. "I'd like to finish the roof. How about next week?"

"That would be fine."

They walked back to her apartment in companionable silence. If anyone could give Gus confidence it was J.T. She trusted him fully with her brother. Whether she could learn to trust J.T. with her heart, and whether J.T. could learn to trust God, remained to be seen. Until then, she'd keep her feelings and her memories tucked safely away.

Chapter Eleven

On Sunday morning, J.T. put on his best clothes and went to church. He wanted to think he'd come to see Mary, but he knew otherwise. Since their talk, he'd felt like a stranger in his own skin. This morning when he'd shaved, he'd seen a man he didn't know anymore. He looked younger, almost happy. He was more excited than Gus about the camping trip, and yesterday he'd caught himself humming "Pop Goes the Weasel" while he pounded nails.

Something crazy was happening to him, and he didn't like it. If he lost his edge, he'd be a dead man. Yesterday on the roof, he'd glared at the clouds and muttered a foul word just to prove he could do it. It had sounded hollow, and he'd felt an emptiness that had nearly knocked him to his knees. He'd muttered a second oath. *If You're real, God, I want to know it.*

Nothing.

Silence.

He'd felt the weight of his guns and made a decision. If God wouldn't show Himself, J.T. would go hunting for Him. That's why he was sitting in Brick's Saloon on Sunday morning, cleaned up and smelling a little too good because he'd come to see Mary, too. He'd arrived early to be sure he got a seat near the back. Fancy Girl lay at his feet, the recipient of a special invitation from Josh. He smiled at the memory of the minister telling him God loved all creatures great and small, and that Fancy would be welcome anytime.

Keeping an eye on the back door, he saw all sorts of folks coming to church. He recognized a couple of men from the building, three ladies who'd brought lunch and Bessie from Swan's Nest. The nurse had come in with another woman, a brunette who had to be her sister. Bessie saw him, waved and took a seat near the front.

Josh came out of a back room and strode to the podium. A fiddle player struck up a melody and the room quieted. J.T. hadn't seen Mary since Wednesday, and he wanted to know what had happened with Gertie and Roy. Gus had been coming with Josh to work on the roof, but J.T. hadn't quizzed him. It would have been unfair to the boy.

With no sign of Mary, his nerves prickled. He was about to leave for the café when Gus, squeaky clean but out of breath, pushed through the doors.

J.T. motioned to him. "Hey, partner."

The boy's face lit up. "C-c-can I sit with you?"

"Sure." J.T. appreciated the company, another sign he wasn't himself.

As Gus joined him, Gertie sauntered in with her nose in the air. Mary rushed in behind her, looking more harried than he'd ever seen her. Gertie slipped into a seat in the corner opposite from him and put on a pout. Mary walked to the front of the church and whispered something to Josh, probably an apology for arriving late. The minister said something back, maybe asking if she needed time to compose herself. When she shook her

head, Josh nodded to the fiddler. The musician raised his
bow high, then brought it down with a slash that began
a storm of beautiful music. J.T. sat riveted, both by the
melody and by Mary. When the sharp notes trickled to
silence, she began to sing.

He didn't pay attention to the words, but the tune
matched the one she'd been humming on Wednesday
night. The music connected him to her, but he didn't see
the Almighty anywhere in the room. Josh was the same
man who'd hired J.T. and got annoyed at crooked nails.
His eyes wandered to Bessie and her sister. They were
singing the words, but they were still just people.

Mary finished the song with a long "Amen." On a
signal from Josh, the congregation rose to its feet. J.T.
stood out of respect for Mary and Josh, not reverence for
God.

"Ladies and gentlemen," Josh said in a full voice.
"Let's pray." The minister thanked God for the glorious
day. J.T. had to agree. The July morning couldn't have
been nicer, but so what? Next Josh prayed for God to
bless his sermon. Fine, J.T. thought. He'd listen, but he
didn't expect much.

After a hearty "Amen," Josh looked up. "Our next
hymn is 'Come Thou Fount of Every Blessing.'"

When the fiddler played a run, Mary took a breath.
In the same instant, she saw J.T. and paused with surprise. He thought of the dream he had, the one where
she was singing on a big stage on a Saturday night—the
dream where she sang just for him. The moment matched
exactly, except they were in a church instead of a theater.
And instead of a flashy dress, she had on the lilac gown
she'd worn last week. She didn't look like a schoolmarm
today, and she no longer seemed harried and worn out.

She couldn't have been more beautiful to him. Just like in his dream, she smiled and began to sing.

J.T. didn't understand the words about streams of mercy. They made no sense at all, but then he heard a voice coming from the seat next to him. It belonged to Gus, and the boy wasn't stammering. J.T. looked at him, amazed at the clear tones. Gus couldn't talk right, but he could sing perfectly. In the boy's eyes, J.T. saw the innocence of a child and the marks of suffering. He saw himself in those depths. He also saw something that scared him half to death. He saw the goodness Mary saw in *him*.

He saw the love of God.

Had the Almighty just shown Himself? It seemed so, but J.T. couldn't believe it. A God with any sense would have been spitting fire at a man like him. He wanted to fight with an enemy. Instead he was looking at Gus with a brotherly love he'd never felt before. The boy needed him, but J.T. needed the boy just as much, maybe more. Gus gave him a purpose, a reason to be an honorable man.

The next words of the hymn made a little more sense. *Jesus sought me when a stranger, Wandering from the fold of God.* J.T. didn't know if he'd wandered from God or not. Could a man wander from someone he'd never known? His mother had owned a Bible and she'd read it, but it had been lost when he and his brothers had been tossed out of their meager apartment. He'd never forget that awful day. A minister with droopy eyes had tried to take J.T. to an orphanage, separating him from his brothers because he'd been the youngest. He'd fought and so had his brothers, though later he'd wondered why.

The stealing had started right away. The fighting got worse and his oldest brother had cut him with a knife.

With the blood running down his scrawny chest, J.T. had made a decision. He'd kill before he'd be killed; he'd hurt others before they hurt him. For close to twenty years he'd lived that way with great success, but today he felt like that boy pinned to the hard ground.

He turned to the front of the room with a scowl. When Mary finished the song, he sat. Josh went to the podium, greeted him with a discreet nod and started talking about love. The minister didn't dwell on the love of a man for a woman or brotherly love. He'd talked about the love that made a man willing to die for others, to make sacrifices and stay decent even when others weren't. Because of his feelings for Mary, J.T. felt the truth of every word.

The truth stopped when Josh got to the part about forgiving his enemies. "We can forgive others because God forgives us," the minister said.

J.T. had no desire to forgive his brothers. Why would he? They'd beaten him black and blue. He refocused in time to hear Josh talk about turning the other cheek. No way on earth would J.T. let someone beat him up, or worse, beat up someone he cared about. Hadn't Josh seen Gus's black eye? Clearly the man didn't know how it felt to be held down and kicked in the ribs. When J.T. had refused to steal, his oldest brother had pressed the knife into his shoulder and twisted it until he screamed.

He'd come to church today to smoke out the Almighty. Instead he'd been introduced to a fool. With his muscles taut, he stopped listening to Josh and stared at Mary, wondering what had happened with Roy and Gertie and what she'd say when he insisted on walking her home. Just as he'd once vowed to hurt others before they hurt him, he made a mental promise to keep Mary and her sister safe from Roy Desmond. If Mary's God didn't want the job, J.T. would gladly take it.

* * *

When she finished the opening hymn, Mary sat in the front row with Adie. Could her life be any more complicated? God had created the world in seven days. J.T. had been in Denver for the same amount of time, and her world had gone to pieces. She and Gertie weren't speaking, and yesterday Caroline had quizzed her about J.T. Mary hadn't given her the details about what had happened in Abilene, but her refusal only added to the air of mystery around him.

Today she expected the talk to get worse. J.T. had come to church looking both handsome and skeptical. At the end of the sermon, Josh would invite everyone to Swan's Nest for supper. If he came, her friends would see them together. Good-natured or not, she dreaded the speculation. To end it, she'd be J.T.'s friend today and nothing more.

Another threat to her secret came from Roy. Three days ago she'd turned down his offer. Instead of accepting her decision graciously, he'd taunted her in a sly tone. Predictably, Gertie had been furious.

But why! You said—

I know what I said. I made a mistake. I got carried away. You're too young.

It's because of what J. T. Quinn said, isn't it? Who is he, anyway? He's practically a criminal!

To her shame, Mary had said nothing in J.T.'s defense. He'd acted honorably, but she couldn't defend him to Gertie. Her sister would ask too many questions…questions Mary didn't want to answer. She desperately wanted to put Gertie on the next train to New York, so yesterday she'd gone to the bank to borrow money. The banker had turned her down, kindly suggesting that patience was a better investment. If only Gertie had agreed. The girl hadn't spoken to Mary in two days. She'd come to church this morning, but only because Gus had asked.

Mary tried to focus on the sermon just as Josh closed his Bible. As expected he invited everyone to Swan's Nest, then motioned for Mary to come forward for the closing hymn. She sang the same song every week, so the words came easily even though her thoughts remained scattered. After the last note, the crowd broke apart. As men put back the chairs, the women drifted to the refreshment table.

Mary spotted J.T. and Gus at the back of the room. The boy looked happy, but the man had an angry gleam in his eyes. Gertie was heading for the door, and she looked smug. Mary couldn't stop her sister, so she approached J.T. and Gus.

J.T. scowled at her, but Gus smiled. "H-h-h-i!"

"Hi, there," she replied. His hair had fallen in his eyes. She itched to smooth it back but stopped herself. J.T. was right. Gus needed to grow up.

"W-watch this." He gave Fancy the signal to sit. When the dog obeyed, he fed her a cookie.

Mary smiled at J.T. Instead of enjoying his dog's talent, he looked ready to kick a chair across the room. "You don't look happy," she said mildly.

"I'm not."

He was glowering when Caroline approached. "I haven't officially met Mr. Quinn," she said to Mary.

She did *not* want Caroline asking questions *or* playing matchmaker. "J.T., this is Miss Caroline Bradley. Caroline, this is Mr. J. T. Quinn."

J.T. lost the scowl. "It's a pleasure to meet you, Miss Bradley."

"Call me Caroline. I hope you're coming for supper."

J.T. looked peeved. "I don't think so."

"Jake plays a mean jig," Caroline said with a teasing air. "You should see Mary dance."

"I've had the pleasure," he replied. "We were acquainted in Abilene."

Mary was the actress, but J.T. delivered the explanation of their past in a perfectly casual tone.

Caroline smiled at him. "I'd love to hear more about those days. Mary has such a beautiful voice. I bet she was famous."

Infamous had been more like it. She traded a look with J.T., one that would have seemed bland to an observer but held all the ties of the past. *Please don't reveal anything. Please keep quiet.*

Looking almost bored, he turned to Caroline. "Mary had quite a career. But like she said, it was a long time ago."

Caroline wasn't appeased. "How did you two meet?"

Annoyed, Mary cut in. "We met at the theater. That's all there is to it."

"That's right," J.T. said mildly.

Bessie approached from the side. "Good morning, Mr. Quinn. I hope you'll join us for supper this afternoon."

He shook his head. "I don't think—"

Gus interrupted. "P-p-lease, J.T.? It'll be f-fun."

A week ago her brother had been silent and sullen. Today he had spunk. J.T. shot her a look. He had no desire to go to supper, and he knew his presence would raise questions for her, but he also wanted to please Gus. To keep the talk to a minimum, they needed to appear to be friends. Mary offered a warm smile. "You're more than welcome, J.T."

"All right," he said. "I accept."

Bessie, always a nurse, tipped up Gus's chin and looked at his black eye. "You've got quite a shiner."

"Yeah."

"How's the rest of you?"

"G-g-good." He wanted to say more but couldn't.

J.T. filled in. "Gus is working with me on the new church."

When Mary smiled her appreciation at J.T., Caroline saw and got a mischievous look. The woman was an unstoppable matchmaker. Mary could have been angry, but her heart ached for her friend. Of the five women from Swan's Nest, Caroline had been the most eager to have a family of her own. A young widow, she'd suffered in ways no one else had. No matter what Caroline did, Mary loved her.

Bessie indicated three men leaning against the wall. "I believe those gentlemen need refreshments, Caroline. Shall we?"

"I—I—I want more, too," Gus added.

"Then let's get you some." Caroline motioned to Gus, and the three of them left. Fancy stayed with J.T.

Frowning, he scratched the dog's ears. "Sorry about going to supper. I hope it's not awkward for you."

"We can handle it." *We.* When had they gone from enemies to allies? Mary didn't know, but she appreciated his consideration.

Still looking down, he spoke to his dog. "What do you say, Fancy? Can we handle supper with church folk?"

When the dog wagged her tail, J.T. chuckled. "I guess so." He looked back at Mary. "I'll do my best to keep talk away from Abilene, but Caroline's determined to find out what happened between us."

"I know." She grimaced. "If you want to back out, I'll make excuses for you."

"Not a chance," he muttered. "Gus needs to know a man keeps his word." His tone implied that *she* needed to know he'd keep *his*.

Her brother came back with more cookies. "Wh-where's Gertie?"

"She went home."

He turned to J.T. "My s-s-sister's mad."

"Yeah, I saw."

Mary couldn't go into details with Gus present, but J.T. deserved to know she'd taken his advice. "I told Roy no for both of us."

"I want to hear about it," he said casually. "I'll walk you home."

She didn't want to be seen leaving with him. "I wish I could say yes, but—" she indicated the crowd in the room "—well, you know."

"Yeah. I understand." He sounded snide. "I'll go with Gus. You can deal with Gertie."

"That would be nice."

The boy grinned. "We can teach Fancy a new trick."

Had she imagined Gus's smooth speech, or had the stammering eased? J.T. looked at him with the same question, then he turned to her. "I'll see you in a while. Be ready, because I want answers."

"You'll get them."

Somehow she had the feeling he was talking about more than her dealings with Roy. He'd come to church today, something she'd never expected. He'd also been gracious to her friends and careful with the past. It was getting harder not to trust this man. With a final nod, she left him and went home to smooth the waters with her sister.

Chapter Twelve

J.T. watched Mary pass through the door, silently wishing her luck as she went to check on her sister. He'd seen the girl leave the church, and he'd been struck by the cocky tilt of her chin. Gertie had Mary's fire but none of her experience. She'd be easy prey for Roy, a thought that filled J.T. with familiar bitterness. He didn't want Gertie or anyone else to have scars like his own.

It was a long walk to Swan's Nest, so he decided to fetch his horse from the livery and ride double with Gus. After he spoke with Mary about Roy, he'd get ready for the camping trip. Yesterday he'd finished the roof except for the bell tower, which required a batch of smaller shingles that had to be cut. Josh had been pleased to hear about the trip with Gus and had offered to loan them fishing poles.

Until this morning, J.T. had liked the minister, even respected him. While working on the church, Josh was just…Josh. He laughed when other men laughed, and he sympathized with their troubles. That man had preached today, and he'd thrown down some hard words. Halfway through the sermon, J.T. had been so angry he'd stopped listening. "Come on," he said to Gus. "Let's get out of here."

They were close to the door when Josh blocked their path. "Good to see you, J.T."

J.T. scowled. "Reverend Blue."

Josh's lips tipped up. "I wear a preacher's collar for church, but that's the only difference from the rest of the week. I'm still Josh. Do you have a minute?"

"Nope." He turned to leave, but the minister gripped his arm. No one stopped J.T. from leaving, and he indicated that fact to the good Reverend Blue with a steely look. "What do you want?"

Josh released his arm. "A minute of your time."

"What for?"

"You started snarling halfway through the sermon. I want to know why."

J.T. put a hand over his heart. "You gave a *fine* sermon, reverend. It was downright glorious, chock-full of sweetness and light. I was blessed indeed to hear you talk about turning the other cheek."

Josh raised one eyebrow. "You're good at sarcasm."

J.T. said nothing.

"There's more to this message," Josh said in a firm tone. "Next Sunday we're going to talk about when it's right to fight. I suspect you know something about that."

"I do."

"Good," he said. "Come back. You can tell me if I'm getting it right."

The minister was toying with him. Fine. If Josh wanted to argue, J.T. would give him an earful at Swan's Nest.

As the man stepped aside, J.T. muttered, "See you later," and headed for the door. Gus, imitating him, repeated his words and they left, walking in silence until they got to the livery. The old man running the place saddled J.T.'s horse, brought it out and accepted a tip. J.T. swung into the saddle and pulled Gus up behind him. He could feel the buckskin prancing as they passed the alley where Gus had been attacked.

The boy tensed. "L-l-ook!"

Turning, J.T. saw the three boys who'd beaten Gus, no doubt lying in wait for him. He reined the buckskin to a halt. "What do you want to do, kid?"

"I w-w-want them d-d-dead!"

J.T. knew the feeling. He also wanted Gus to become a far better man than himself. He thought of Josh's sermon about cheek-turning and his mention of a time to fight. How did a man put the pieces together? J.T. didn't know, but he knew one thing with certainty. He didn't want Gus to be like him. Before he influenced the boy for the worse, he needed to puzzle out what he'd heard today.

He spoke more to himself than Gus. "Maybe later, kid."

"Yeah, later."

As they rode past the alley, J.T. felt none of the rage that should have spurred him on. What kind of mess had he gotten himself into? Not only had he given up liquor and cards, he'd lost some of his meanness. A month ago he'd have bullied the bullies with pleasure. Today the rage was a mountain in the distance, no less real than the dirt below his feet but somehow less personal. The thought made him ornery. By the time they arrived at Swan's Nest, he wanted to fight someone. Gus slid off the buckskin first, followed by J.T., who tied his horse to a fence. His gaze skipped the front porch and went to a garden where he heard conversation.

Gus scampered down a narrow path. "Th-this way."

J.T. followed him past a vegetable garden, then to a cut in a hedge of blooming rosebushes. The sweet fragrance filled his nose, but he refused to enjoy it. Gus indicated the house. "I—I have to h-help carry food."

"Go on ahead," J.T. replied.

With Fancy Girl at his side, he looked around the garden. Tables and chairs had been set up, but what caught his eye was a white marble bench. It reminded him of the gravestones he'd seen in a New York cemetery, not the paupers' field where his mother had been laid to rest but the church cemetery two blocks away. Covered in lush grass, it had been surrounded by a black iron fence two feet taller than he'd been. Behind it he'd seen markers the color of the bench in this garden. When he'd asked why his mama couldn't have a nicer resting place, the minister who'd buried her told him there were different places for rich people.

That day J.T. decided that the Almighty didn't deserve respect. If his mother wasn't welcome in that sacred place, he wanted nothing to do with the God who owned it. He still felt that way. Looking at the bench in Josh's garden, he saw swirls of gold in the white marble. Superior and unwelcoming, the stone gleamed in the heat of the day.

Feeling smug, he walked to the bench and sat on it. As Fancy laid at his feet, the heat of the stone went through his trousers. It was a bit too hot, but he stubbornly stayed in place. No one, not God or the sun, was going to tell him where to sit. Hunkering forward, he looked at the people chattering to each other. Josh had spotted him and was coming at him with a glass of lemonade.

The preacher bit off a grin. "Comfortable?"

"More or less."

"That bench gets a tad hot this time of day." He held out the dripping glass. "Have some."

The lemonade looked delicious, but J.T. hesitated. He didn't want to talk to Josh, not with his backside on fire. He wished he hadn't sat down. He wished other things, too—that Josh hadn't talked about turning the other cheek, and that his mother had been buried in a cemetery with an uncomfortable bench. He hadn't been expecting such thoughts. They'd come from nowhere, but he couldn't shake the old anger, or the picture of that droopy-eyed minister telling him the nice cemetery was for rich folks.

He was thirsty, so he accepted the glass with a snide look. "Hoop-di-doo. Christian charity." He raised the lemonade in a mock toast. "Thanks, preacher-man."

Josh had the nerve to look pleased. "The sermon got to you, didn't it?"

He could say no and hide behind the lie, or he could admit that the sermon had upset him. Neither choice appealed to him.

Josh stepped slightly to the side, casting a shadow across J.T.'s face. Memories spun through his mind, joining with fragments of the past week to create a disjointed picture of his entire life. He thought of the good times with Mary and then about the men he'd killed. He thought of Gus, then about Fancy Girl and playing fetch with a stick, and how he used to wonder if she'd really come back. When he thought of his mother's last breath, and then his brothers holding him down and the knife cutting his flesh, his thoughts turned black.

He shoved to his feet. With his hands dangling as if ready to draw, he squared off with Josh. "Tell me, preacher-man. Why all this?" He waved his arm as if swatting away his life. "Why can't Gus talk? Why do mothers get sick and die, and why do brothers hurt each other?"

Sadness filled the minister's eyes, but they were still blue like the sky. J.T. didn't usually notice such things, but he felt as if the sky were falling down around him.

Josh spoke in a hush. "You've seen a lot of life."

"You bet I have," he said, dragging out the words. "I've seen way too much to believe in turning the other cheek."

"I know."

"No, you don't." He was close to shouting. He never shouted, but he couldn't stop his voice from rising. "Tell me, preacher-man. Have you been pinned like a bug on your back? Maybe shot or cut with a knife?"

"No knives," Josh acknowledged. "But I've been shot and beat up."

The answer caught J.T. off guard. He thought of Gus wanting to kill the boys who'd hurt him. For Gus's sake, he'd give the preacher a chance. "What did you do?"

"I protected Adie." He stared hard at J.T. "I'll choose talking over fighting every time I have a choice. But if a woman's being hurt, or a child, I'm going to protect that person any way I can. If it means inflicting a bit of pain, I'll do it. If it means dying to save them, I'm willing."

J.T. felt the same way about Mary.

The minister's eyes turned to blue fire. "It's a choice a man makes on the fly. I've made it. You have, too. Don't think God doesn't understand. He knows more about justice and suffering than you or I ever will."

J.T. didn't know what to make of Josh's little speech, especially the mention of justice. J.T. survived by selling his gun. That didn't strike him as especially wrong, but his feelings about it did. He'd enjoyed every battle, every bullet that had drawn blood.

The minister removed a chapbook from his coat pocket and handed it to him. "Here."

J.T. took it and looked at the cover. He saw a picture of a lamb and a title he didn't recognize. "What is it?"

"The Gospel of John. It's a piece of the Bible."

J.T. didn't want it, but he was tired of arguing. Scowling, he tucked it inside his vest next to the Deringer he kept hidden.

A little girl called in their direction. "Pastor Josh! Miss Adie wants you."

"I better get moving." The minister shook his head as if he were henpecked, but J.T. saw through him. Josh loved being needed by his wife. J.T. wanted Mary to need *him* the same way. He expected her any minute, so he kept his eye on the path from the street. Fancy Girl lay at his feet asleep in the shade of the bench. She'd been napping a lot lately, and he was beginning to think they were both getting soft.

Brick walked over and asked how the roof was coming along. J.T. didn't mind chatting with the man, and it helped to pass the time. When the barkeep moved on, Caroline brought him another glass of lemonade and asked if he'd be staying for the fiddle music. J.T. accepted the tea to be polite, but he had no desire to stick around for the music. He wanted to speak to Mary and leave.

Another five minutes passed. Adie and Caroline were bringing food out to the tables, trading whispers and glancing at him until Adie finally walked up to him. They hadn't been officially introduced, so she offered her hand. "I'm Adie Blue, Josh's wife."

"Yes, ma'am," he replied. "I'm J. T. Quinn, Mary's friend."

"Is she here?"

"No, but I'm expecting her."

"Me, too." Adie glanced around the garden. "It's not like her to be late. Would you mind checking the café?"

"I'll go right now." He'd had the same thought. "Will you tell Gus?"

"Sure."

He wasn't coming back, so he woke up Fancy. "Come on, girl."

She jolted awake and followed him to his horse. Eager to be gone, he rode at a gallop until he neared the train depot. Wagons and carriages slowed him down, but his thoughts were running at full speed. Something had kept Mary away from Swan's Nest. It probably involved Gertie, which meant the trouble harkened back to Roy.

J.T. turned on the street where the café sat like a buttercup in row of weeds. Leaping off his horse, he saw that the café windows were dark, so he took the stairs to the apartment two at a time. At the top, he heard Mary weeping. He didn't bother to knock or call her name. He walked straight into the apartment, where he saw her huddled on the divan. Before she could protest, he pulled her into his arms and did what he should have done in Abilene. He held her like he'd never let her go. "Tell me what you need," he crooned. "Whatever it is, I'll find a way."

Chapter Thirteen

She needed a handkerchief, but she doubted J.T. had one. She tried to lift her head to say so, but he held her close, smoothing her hair with the touch she'd enjoyed in Abilene. How could a man capable of such violence be so tender? Through her tears, she saw Fancy Girl drop down in a beam of sunlight and stretch, a reminder that J.T. had changed from the hard man who'd left her.

As her tears dampened his shirt, she smelled bay rum and cotton made warm from his skin. When he'd held her in Abilene, she'd inhaled deeply and enjoyed the scent of him. Today it sobered her and she pulled back, wiping her eyes on her sleeve. She couldn't let him hold her like this. She trusted him with Gus, but her feelings were another matter. If she lost her heart to him, she'd have more heartache than she did right now, which was plenty in light of Gertie's letter. The two-page missive was on the table.

J.T. reached inside his vest and pulled out a bandanna. "Here you go, honey."

She took it and dabbed at her eyes, the endearment echoing in her mind. "You shouldn't call me that."

"I know," he said quietly. "It just slipped out."

She couldn't hold it against him, not when she'd enjoyed hearing it. Deep down, she wanted to hear the sweet name again. It was a foolish notion considering the past, but she couldn't deny the pleasure of being in his arms. They fit well together. They always had.

As he gauged her reaction, she felt the dampness of her tears. Gertie's letter had filled her with guilt, and every regret had come out in a flood. She wished she'd never been with J.T.… She wished she'd told Gertie everything he'd revealed about Roy. But the cost…Gertie would demand to know why Mary believed him, and she'd have to tell her sister everything. She'd have done it in an instant to protect Gertie, but the shame had silenced her. So did the fear that she'd lose Gertie's respect and what little influence she had. She also had to worry about Gus. If Mary told Gertie the truth and Gertie shared the secret with Katrina or anyone else, the gossip would burn like wildfire. Mary's good name would be ruined in Denver, and Gus would be the brother of a scarlet woman.

J.T. studied her as if she'd been injured. "You don't cry easily. What happened?"

"It's Gertie." She handed him the letter.

He took it and shifted forward, holding the pages with both hands. As he read, she recalled walking into her apartment. She'd felt the stillness, gone to the bedroom and flung open the wardrobe. Her own dresses had been untouched, but Gertie's side had been empty. Mary had found the letter on her pillow and read it. Seated next to J.T., she skimmed it again.

Mary,
Forgive me, dear sister. After all you've done for me, a letter is a cowardly way to tell you what I've decided. I should tell you to your face, I know, but

I can't bear to see the disappointment in your eyes. Neither do I want you working your fingers to the bone so I can go to New York, especially when it's not necessary.

Something wonderful happened. I auditioned for the role of Arline and I got it. Roy says I sound just like you. That's high praise indeed. He made it clear you were his first choice, that I'd be your understudy if you changed your mind, but he has high hopes for me. He knows so much about the theater. I'm sure I can learn from him as surely as I could have learned in New York.

I love you, Mary. But I have to take this opportunity. Katrina has invited me to live with her. I hope you and I can be friends.

Your sister,

Gertie

P.S. I'd be honored if you'd come to opening night.

Mary finished reading and looked away. J.T. set the letter on the table. "Roy's using her to get to you."

A shiver rippled down her spine. "I can't sit here and do nothing. Maybe I should take the role." The scandal was likely to find her, but she could keep an eye on Gertie.

"Don't do it," J.T. said, bossing her.

She didn't like his tone. "You don't have the right to give me orders."

"Maybe not, but I'm going to anyway."

"That's ridiculous!"

"It's smart. If you give Roy what he wants, he'll want more. Don't think for a minute he'll leave Gertie alone. He'll use her to manipulate you. Mark my words."

He'd spoken like the cold, calculating man who hired out his gun for money. "I don't want to be around Roy, but I have to find a way to protect Gertie."

"I'll talk to her."

"You can't." Gertie would ask questions. "I don't want her to know about us. She'll tell Katrina everything." And Katrina would tell her customers.

"That's a fact." He looked into Mary's eyes. "I failed you in Abilene. I won't do it again. We'll deal with this together."

She felt protected, but J.T.'s presence would throw kerosene on even a hint of the old rumors. Neither could she risk J.T. learning about the baby and the miscarriage. "I appreciate the thought, but I know Gertie better than you do."

"And I know Roy," he countered. "I won't leave you, Mary. Not with your sister acting crazy. Roy's going to use her as bait. I'm sorry to disappoint Gus, but we won't be going on that camping trip. I need to stay in town."

"That's not necessary." She hated to let her brother down, but mostly she wanted J.T. to be out of the way in case she changed her mind about confiding in Gertie. "Gus is excited."

"He'll understand."

"Yes, but it's not fair." How did she balance Gus's needs with Gertie's? And what about J.T.? She suspected the camping trip meant as much to him as it did to her brother.

Mary faced him. "Do you think Gertie's in danger right now?"

"Not yet." He sounded businesslike. "As long as she's useful, he won't harm her."

"That's not much of a comfort, but I want you to go with Gus."

He thought for a minute. "All right, I'll take him. I don't like Gertie being around Roy, but she might grow up a little. Maybe she'll decide going to New York is best."

"That would be wonderful, but I don't have enough money to send her yet."

"How much do you need?"

"Fifteen hundred dollars." The amount would cover train fare, several months of living expenses, fashionable clothing for Gertie and something for Maude. Mary had some money saved, but it wasn't nearly enough.

J.T. lifted her hand in his and squeezed. "I've got five hundred dollars. It's not enough, but it's yours."

The gesture touched her to the core. "I can't take your money."

"Why not?"

"Because it wouldn't be right."

Suddenly tense, he loosened his grip on her hand, paced to the window and stood with his back to her and his arms crossed as he looked out the glass. When he turned around, his eyes were like blue stones. "So my money's not good enough for you. It's tainted, and so am I. Is that it?"

"Tainted?"

"Yeah." He smirked. "We both know how I earned it."

Mary finally understood. By rejecting J.T.'s money, in his mind she was rejecting *him*. "That's not it." She stood and went to his side. "If I worried about how my customers earned a living, I'd have to quiz each one at the door. If you feel bad about the gambling, give the money to charity."

"I do feel bad," he said quietly. "I want to give it to *you*."

Her heart stretched with each beat, making room for this man who failed her but wanted to make things right. She couldn't change the past, but she could respect his effort to be a good man. "Do you mean it?"

"I do."

"In that case," she said. "I accept."

He took her hand again and kissed her knuckles. "I'll find a way to get Gertie to New York before Roy does any real damage. I just need some time."

She knew how J.T. made a living. Worry wrinkled her brow. "Time for what?"

"To earn the rest of that fifteen hundred dollars."

She held his hand tight. "Promise me something."

"What?"

"That you won't go gambling for any more of it. That's money I won't take."

He squeezed her hand in reply, but he didn't make the promise. Did she trust him, or should she pressure him to give his word? She couldn't do either, and she wouldn't breathe a hint of his gift to Gertie. J.T. had made a rash promise, and she didn't want her sister to be disappointed if he failed to keep it. The possibility—even the likelihood—of J.T. going back to his old ways had to be considered. Bristling, she went to the divan and sat. Gertie's letter lay neatly on the table, a testament to her sister's naiveté and her own back in Abilene. "I wish Gertie could see what Roy's doing."

"So do I."

She barely heard him. "She's going to make the same mistakes I did. She'll wear costumes that reveal too much, and then she'll wear costumes that reveal more. Men will look at her, and she'll feel beautiful. She'll think she's in love, and then she'll—she'll—" She shook her head to chase away the shame.

"Mary, don't."

Silhouetted by harsh light, he stood tall and bossy and as handsome as ever. "Don't what?" she cried. "Don't remember what *I* did?"

"Don't blame yourself for Gertie's choices." He paused. "Or for what *I* took from you. You were innocent. I wasn't."

She couldn't hear this, not now. "It's over, J.T. *Over.* I'm forgiven. I forgive you. That's enough."

"Not for me."

"It should be," she said angrily. "We sinned. I regret it. Apparently so do you."

"I do." He paced across the room and stood in front of her. "I pressured you. It was gentle, but it was still wrong."

She'd given herself to him freely, but he was right. She'd been naive. She hadn't expected to conceive, and she wondered now what he'd say if she told him about the miscarriage. She didn't know, and she was afraid to find out. Hurting for them both, she reached for his hand. "We can't change the past, but we can put it behind us."

He looked at their fingers laced in a pledge of sorts. "Do you really believe that?"

"I do."

He shook his head. "I wish I could."

"You can," she said gently. "It's a choice."

"What is?"

"Starting over."

"Not for me." He looked into her eyes with a bleakness she'd hadn't seen in Abilene, then he released her hand. "Do you really think I can hang up my guns? That I can just *decide* to be someone new?"

"I did," she said. "You're situation is more complicated, but no one knows what tomorrow holds."

"That's a fact." He looked around the room, taking in the trinkets of her life both past and present. His eyes lingered on a vase she'd brought from Abilene, then he studied the animals Gus had carved and an embroidered sampler of a Bible verse. It had been a gift from Josh and Adie. Without her faith, her family and her friends, her apartment would have been a very different place, and J.T. knew it.

She'd given him all she had, so she held out her hand. "Let's go to Swan's Nest."

He hesitated, then clasped her fingers. "I was going to skip supper, but I'm feeling hungry after all."

As he helped her off the divan, Mary noticed Fancy Girl lying on her side in the sun. Her belly was round and firm, and…moving.

J.T. looked at the dog with affection. "I've been in town too long. She's getting fat and lazy."

Mary touched his arm. "I don't think that's it."

He watched Fancy Girl, scowling until her tummy did a little roll. He looked closer, then his eyes widened. "Well, I'll be. She's having puppies." He walked to the dog's side, dropped to a crouch and put his hand on her belly. Mary stood watching, feeling the warmth along with him, then the beginning of new life when a puppy moved and a smile spread across his face. She'd seen J.T. smile before, but it had been nothing like the one she saw now. It came from the inside, some place hidden but full of life.

He pushed to his feet, then looked at her with awe. "I've never felt anything like that."

"It's amazing, isn't it."

"Yeah." He chuckled. "I wonder when it'll happen."

"I'd guess a week or two." She'd grown up around farm animals.

J.T. rubbed his neck. "Will she be all right with Gus and me on this trip?"

"I think so."

He blew out a breath. "If that doesn't beat all. My dog having puppies… Can Gus keep one?"

She felt rosy inside. "We'd both like that."

J.T. clicked his tongue to the dog. Fancy lumbered to her feet, and the three of them left the apartment. Mary saw his horse in front of the café. "I don't want Gus or Adie to worry. Why don't you ride ahead?"

He gave her a look that bordered on scathing. "There's no way I'm leaving without you. We'll both walk."

"That's silly."

His eyes flared with a spark she knew well. "Are you feeling a tad bit bold?"

"Why are you asking?"

"You can ride with me. We'll take a back street so no one sees your petticoats."

She hoisted her lilac skirt above her ankles, put her foot in the stirrup and pulled herself into the saddle. "Hurry up," she teased.

He untied the reins, climbed up behind her and reached around her waist. "How fast do you want to go?"

In Abilene she'd trusted him to lead, and they'd galloped down long and twisting trails to nowhere. Today the path would lead to Swan's Nest, but they could take the long way or a slower one. "You decide," she said, feeling wistful.

He kept the buckskin at a walk until they turned the corner that led to the railroad tracks and a back way to the mansion. With the road empty, he eased the horse into a lope that wouldn't strain Fancy Girl. When they arrived at Swan's Nest, he slid off the buckskin and lifted her out of the saddle. She landed facing him with her hands on his shoulders. The scent of bay rum tickled her nose, and laughter from the garden filled her ears. Rising to her toes, she kissed his cheek.

His gaze hardened, but in a good way. "What was that for?"

"For everything," she said. "For Gus. For Gertie…"

He held her a bit tighter. "I'm watching out for them. I'm keeping an eye on you, too."

A week ago she had given J.T. the cold shoulder. Today she wanted—needed—to trust him. If he hadn't come to Denver, she might have stepped into Roy's trap. Not only did her siblings need this man's influence, but she felt the stirrings of the old attraction. She wanted to hold him close. She yearned to comfort him and lean on him, but she knew how quickly he could disappoint her. She stepped out of his grasp. "Let's find Gus."

Side by side they walked into the garden with Fancy at J.T.'s side. They found Gus finishing his supper and told him about the puppies.

"C-c-can I keep one?"

J.T. grinned. "You get first choice."

Mary left the two of them talking about dogs and camping while she searched for Adie. She found her friend in the house, putting Stephen down for a nap in the nursery. When the boy settled, Adie led Mary to the bedroom she shared with Josh. There she sat on the settee while Mary swayed in an old rocking chair, telling Adie about J.T.'s talk with Roy, Roy's insistence she play Arline and his influence on Gertie.

"I'm terrified for her," Mary finished. "She has no idea what she's doing."

"No, she doesn't." Adie looked peeved. "We want Gertie to come home, but you can't force her."

Mary agreed. "She'd run away again."

"Have you considered talking to her plainly?" Adie meant about the scandal.

"I think about it all the time, but I can't trust her to keep it to herself. And I'm ashamed. I want to be a good example for her. What will she think if she knows the things I've done?"

"It's a tough choice, but one you're going to have to make." Adie straightened a pillow on the bench. "Whatever you decide, Gertie's not the only person you have to worry about."

"There's always Gus—"

"I'm not talking about your brother." She nudged the pillow again. "I want to hear about that handsome man who's obviously in love with you."

"Adie!"

"Well, he is," she said plainly. "Are you in love with him?"

Mary shook her head. "Absolutely not."

"I saw you riding with him." Adie didn't have Caroline's matchmaking instincts, but she could separate truth from wishful thinking with a shrewdness that came from experience. "You looked happy about it, too."

"I was, but I don't want to be. He hurt me terribly. I can't trust him."

"You're trusting him with Gus and Gertie."

"That's different."

"It's also a start," Adie said quietly.

"I will *not* fall in love!" Mary rocked harder in the chair. "Not with J.T. or any other man."

"I said the same thing a year ago. So did Pearl Oliver, and look at her now."

"That's different."

"Is it?" Adie asked. "Do you really think you can choose whom you love?"

Mary wanted to say yes, but she couldn't deny the stirring in her heart. "I don't know."

"God isn't blind to what's happening between you two."

"I don't want *anything* to happen," she insisted. "I don't trust him. Besides, he's not a Christian."

"Neither was I before I met Josh." Adie looked wistful. "He loved me anyway…as a friend."

A lump pushed into Mary's throat. The thought of trusting J.T. even as a friend terrified her. So did the sight of a baby blanket lying haphazardly on the settee and the glide of the chair where Adie rocked her son to sleep. She couldn't love J.T. until she trusted him, and she couldn't fully trust him until she told him her secret. She stared out the open window, listening to the chirp of a sparrow. "It's not that simple."

"Why not?"

The words spilled out before she could stop them. "I was with child when J.T. left me. I lost it."

"I'm so sorry." Adie reached for her hand. "Does he know?"

"No, and I can't tell him. He'd say something mean, and I'd hurt all over again."

"He might surprise you."

He already had. What he'd done for Gus had left her in awe, and he'd been smart about Gertie. Mary knew how to cope with hurt feelings. J.T.'s good intentions unnerved her.

"Pray about it," Adie advised.

Mary didn't want to even *think* about it, but she had to be willing. "I'll try."

"That's enough."

Mary could have stayed in the quiet room for hours, but Gus and J.T. would be looking for her. "We should go back."

The women returned to the garden, where Mary found J.T. seated with Bessie and Caroline, polishing off a meal. The next two hours passed in a blur. She expected him to be remote, but instead he entertained her friends with stories of his travels. He'd been all over the West, everywhere from Texas to Montana, and he'd seen everything from a line of twisters eating up the prairie to a cattle drive bigger than Rhode Island.

Near the end of the afternoon, Caroline and Jake the fiddler coaxed Mary into singing some old favorites. She had a grand time, but the real stars of the day were Gus and Fancy Girl. As the boy showed off her tricks with hand signals, Mary couldn't decide who looked more proud—Gus or J.T.

The last surprise came as they stood to leave. When Josh offered to stable J.T.'s horses at Swan's Nest, J.T. agreed and thanked him. Not once in Abilene had the man accepted a favor from anyone.

They said their goodbyes, then she and J.T. headed down the street, with Gus and Fancy Girl walking several feet ahead of them. If they'd been in Abilene, she'd have been expecting a kiss. She felt the anticipation now, and it was pleasant. She couldn't trust J.T. with her heart, but did the battle have to be won before she kissed him? Common sense told her yes, but he deserved to know she appreciated the changes in him.

When they reached the café, Gus was waiting on the third step. She reached in her pocket and handed him the key. "Go on up. I'll be right behind you."

He hugged Fancy Girl so hard that Mary thought the

dog would pop. J.T. watched with a smile. "Hey, girl. Kiss goodnight."

He'd spoken to the dog, but his eyes were on her as Fancy licked Gus's face with abandon.

"Good night, Fancy," Gus said easily.

J.T. offered his hand to the boy and they shook. "Get some sleep, partner. We're leaving early."

The boy raced up the steps, leaving her alone with this man who confused her and dusk falling like a curtain. She knew J.T.'s ways. If she stayed, he'd kiss her. With streaks of pink coloring the horizon, a kiss seemed like a precious gift, a reminder that love trumped a man's mistakes. She couldn't trust J.T. completely, but he needed to know people cared about him. Feeling shy, she tilted her face up to his. He looked into her eyes like he'd done in Abilene, but he didn't move. Instead he inhaled softly, then he kissed her on the cheek. "Good night, Mary."

She'd expected more, wanted more. "You're leaving?"

"Yeah."

She didn't know what to think.

"Go on, now," he murmured. "Get upstairs before I kiss you the way I want."

She couldn't move her feet, couldn't think beyond the shock of J.T. resisting the kiss she'd been willing to give. If he'd kissed her, her heart would have sped up. Without the kiss, it wanted to fly out of her chest. Instead of taking the gift she had freely offered, he'd chosen to protect her from possible regrets. She'd been ready to forget herself. Tonight J.T. had been strong.

She cupped his cheek. "There's goodness in you, Jonah. I see it."

He looked like he wanted to argue. Instead he murmured, "Good night, Mary. Pleasant dreams."

She turned and went up the stairs, his presence gentle in her mind as he waited for her to step inside the apartment. She closed the door, then went to the window and looked down. Her eyes found his, and he acknowledged her with a nod. Touching the glass, she whispered a prayer for him, then watched as he walked down the street. She prayed for him until he vanished from sight, then she kissed her fingers and pressed them to the window, leaving a mark on the glass shining darkly between them.

Chapter Fourteen

Early the next morning J.T. had breakfast with Gus at the café, then the two of them rode to the stream past the Slewfoot Mine. They spent the day shooting at cans and laughing at stupid jokes, then they fished for their supper. They caught enough trout to feed themselves and Fancy Girl, burned a can of beans and ate all the biscuits Mary had tucked into Gus's pack.

Full to the brim and tuckered out, Gus spread his bedroll on one side of the fire and climbed in. Fancy was stretched at his side. Yawning, the boy stared up at the stars. J.T. wasn't ready to settle down. Sitting on a rock by the campfire, he refilled his coffee cup. The day had left him pleasantly worn out, but he was worried. When he and Gus first set up camp, he'd found two whiskey bottles, a sign someone had camped here last night. Whoever he was, he'd used the brand preferred by Griff Lassen. J.T. had tossed the bottles aside, but the smell had reminded him of the things he'd denied himself. In particular he was thinking of last night's kiss…the one he'd held back.

In Abilene he'd have kissed her until she told him to stop, and he'd have made sure she didn't want to stop.

Last night he'd stopped for them both. It made no sense. For six months he'd imagined holding her close. She'd given him the chance and he'd stepped back. He had to be crazy or stupid, maybe both. He picked up a rock and heaved it into the dark.

Gus turned over in his bedroll. "A-a-are you all right?"

"Sure."

"Y-y-you look mad."

"Nah." He dumped his coffee to do something. "I was just thinking about stuff."

"Yeah. Me, too." Looking slightly nervous, the boy propped himself on one elbow. "C-can I ask you something?"

"Sure."

"It's about…where p-p-uppies come from."

"Puppies?" J.T. almost stammered like Gus. "You mean like…where babies come from?"

"Sort of."

No one ever got the jump on J.T., but Gus had caught him completely off guard. He had no desire to have this particular talk, but he also saw a need. What twelve-year-old boy wanted to ask his sister about such personal things? J.T. saw a chance to man up and do something good. He tossed a second rock. "So you want to know about babies and stuff."

"S-s-sort of."

The boy stammered more when he was worried, so J.T. took the bull by the horns. "It's nature's way, kid. A man and a woman—"

Gus shook his head. "I—I—I already kn-n-ow *that* part."

Relief washed over J.T., until he realized Gus's real

question might be even harder to answer. "What do you want to know?"

"I know where b-b-babies come from. I just don't know *why.*"

"Why what?"

"Why it happens."

Six months ago, J.T. would have said nature took its course. Tonight he recalled *not* kissing Mary, and he knew he had to give Gus an honest answer. What he said would influence the boy for the rest of his life. J.T.'s own education on the matter had come from his oldest brother, and it had been crude. Even at a tender age, he'd known his brother was wrong-minded about women.

He saw a chance to give Gus something better. "The best way it happens is when a man and woman love each other and get married." He didn't bother telling the boy about the other ways it happened, or the worst ways.

"Wh-why do they love each other?"

"That's a mystery to me, too." He tapped his fingers on the enamel cup. "A man meets the right lady, and it just happens."

"H-h-has it happened to you?"

The meaning of the question hit J.T. hard. For six months, he'd thought about finding Mary and being with her. He'd recalled how she'd cared for him in Abilene and how she'd made him smile. Not once had he thought beyond giving her a place to sing. Marrying hadn't been in the plan, and neither had giving her children. He'd been too selfish to think about anything except his own wants. Last night when he hadn't kissed her, he'd done it for her…he'd done it for *them.* The meaning of that choice hit him hard.

He kicked the dirt. "Yeah, I've been in love."

"Do you l-love m-my sister?"

He saw *that* question coming. Looking stern, he stared at Gus across the fire. The boy stared back with a daring J.T. had to admire. Instead of telling Gus that some questions were too personal, he laughed out loud.

Gus glared at him. "Well, do you?"

He knew better than to involve the boy. Yes, he loved Mary. He could admit it to himself, but what did he have to give her? His guns, two good horses and a talent for faro. And his bad name. No woman in her right mind would want J. T. Quinn for a husband, but he felt a yearning he couldn't deny. He wanted to spend the rest of his days with Mary Larue, and he wanted to give her the respect of a wedding ring.

He felt Gus's eyes on his face and hoped the boy couldn't read his thoughts. He picked up another rock and hurled it at a distant shadow. "If I talk to anyone about that, it should be your sister."

"But you like her, don't you?"

"Yes, Gus. I do. I like your sister a lot." He felt a lot more than *like,* but *like* would do for a twelve-year-old. "It's late, and we're hunting rabbit tomorrow. You need to get some sleep."

"Yeah." The boy hunkered down in his bedroll.

J.T. spread his own blankets, then stretched flat and stared at the sky. He didn't doubt his love for Mary, but what could he do about it? Even if he found a way to make a living—he enjoyed roofing—other differences kept them apart. She believed in God, and he didn't. No way would J.T. ever turn the other cheek to an enemy. Looking at the patchwork of clouds and sky, he began to wonder—did it matter what he thought about God? He couldn't share her faith, but maybe he didn't need to compete with it. All couples had their differences. She liked rhubarb and he didn't. He liked his coffee hot and strong. She ruined hers with cream. Did their differences really matter? He'd cleaned up his life. He was willing to die for her. Surely that was enough to earn back her trust.

He was pondering the possibility when he heard scuffling in the brush. Bolting upright, he grabbed his gun and took aim. Fancy Girl jumped to her feet and growled. When the noise faded completely, he uncocked the hammer.

Gus sat upright. Sleepy but wide-eyed, he looked at the gun in J.T.'s hand. "Did you hear something?"

"Just a coyote."

The boy patted Fancy Girl, then glanced at the sky. He looked nervous, and J.T. regretted scaring him. It would have been worse, though, if someone had snuck up on them.

Gus looked at him from across the dead campfire. "C-c-an I asked you another question?"

"Sure." It couldn't be worse than the ones about love.

"D-do you ever pray?"

He was wrong. This question was harder. Gus looked up to him. What he said would matter, and J.T. didn't want the boy to be like him. He also had to be honest, because anything less would insult them both. He put the gun back under the blanket he used for a pillow. "I prayed when I was your age."

"What about now?"

"Not much." *Not ever.*

"I-it's not hard." Gus sounded confident. "M-my mama taught me special words to s-s-ay, but mostly I th-think them."

J.T. had no idea what to say, but he wanted to encourage the boy. "That's good."

"I—I don't stammer when I t-t-talk in my head."

What would that be like, J.T. wondered, to hear yourself right but have the words come out wrong? Every man had flaws, but Gus lived with constant failure. It had to hurt.

The boy seemed to be talking to the dark. "M-ary says my stam-m-mer doesn't m-m-matter to God, but I w-wish i-it would stop."

"I know the feeling, Gus." J.T. had wishes of his own. "I've never had a stammer, but there are things about myself I don't much like."

He had no desire to share his regrets with Gus. The boy had been far too protected to understand J.T.'s choices. To his relief, Gus lay back down. So did J.T., but he felt as if the stars were pinning him down. Since he'd dared God to show Himself, he'd had been pestered by clouds and curious boys, hot benches, friendly people, puppies and most dangerous of all, the notion of being in love. If the Almighty had taken J.T.'s challenge to show Himself, He'd done it in curious ways.

Gus's voice came out of the dark. "J.T.?"

"Yeah?"

"Do you think G-God listens?"

A week ago he'd have said no. Tonight he was asking the same question. "I don't know."

"I do," Gus said with certainty.

As if that were enough, the boy fell asleep, leaving J.T. to stare at the sky. He shut his eyes to hide the stars, but he couldn't shake the feeling he was being watched, or watched over, so he opened them again. A falling star shot across the black expanse, leaving a trail that faded to nothing. He imagined his own life ending the same way. He wasn't afraid of dying. He wasn't afraid of anything.... Except he was. He was terrified of small dark places and being pinned on his back. He was worried about Fancy Girl having puppies, and he feared what Roy Desmond would do to Gertie. And Mary. He was afraid he'd lose her again before he could fully earn her trust.

A cloud obscured the top half of the crescent moon. As the shadow passed, Fancy Girl lumbered to her feet and came to him. Leaving Gus to his dreams, she took her usual spot and rested her head on his chest.

"Hi there, girl." He scratched her neck the way she liked, then rested his hand on her belly. The puppies were quiet now, but he could feel the promise of life and it humbled him. There were things a man could do, and things he couldn't. J.T. could take a life, but he couldn't give it back. He hoped Mary would be around when Fancy's time came. The dog would do all the work, but he knew that birth and death were a breath apart.

"Rest up, girl," he murmured. "You're going to be fine."

The dog's tail whapped.

"I know," he said to her. "Strange things are happening to both of us."

J.T. didn't have new life growing in his belly, but he felt the stirrings just the same. With Fancy at his side, he closed his eyes and thought of what he'd do with Gus tomorrow. They'd hunt rabbit so the boy could practice with a rifle, then they'd do some more boxing. Lost in pleasant thoughts, he fell into a deep and comfortable sleep.

On Wednesday morning Mary finished cleaning up after breakfast, locked the café and went to Swan's Nest to borrow a buggy. In her arms was a picnic basket, and in her pocket was the map J.T. had left to the stream where they'd be camping. He'd given it to her without being asked, and she'd been impressed. After a chat with Adie, she left Denver with a sense of pleasant anticipation.

She'd had plenty of time to think about her feelings for J.T. She didn't feel ready to tell him about the miscarriage, but she liked the idea of being his friend. Adie had helped to open Mary's eyes, but sadly so had Gertie. While praying for her sister, Mary had seen herself even more clearly in Gertie's determination to ignore the facts about Roy. Mary couldn't deny that J.T. had changed.

She'd seen the evidence for herself and no longer questioned his good intentions, but his place in her life was another matter. Regret changed a man's heart, but faith changed his ways. With faith, a man could love a woman more than he cared about himself. Without it Mary couldn't trust J.T. fully, but she hoped they could be friends. To show him she'd crossed a line, she'd packed a picnic lunch with cobbler and other goodies, and she planned to surprise him at the stream.

With the sun bright, she passed the Slewfoot Mine and turned down the road that led to Cherry Creek. It wound past boulders and cottonwoods, around a bend and ended at a clearing. She saw ashes in the fire pit, bedrolls, neatly stacked cookware and their horses grazing nearby. J.T. and Gus had to be close, so she climbed out of the buggy. Heading toward the creek, she heard J.T. making playful threats, Gus's high-pitched shouting and the furious splashing of a water fight.

Enjoying the happy sounds, she ambled down the trail until the sparkle of amber glass stopped her in her tracks. Looking more closely, she saw a whiskey bottle in the brush. Not just one bottle, but two. Trembling, she bent down and inspected them. They were both clean, unmarked by rainwater or dirt. One of them had no odor, but the other still reeked and was marked with fingerprints. It hadn't been there long. Maybe hours... no more than a day or two.

J.T. had let her down...again.

She wanted to go back to the buggy and leave, but she couldn't leave Gus in the care of a drunken gunfighter.

Furious, she picked up the bottle and marched to the stream. From the top of a small rise, she saw the man and the boy waging war with water and buckets. She saw J.T.'s shaving tools on a rock, his shirt hanging on a willow branch and Gus's shirt next to it as if they were cut from the same cloth. She stood with the whiskey bottle in her hand, watching and crying and wishing J.T. had never come back to Denver.

With her eyes on J.T.'s face, she navigated between the rocks and weeds. He didn't see her and neither did Gus. She watched her brother dump a bucket of water over J.T.'s head. The clear liquid sparkled on his hair and face, then ran in streams down his chest, washing him clean but not really.

"Why, God?" she murmured. "Why did You bring him back just to fail me?"

As if to answer her question, J.T. suddenly spotted her and smiled. Gus took advantage and knocked him off his feet. He went under and came up sputtering and laughing and happier than she'd ever seen him. With a disgusted look, she held up the whiskey bottle. She waved it for him to see, threw it as far as she could and went back to the buggy to wait.

Chapter Fifteen

J.T. didn't see the bottle until it flew out of Mary's hand. Sloshing out of the stream, he shouted at Gus over his shoulder. "Stay here, kid. This is between your sister and me."

Dripping wet, he grabbed his shirt and charged barefoot up the steep incline, dragging his shirt over his head as he chased her. A thorn dug into the sole of his foot, but he ignored it. At the top of the hill, he saw her twenty feet away. "Mary, wait! It's not what you think."

She whirled and faced him. "Yes, it is. It's whiskey."

"It's not mine."

"Do you expect me to *believe* you?" She laughed bitterly. "I smelled the bottle. It's fresh. It has fingerprints on it."

"I know. I threw it away."

She huffed. "Of course you did."

"You've got to believe me." He paced closer, a step at a time, giving her a chance to back off if she was going to run. Crowding her wouldn't help his cause. She had to come willingly. She had to choose to give him a chance. Fighting both the fear that she'd run and the anger of being falsely accused, he held his arms to the side to open himself fully to her view.

"Do I look drunk?" he said mildly.

Her eyes dipped to his bare feet, dirty now and stinging from the thorn. She took in his wet trousers and the damp shirt, and finally she looked into his eyes. J.T. knew they were clear and bright. They were also full of hope, because he really did have a clean conscience. It felt good.

He took a step closer. "Am I slurring my words?"

"No." She bit her lip. "I want to believe you, but I saw the bottle. I smelled it."

He took another step, a larger one.

Mary stayed in place.

He came closer still, holding her gaze until they were a foot apart. If she wanted to smell his breath, the choice was hers. Understanding his intention, she leaned slightly forward and inhaled. So did J.T. He smelled the rosy soap Mary used in Abilene and sun-warmed cotton. When her eyes went wide, he lowered his arms. "What do you smell?"

"I smell…water."

He wanted to kiss her for the joy of it, but he settled for enjoying her surprise. "I found the bottles by the fire pit. I tossed them so Gus wouldn't find them."

The next thing he knew, Mary had her hands on his shoulders and was clutching his shirt. The wet cotton dragged against his back, pulling them closer as she matched her mouth to his in a kiss that erased every thought except one—he loved this woman. She didn't seem to care that he was sopping wet, so he put his arms around her and drew her close. When she made the kiss bolder, so did he. Her straw hat was in his way, so he loosened the ribbons and took it off her head.

He wanted to give more than he took, but he wouldn't give more than Mary wanted. He matched her breath for breath but offered nothing more. She ended the kiss with a sigh, then rested her head on his shoulder. He thought of his demand that God show Himself. This was forgiveness. This was mercy. Mary trusted him again, but now where did they go? He wasn't the only person who had to decide, so he loosened his arms enough to see her face. She looked like a woman who'd been thoroughly kissed and now regretted it. Troubled, he used both hands to put the hat back on her head.

"What happens next?" he asked.

"I don't know." Backing away, she hastily tied the satin ribbons. The patches from his wet shirt showed on her dress, leaving an imprint of the embrace. The sun would dry the dress in minutes. The kiss couldn't be so easily erased, but Mary looked like she wanted to try. She finished the bow with a snap, then squared her shoulders. "I shouldn't have kissed you."

"Oh, definitely not," he said, teasing her.

"I mean it." She started to pace. "I came out her to tell you how much I appreciate what you've done for Gus and Gertie. I brought bread and chicken and…and cobbler. I thought we could be friends, but that kiss—" Groaning, she turned her back. "You've *always* done that to me. It's just not fair!"

"It's fair, all right."

"Oh, no, it's not!"

He walked up behind her. "You do the same thing to me, probably even stronger." He wanted to turn her around, but the choice to come into his arms belonged to her.

"I'm so confused!" she said to the sky. She pressed

her hands to her cheeks, moaned, then lowered her arms and faced him. "I have to be honest with you."

"I'm listening."

"Kissing you was as wonderful as ever."

He'd been expecting her to call him a good-for-nothing. Instead she'd given him a compliment. "I can say the same to you."

"Some things don't change," she said quietly. "But others do. I can't kiss you again. Not like that. I was caught up in the moment. It shouldn't have happened."

"Why not?"

"Because I'd be lying."

"Lying?" He didn't understand at all.

"I don't want to repeat the past, and right now that's all we have." She looked stronger now, as if she'd found her purpose. "I'm not the woman you knew in Abilene. It might not look like it from the outside—"

"It shows," he interrupted. "I see the changes."

"They're on the inside, too." She lifted her chin even higher. "My faith is important to me, but I'm human. I like kissing you, but we can't be more than friends. The differences between us matter."

When he finally understood, his eyes narrowed. "You love God and I don't." He calmed his voice. "I don't see why it's a problem. You can go to church all you want. It doesn't bother me a bit."

Her expression told him that he'd missed the point.

He felt like throwing a rock at a cloud, climbing up to one and pummeling it into smoke. He cared about Mary. He loved her. He'd have told her if he thought she'd be happy about it, but loving her only added to the wedge between them. He was beginning to feel like a puppet on a string, and he didn't like it. He was also starting to worry about Gus. The boy had seen the start of the quarrel and would be concerned. "This needs to wait," he said coldly. "Gus is still at the creek."

Mary looked pained. "I didn't forget him."

"Neither did I."

She lifted her chin. "He'll be hungry. We can still have lunch."

J.T. wanted to get away from her, but she had a point. "I'll get him. Wait here."

"I'll go," she insisted. "I want to see him."

"No!" He'd had all he could stand. "I'm soaking wet, and I've got a thorn in my foot. You accused me of getting drunk in front of Gus, then you kissed me like you meant it, but you didn't. And *now* you want to give me cobbler. Right now, all I want is to put on dry clothes and *not* talk."

With that, he headed for the stream to get Gus.

As Mary handed out sandwiches, she couldn't stop remembering the picnic in Kansas. That day she and J.T. had talked for hours and kissed like fools. Today they weren't speaking to each other. Instead they each focused on Gus. She listened to the boy's tales about shooting and boxing lessons, while J.T. ate in silence except to praise her brother. After the cobbler, Gus asked J.T. if they could go home today instead of tomorrow. He agreed, and together they packed while Mary washed dishes at the stream.

With the water rippling around the rocks, she thought of her decision to be J.T.'s friend and the kiss that revealed her deeper feelings. Adie was right. Love wasn't a choice, and she loved J.T. She couldn't tell him, though. Not only did her faith matter, but she'd didn't trust him with her feelings about the past.

A lean shadow fell on the sand next to her. Abruptly,

she turned and saw J.T. several steps away. "We're packed and ready."

She had one more plate to rinse. "I'll be up in a minute."

She hoped he'd linger so they could patch up the quarrel, but he walked away. She finished scrubbing the last dish with sand, rinsed it, then gathered the plates and went back to the campsite. To her surprise, the buckskin was tied to the buggy, and J.T. was waiting with his hat pulled low. Gus, mounted on J.T.'s extra horse, looked pleased. When she reached the rig, J.T. took the basket, shoved it under the seat and then offered his hand. "I'm driving you home."

"You don't have to."

"Tell that to Gus," he said drily. "He accused me of not being a gentleman."

She gave J.T. a sympathetic look and then took his hand and climbed into the buggy. He motioned for Fancy Girl to jump in next to her and then walked around the rig and joined her, the seat squeaking with his weight. He took the reins, and off they went.

One mile of silence.

Two miles of silence.

Three miles of silence. Fancy Girl leaned against Mary, pushing her into J.T.'s ribs. If he'd put his arm around her, they'd have been as close as they'd been in Abilene. Instead, he kept his spine rigid, and so did she. The silence troubled her even more than the kiss. They couldn't be in love, but she wanted to be his friend. She was close to bursting when he shifted his boots and their feet touched. When he didn't pull back, neither did she. The touch wasn't the conversation she wanted to have, but it was a start.

"Any word on Gertie?" he finally asked.

"I haven't seen her." She stared down the empty road. "If I don't hear from her soon, I'm going to visit her."

"We need to get her to New York."

"I wish I could."

His eyes glinted with the toughness she recalled from Abilene. "Give me a few days."

That was all he said until they arrived at the café. He unloaded Gus's things, then he and the boy cleaned the guns they used, including a .22 rifle he gave to Gus to keep. They talked about bullets and whatnot until J.T. left to return the buggy to Swan's Nest with Fancy Girl riding next to him.

As he rode off, Mary wondered if his plan to get the money for Gertie included a turn at a faro table. He knew how she felt about gambling, so she said nothing. The decision to gamble belonged to J.T. The choice to refuse the money was hers, and that's what she intended to do.

At Swan's Nest J.T. cared for his horses and put up the buggy. No one pestered him, so he finished fast and went straight to Sixteenth Street in search of a faro parlor. He'd earn that money for Gertie and he'd do it tonight. He knew Mary objected to gambling, but he hoped she'd take the winnings for Gertie's sake. After today's craziness, he felt more compelled than ever to keep his promise. With his saddlebag over his shoulder—the bag with his clothes and all his money—he pushed through the door to a gaming hall called the Bull's Eye.

"This won't take long, girl," he said to Fancy.

He had his whole stake with him. With a little luck, he'd triple it in an hour…

Two hours later, he walked out the same door shaking his head. He'd never had such awful luck. The dealer hadn't minded Fancy Girl at all, especially once J.T. started losing. To make up for the losses, he'd upped his bets. He'd quit before he lost everything, but he had less than half of what he'd started with.

The run of bad luck made him mad. Being mad reminded him of Mary and how she'd kissed him and backed away. What did she want from him, anyway? Whatever it was, he didn't have it to give. With his saddlebag lighter, he headed to the boardinghouse and went to his room. Leaving the door wide to catch the light in the hall, he dropped the saddlebag on the floor and lit the lamp. Once it flared, he shut the door and locked it.

Fancy headed for a corner she never used, dropped down and looked at him with sad brown eyes.

"I know." He grumbled. "I made a fool of myself."

Thoroughly annoyed, he plopped down on the bed. Faro dealers were notorious cheats, and J.T. was rusty. He considered trying a different faro parlor, but he didn't want to leave Fancy Girl alone. Trapped and too angry to sleep, he wedged a pillow against the wall and sat up on the bed. He needed something to do. Even a button to sew would have been a distraction. Something to read would have been better, even a stupid dime novel.

Desperate, he glanced around the room and saw the chapbook on the nightstand. He blinked and was on the white stone bench in Josh's garden. If he didn't fill his mind with something, he'd end up in that alley in New York, on his back and feeling his brother's knife. Even with the light on, the room felt small and tight. Needing to escape—in his mind, since he couldn't leave Fancy— he opened the chapbook. His thumb pointed to a single sentence. *And the light shineth in darkness; and the darkness comprehended it not.*

J.T. knew the power of darkness. He knew how it felt

to be trapped by it, caught between walls and rendered helpless and blind. It was light that befuddled him. He didn't understand where it came from, but he could see it. He'd seen the light in the way Fancy Girl loved him. He'd seen the light in Gus, too. Today he'd seen the brightest light of all in Mary. She'd taken back the kiss, but not before she'd come willingly into his arms. The light, he realized, was love. Not only had he seen the light…he'd felt it. He loved Fancy Girl and Gus. He loved Mary most of all, and today he could believe she loved him back.

Him, J. T. Quinn, a killer by trade and a gambler by choice. A man who'd spilled blood and enjoyed it. Mary cared for him. How could that be? He read more of the little book, comprehending just enough to know that he wanted to know more. He didn't understand most of what he read, but Mary did. The light lived in her. More than anything, he wanted to feel the brightness for the rest of their lives. He'd do anything to earn that privilege, but how? What did he have to do? A thought came out of the blue, and he smiled. Tomorrow Mary would get a surprise.

J.T. set down the book. As he turned down the lamp, Fancy Girl jumped on the bed and curled against his leg. With his hand on her belly, he thought about puppies and cobbler, kisses, love, cheating faro dealers and the strange twists of a hard day.

Chapter Sixteen

~~~

"Where are the aprons?" said a male voice.

Mary turned from the stove and saw J.T. and Fancy Girl both looking at her with concern. She'd been racing around the kitchen, and her cheeks were flushed. The waitress she'd hired to replace Gertie hadn't shown up, and Enid was complaining loudly. *And* the train had arrived early, filling the café with hungry patrons. "What are you doing here?" she asked.

"I'm your new dishwasher."

"You're *what?*"

"I'm washing dishes for you." He cast a wary eye at a tub full of dirty plates. "You need help. Here I am."

She didn't know everything he was thinking, but she recognized his effort as a peace offering for yesterday's quarrel. As much as she needed help, she worried about his commitment to finishing the church. "Isn't Josh expecting you?"

"Not today."

She smiled at him. "In that case, the job's yours. In fact, I'm grateful. The aprons are next to the pantry."

Fancy found a comfortable corner, and J.T. went to the row of hooks with kitchen apparel. He selected a white bibbed apron, tied the strings over his gun belt and went to work on a stack of greasy plates. Between the sizzling bacon and the clatter of dishes, Mary thought about yesterday. The kiss had to be forgotten, but she needed to talk to him about earning the money for Gertie. Yesterday she'd let him leave without speaking her mind. This morning she felt compelled to bring up the matter.

She spoke to him from the stove while flipping hotcakes. "We need to talk about Gertie and New York."

When he didn't reply, she looked over her shoulder. Not many men could wear an apron tied in a bow and still be menacing. Somehow J.T. looked as if he were commanding the dishes to wash themselves. Mary wished she could control Gertie with that kind of authority, but her sister would have stared back.

She added a rasher of bacon to a pan. "I want to be sure you know, I won't take new gambling money."

He still didn't respond.

"It wouldn't be right," she insisted. "I'd feel—"

"You don't have to worry," he said, almost growling at her. "I lost my shirt at the Bull's Eye. I won't be going back."

"Oh, dear." She felt both bad for him and relieved. "How much did you lose?"

"A lot."

She didn't want to embarrass him, but she needed to understand. "Are you washing dishes because you need the job? I'll pay you."

He faced her with a dripping plate in one hand, a rag in the other and a stare that would have made a wolf cower. "I'm not doing this for money."

"I just thought—"

"I didn't lose everything." He plunged the plate in the soapy water. "I failed you, Mary. I didn't get drunk, but

I gambled and lost half of what I had. Instead of getting Gertie to New York, I made things worse."

"No, you didn't." His method had been all wrong, but she couldn't ignore his good intentions. She saw the losing streak as a blessing and smiled. "The way I see it, I got a dishwasher out of the deal." She winked at him for fun. "A handsome one at that."

His brows snapped together. "Don't tease me."

She turned red.

"I like it too much," he muttered. "And losing's no fun."

"I'm sorry." She should have considered his pride. "It was thoughtless of me, but I'm not sorry you had a bad night at faro. Winning would have hurt you more than it would have helped Gertie."

He shook his head. "I feel like a fool."

She crossed the room and stood in front of him, clasping his biceps as she looked up. "You made a mistake, Jonah. It'll be okay."

His hands, dry but still warm from the water, came to rest on her waist. Neither of them took the kiss dangling between them. It hung like hard, green fruit, full of promise but far from ripe. With her eyes bright, she kissed his cheek and went back to the stove.

"Mary?"

She looked over shoulder. "Yes?"

"Thank you."

"For what?"

"Understanding." Silent again, he dipped a plate into the rinse water.

For the next two hours, they worked as a team with Enid serving, Gus clearing tables and Fancy Girl getting scraps from Gus. When the last customer left, Mary began scraping grease from the stove. Gus came up behind her. "G-Gertie's here."

The stove could wait. She reached around her back to untie the apron. "I'll be right there."

Gus paused. "Sh-she's with th-that man."

Mary wanted to lock Gertie upstairs and give Roy a piece of her mind, but the strings had turned into a knot. Before she could untie it, J.T. had removed his own apron and wadded it into a ball. "You're not going out there alone."

"But—"

"The four of us need to have a civilized conversation," he said amiably. He looked at Gus. "Take Fancy Girl upstairs."

"Sure."

The boy left with the dog, and Mary spoke briefly to Enid. The waitress promised to bring a friend to help serve lunch and went out the back door.

J.T. indicated the entry to the dining hall. "Shall we?"

"Certainly."

She stepped into the room with J.T. behind her. Gertie's eyes widened at the sight of him, but it was Roy's expression that told a story. He clenched his jaw, then put on a smile. The surprise gave Mary an advantage, and she intended to keep it by being hospitable. She crossed the room as if she'd been expecting them and greeted Gertie with a hug.

"Shall we sit?" she said graciously.

Gertie feigned a dignified nod. Roy looked less agreeable, but he helped the girl with her chair. J.T. seated Mary next to Gertie, then pulled out a chair for himself.

Mary smiled a bit too cheerfully. "I'm done serving breakfast, but I can offer coffee or tea?"

Gertie squirmed, then shared a glance with Roy that sent bolts of fury down Mary's spine. She did *not* want her sister trading secretive looks with Roy. She shot a look of her own at J.T. He seemed completely at ease, except that he was drilling Roy with his eyes.

The theater manager cleared his throat. "Gertie asked me to call on you today, Mary. She says you're worried about her joining my theater troupe, that you think she'll grow up too fast. I can assure you, I'll treat her like my own daughter."

He'd said the right words, but his dark eyes had no life. How could she have trusted this man?

Gertie smiled at him gratefully and then faced Mary. "There's no reason for me to go to New York. Roy's been so kind, and I'm learning from the other actresses. I want you to be happy for me."

Mary knew her sister. Gertie would rebel if she spoke her mind, but neither could Mary offer the approval the girl wanted. She had to tell the truth. "I will always love you, Gertie."

"I know, but—"

Mary shook her head. "There are no 'buts' when it comes to family. I want you to go to New York. It's just a question of when."

Gertie pulled back from Mary and faced Roy. "I told you she wouldn't understand."

"But I do," Mary countered.

"So do I," J.T. added.

Glaring at him, Gertie took a hankie from her reticule and dabbed at her moist brow. Mary didn't recognize the fine linen and wondered if Roy had given it to her. The theater manager looked pointedly at J.T., then took the girl's hand. "It'll be fine, Gertie. I promise."

Mary wanted to give Roy a piece of her mind, but J.T. looked as cool as January. It was easy to imagine him killing Roy in cold blood, a thought that horrified her. If he harmed Gertie, she'd want justice to be served but only by the law. She turned to her sister. "I care about you. You *know* I want what's best for you."

Gertie sniffed.

Roy pushed to his feet. "I think it's time we left."

J.T. stood but said nothing. Gertie rose more slowly and so did Mary. She wanted to hug her sister, but the girl paced to the door. Mary followed, vaguely aware of Roy saying something to J.T. Gertie left without a goodbye, her shoes tapping angrily on the boardwalk.

Roy followed her, stopping in front of Mary and leaning too close. "Take the role, and I'll leave your sister alone."

"How dare you!" she hissed. "She's a *child!*"

"She's old enough. Just remember, you can change your mind anytime you want."

"I won't."

An ugly smirk curled on his lips. "It would be a shame to have word get out about your sordid past. I wonder what little Gertie would think about you and J. T. Quinn?"

An actress at heart, Mary feigned disinterest. "That's old news, Roy. No one cares but you."

"I doubt that." Looking smug, he walked out the door.

Mary wanted to throw a plate. "The nerve of that man!"

J.T. had stayed at the table, and he stood there now with a look of cold disdain. How could he be so calm?

Mary wanted to drag Gertie home by her hair. Instead she massaged her temples. When she remembered Roy had spoken to J.T., she stopped rubbing at the headache and looked up. "What did he say to you?"

"He wants to talk to me alone."

"About what?"

"I'll find out tonight. We're meeting during the show."

"At the theater?"

"His office," he replied.

She hated giving Roy an advantage, even a territorial one. "I want to go with you."

He lowered his chin. "No."

"But—"

"He's a snake, Mary. You go near him, and he'll bite you."

"But he's got my *sister*." If she told Gertie everything—her own secret and what J.T. had said—maybe the girl would listen. It was her last resort.

He crossed the room and stood nose to nose with her. "If you go *near* that theater, I'll throw you over my shoulder and carry you home."

He was teasing, sort of. "You wouldn't dare."

"I'd dare, all right." The playfulness left his eyes. "Whatever it takes to keep you away from Roy, I'll do it."

She felt the weight of his words, the caring in them. She trusted J.T. with Gus and Gertie, even her own life, but her heart was another matter. "You're right," she murmured. "I won't go near the Newcastle."

Stepping back, he indicated the weapon that never left his hip. "My gun is staying right here. If Roy harms you or Gertie, I'll use it."

Mary abhorred violence, but she valued his protection.

"If you fire that thing at Roy in self-defense, I might not mind. But I hope you don't have to."

"Me, too."

His answer surprised her. In Abilene he'd been quick to shed blood. "Do you mean that?"

"I do." His mouth leveled into a line. "I'm tired of fighting, but that doesn't mean I can stop."

"Why not?"

He shook his head. "A man's reputation stays with him."

So did a woman's. Mary knew that fact well. "I made a fresh start. So can you."

"Not with men like Griff Lassen after me." He looked more tense than ever. "It'll be a long time before they all forget I'm alive."

Mary had the same problem. People would talk about the Abilene scandal as long as someone would listen. "I understand. It's why I'm so careful with my reputation."

His jaw muscles tensed. "If anyone pesters you, they'll regret it."

He'd always been protective of her. "Thank you."

"The same goes for Gertie. If Roy touches her, he'll pay."

Mary believed in justice, not cold-blooded killing, but she'd be as quick as J.T. to protect Gertie. "Let's hope nothing happens to her."

He got down to business. "Tonight I'll hear what Roy has to say. I have a feeling something happened we don't know about."

"What makes you say that?"

"He came here to bargain with us. That means he's not getting what he needs from Gertie. You didn't give in, and we know he needs money for his so-called investors. Now he wants to talk to me." J.T.'s eyes took on an amused light. "Since I can't sing a lick, there's got to be another angle."

"Like what?"

He took his gun from the holster, spun it fast and dropped it back in place. "Maybe he wants someone dead."

"J.T., no!"

He acted as if he hadn't heard her. "We'll talk after I see him, either tonight or tomorrow."

"Tonight," she insisted. If Roy and J.T. tangled, she wanted to know about it. And if he had news on Gertie, she needed to hear that, too.

"I better go," he said. "I've got a little work left on the roof. Mind if I take Gus?"

"I'll get him."

Mary went up the stairs. She saw her brother sitting with Fancy Girl in a dark corner. Unless Mary missed her guess, the dog would have her puppies in a day or two.

She spoke to Gus. "J.T.'s waiting for you. Tell him I'll watch Fancy while you two work."

"O-okay."

Gus left in a hurry. Mary took an old blanket from under her bed and gave it to the dog for a nest. Rubbing Fancy Girl's belly, she remembered her own few months of being with child. She didn't feel ready to tell J.T. about the baby they'd lost, but Roy's threat to expose the scandal put pressure on her. She also knew Roy would keep her secret as long as it gave him an advantage. She had time to decide, and she wanted to take it. She needed J.T.'s friendship too much to risk losing it.

"What do you think?" she said to Fancy Girl. "Do you think he'll understand?"

The dog sighed, then closed her eyes. Mary had the same inclination.

* * *

As J.T. approached the side door to the Newcastle Theater, he passed the scaffolding he'd climbed this afternoon while working on the roof with Gus. Moonlight lit up the planks where he'd stood with the boy, giving them the look of a ladder to the sky. He liked being high, but tonight he had to go low, as low as Roy Desmond.

This afternoon he'd seen Gertie sashay into the theater. He'd also observed other actors as they'd come and gone, and they'd mocked her unmercifully. The girl didn't have Mary's talent. Roy needed Mary, which meant Gertie was bait. Like a worm on a hook, she'd be sacrificed in Roy's quest to satisfy his investors. J.T. didn't have the details, but he figured Roy had two options. He could pay the money he owed, or he could eliminate the threat of someone coming to collect it.

Applause burst from the open windows of the theater. J.T. glanced up, then knocked on the side door. Roy opened it immediately, a sign he'd been waiting and didn't want to be seen.

"Come in, Quinn."

J.T. stepped into a long hall lit by six wooden sconces. In the distance he heard an actor's booming voice and an answering rumble of laughter. He wondered if Gertie was backstage or in the audience, and if she'd come to the theater alone or with Katrina. Roy opened the door to his office, a square room with a massive desk, a sideboard set with crystal and whiskey and a divan upholstered in red velvet. He indicated the divan. "Have a seat."

"No, thanks."

"Whiskey?"

The liquor didn't tempt him at all. "Not tonight."

Roy poured a glass for himself. "I guess the rumors are true."

"What rumors?"

"That you've gotten soft."

If J.T. lost his reputation, he'd be an easy target for any young buck wanting to prove himself. The thought shook him up, but he put the reaction aside. He had to focus on Mary and Gertie. "What do you want, Roy?"

"I have an offer for you." Seated behind the desk, Roy swirled the whiskey and downed the contents. Men drank for a lot of reasons, including for courage. Something had put Roy on edge. If the right person was making the man nervous, J.T. would have an ally.

Roy set down the glass with a thud. "You don't like me, Quinn. And you don't want Mary Larue singing in my theater."

"That's right."

"She doesn't want her baby sister here, either."

"Right again."

"I propose a trade." He steepled his fingers over his chest, tapping them in a rhythm meant to make J.T. nervous.

It wouldn't work, because J.T. refused to let it. "I've been working all day, Roy. Say your piece or I'm gone."

"You won't leave."

"And you don't want me to. Get on with it."

"All right." He leaned forward. "I told you I have investors. That's not exactly true."

"I figured."

"I won a considerable amount of money playing poker on Mississippi riverboats. I figured I could go legitimate." The man looked pale. "I'm not getting any younger, and I like the idea of settling down, even taking a wife."

J.T. had had similar thoughts.

"Contrary to what you think," Roy continued. "I'm very fond of Mary Larue."

"So am I. "

"I figured that out. Don't worry, Quinn. You can have her."

J.T. felt no relief. The man still had a hold on Gertie. "What do you want?"

"I need someone to do a job for me."

He had no desire to do Roy's dirty work, but he liked the idea of negotiating to keep him away from Gertie, maybe for the money to send her to New York. "What kind of job?"

"The kind that requires your particular talent. The men who lost to me on that riverboat didn't do it graciously. They said I cheated."

"Did you?"

"Maybe."

Of course he'd cheated. J.T. had seen Roy do it in Dodge. He wasn't a good enough gambler to earn enough to invest in a high-class theater. No man liked being cheated. A rich one had the power to seek revenge, sometimes by hiring a man like J.T. to do the job. "What do you want from me?"

"Someone's looking for me, and he's in Denver. I got wind of it from one of my actors. The fellow's a hired gun like yourself."

"Who is he?"

"Griff Lassen."

J.T. could have lived the rest of his life without seeing Griff. He weighed the odds of the man already knowing he was in Denver and decided it wasn't likely. J.T. had spent less than two hours in a single gaming hall. Otherwise he'd been pounding nails at a church and washing dishes. Griff wouldn't find him easily, but the possibility had to be considered.

"I know Griff," he said to Roy.

"He's a mean one."

"So I've heard."

Roy got up and poured more whiskey. "If you kill Lassen, I'll pay you well."

J.T.'s conscience twitched, but not because of Lassen. The man deserved to die. Not only had he wanted to kill a dog, J.T. had seen him torment an expecting woman until J.T. stopped him. Lassen had no scruples, but J.T. had acquired some of his own. What would Mary think if he took this job? He'd demand enough from Roy to get Gertie to New York, but he doubted she'd take the money.

On the other hand, who could object to letting two scorpions sting each other? If J.T. did nothing, Griff would take care of Roy. The theater manager would end up dead with no help from J.T. He'd have to stay low until Lassen did the dirty work, and he'd have to keep a close eye on Mary and Gertie, but the idea had merit. In no way did it violate Mary's beliefs. The longer he waited to give Roy an answer, the more time Lassen had to do his job.

J.T. stood. "I'll think about it."

"I want an answer tonight."

"Tomorrow."

Roy hesitated, then nodded because he had no choice. "Tomorrow it is, but know this, Quinn. If you don't do what I'm asking, Gertie Larue is going to find out more about men than she's ready to know."

"Are you threatening—"

"You bet I am." He looked as filthy as his thoughts.

"The girl's worthless to me. I might as well get some use out of her."

J.T. wanted to beat Roy to a pulp. Turn the other cheek to a man who'd abuse a young girl? No way. Seething inside, he blanked his expression. "I'll give you an answer when I'm ready."

Roy gave him a critical look. "I hope it's not true about you."

"What?"

"That you've lost your edge."

"I haven't." Keeping his eyes on Roy, he left the office. Satisfied the man wouldn't try something, he turned down the hall and left the theater.

In the shadow of the church, he considered Roy's claim that he'd lost his edge. He hadn't fired at anything more threatening than a tin can in six months. Suddenly jittery, he headed for the café. With his boots thudding, he thought about Mary and how she'd trusted him with Gus and Gertie, and how she believed there was good in him. Here he was, a cynical man charged with protecting Mary and her family. He had no interest in a God who ignored boys in alleys, but he could respect a God who cared about good women and kids who stammered, foolish girls and dogs having puppies. It was almost enough to make him grab the same branch Mary had grabbed when she'd come to Denver.

As he neared the apartment, he saw her in the upstairs window. She dropped the curtain and disappeared into the dark. Before he reached the steps, she flung open the door. "Hurry, J.T.! It's Fancy Girl. The pups are coming, and she's in trouble."

J.T. bolted up the steps. If God cared, he had a terrible way of showing it.

Chapter Seventeen

J.T. hurried to Fancy Girl and dropped to his knees. He examined her with his eyes but didn't touch her. "How long has she been laboring?"

"Too long."

She told him about the past five hours. Fancy had gone into labor in the later afternoon, and she'd been panting and tense without giving birth. Looking into the dog's eyes, he saw the glaze of pain. Did dogs fear death? He didn't know, but he deeply feared losing her.

Mary took his hand. "I sent Gus to fetch Bessie."

J.T. rubbed Fancy's ears, crooning to her until his voice cracked. He wanted to scoop her into his arms and carry her to someplace bright and safe. Instead he watched as she panted with another contraction. When it passed, she raised her head to him and whined. Fancy never whined.

Mary put her arm around his shoulders. "I'm praying, J.T. It's all I can do."

Needing to give comfort as well as receive it, he cradled Mary's head against his chest. They were like two birds huddled against the cold, lifelong mates sharing warmth and hope and the love he was tired of holding back. Together they dropped to a sitting position. Staying close to him, Mary rested her palm on Fancy's belly.

"Come on, sweetheart," she pleaded. "Push those puppies out."

J.T. would have given anything to command the dog to give birth the way he told her to sit. A hand signal, a few words. But he didn't have that ability. He could take a life, but he couldn't order the puppies to be born. Looking at Fancy, her belly tensing as she panted and suddenly pushed, J.T. felt a jolt of understanding. The puppies would emerge from darkness into light. He was making a similar journey and fighting every step just as they were. Why would he stay in the dark when the light was just a breath away?

The puppies had no idea what goodness awaited them. Their mother's milk would nourish them. Fancy would lick them clean with her rough tongue. In a few weeks they'd be tumbling all over each other, and one special pup would belong to Gus and be loved more than it could imagine. J.T. wanted these puppies to be born. *He* wanted to born again, in much the same way.

Tears leaked from his eyes. "Please, God," he murmured. "Help my dog.… Help me."

Mary gripped his hand…his shooting hand. She squeezed so hard she nearly broke the fingers, and he didn't care if she broke them all. He touched Fancy's belly and felt a contraction. The dog stopped panting and started to push. She pushed and pushed…until life emerged from the darkness of her womb into the light. At the sight of the sac holding the puppy, J.T. couldn't move. Fancy turned and licked, breaking the covering and then licking the puppy until it breathed. He started sobbing like a baby, and he didn't care.

With Mary next to him, he watched as Fancy gave

birth to four more pups for a total of five. Three of them had her blond coloring. The other two were black and white. Wondering about the father, he thought of his talk with Gus about babies. A man had responsibilities to a woman, but dogs would be dogs.

"Are there more?" he asked Mary.

"I think she's done."

They sat side by side, sharing the miracle while J.T. got a hold of his emotions. Finally, he said, "Something amazing just happened."

"Yes."

"I don't mean just the puppies," he said in a hush. "I prayed to your God and He listened. I guess that makes Him my God, too."

Breathing softly, she put her palm on his jaw and turned his face to hers. He felt the warmth against his day-old whiskers. When she spoke, her voice quavered. "I'm happy for you."

"I love you, Mary."

He wanted to hear the words back. Instead she sealed her lips. He'd never needed to be loved before, but tonight he needed *her*. She pressed her fingers tight against his jaw. In return he matched his mouth to hers. They'd kissed before, but it hadn't been like this. He desired her as a woman, yes. But tonight he wanted to belong to her…. He wanted to marry her. The commitment scared him, but not as much as losing her.

Full of hope, he deepened the kiss. To his dismay, Mary pulled back. "I don't know what to say."

Say you love me. Say you trust me. Instead, she seemed troubled. Hadn't he just crossed the last hurdle between them? At the stream, he'd earned back her trust. Tonight he'd embraced her faith. What more did he need to do? He didn't understand. "What's wrong?"

She stared at Fancy, sleeping now with the puppies tight against her belly. "This has been quite a night."

If she needed to beat around the bush, he'd wait for her. "Yeah."

"Fancy's a mother." Her eyes took on a curious light. "I wonder who the father is."

"Just some mutt." The pieces of the puzzle didn't fit. "It doesn't matter. The puppies belong to Fancy."

She rubbed the dog's neck. "It doesn't seem fair."

"What doesn't?"

"She does all the work, and the father gets off scot-free." She looked at him. "Do you think that's right?"

"It is for dogs."

He was more confused than ever. What did dogs and puppies have to do with them?

Mary opened her mouth to say something else, but Gus burst into the apartment. "H-how is she?"

"She's fine." Mary pushed to her feet, stepping away when he wanted to have his arm around her.

Feeling slighted, he stood next to her but kept his hands loose. Bessie came through the door behind Gus, followed by Josh and Adie. J.T. hadn't heard the carriage, and he counted it as a mistake. Was Roy right? Had he lost his edge? The night had been full of changes, and he'd hadn't even told Mary about his talk with Roy.

She stepped away from him to make room for Bessie. "Fancy had the puppies on her own. I think everything's fine."

The nurse smiled. "I'm glad to hear it."

Adie congratulated J.T. as if he were a father and then joined the women. They started talking about Fancy, with Bessie asking questions about medical things that J.T. did *not* want to hear about. Josh looked just as pinched. Gus stayed with them, clearly counting himself as one of the men. J.T. clapped the boy on the shoulder. "Thanks for getting Bessie."

"When I went to g-get her, I s-s-saw those b-boys."

He meant the bullies. "What happened?" J.T. asked.

"The b-b-big one told me to stop, but I k-kept running. If they'd followed me, I'd have f-fought them all."

Ten minutes ago J.T. had cried out to God for mercy. Now here was Gus, stammering and afraid. Had anything really changed tonight? Suddenly solemn, the boy studied the five puppies. "I—I want one that looks like F-Fancy."

Josh glanced at J.T. "Pretty amazing, isn't it?"

"That it is, Reverend."

The minister raised an eyebrow. "You said *reverend* like you meant it."

"I do." J.T. turned to Gus. "Keep an eye on her, okay? I need a word with Josh."

Heading for the door, J.T. caught Mary's attention. "I'll be back. Then we'll talk about Gertie."

"All right."

She sounded guarded, and he wanted to know why. He'd told her he loved her, and she hadn't said it back. He didn't understand her reaction at all. He wanted to throw everyone out of the apartment and talk to her, but he had business with Josh—both personal and professional. He followed the minister down the stairs. When they reached the bottom of the steps, Josh sat on the third one up while J.T. roamed to the street, looked up and down out of habit, then faced the minister. "My dog almost died tonight."

"I hear it was close."

"Too close. I've seen death."

"Me, too."

"I prayed." His jaw tightened. "I don't understand why,

but God was merciful. I'm done fighting Him. What do I have to do?"

Josh stood and bowed his head. J.T. had never bent his neck to anyone, but he did tonight. In a conversational tone, the minister asked God to forgive J.T. of his sins and to welcome him into the Kingdom. When Josh said "Amen," J.T. echoed him. He didn't feel anything new, but he understood that he'd made a decision that mattered. As long as God didn't get in his way. J.T. figured they'd get along just fine.

The minister stepped back. "I feel compelled to warn you about something."

"What?"

"Becoming a Christian is like lighting a stick of dynamite. If the fuse doesn't fizzle out, it goes off with a bang."

J.T. didn't care about dynamite. He had business with Roy, and he wanted Josh's help. "The *bang* I want most is one that'll get rid of Roy Desmond."

Josh's eyes glinted. "What's new with Gertie?"

J.T. described his meeting with Roy. "With Griff Lassen in the picture, there's been a shift in what Roy wants. Instead of getting Mary to sing and earn him a pile of money, he wants me to take care of Lassen. If I do his dirty work, he'll leave Gertie alone."

"And if you say no?"

"He'll hurt her." J.T.'s blood turned to ice. Maybe he hadn't lost his edge after all.

Josh's expression hardened. "What kind of man threatens a seventeen-year-old girl?"

"An evil one."

"Gertie needs to come home *tonight*."

"If she will." J.T. had seen her stubborn side. "When we finish here, I'll take Mary to find her."

Josh eyed him thoughtfully. "Then what?"

A smile played on J.T.'s lips. "We let Lassen take care of Roy."

Josh clapped him on the back. "You know that stick of dynamite I mentioned?"

"Sure."

"Get ready, because it's burning fast. Have you told Mary any of this?"

"Not yet."

"It's up to her to convince Gertie to come home. While we're waiting for Lassen to strike, we'll both keep an eye on Roy."

Tomorrow J.T. would be working on the bell tower. It rose even higher than the Newcastle and gave him a perfect view of the surrounding streets. He'd see Roy coming and going. He'd also be able to spot Griff Lassen if he approached Roy. "I'll be watching."

"So will the Lord," Josh added.

J.T. believed God had saved his dog's life, but he had a hard time imagining Him anywhere except in the clouds. In general he preferred to work alone, and that's what he intended to do.

"We better get inside," Josh said. "Mary needs to have that talk with Gertie."

And J.T. needed to speak with *her*. She'd kissed him like she meant it, then she'd backed away for the second time. Before the night ended, he intended to find out why.

Chapter Eighteen

With the men outside, the women were sitting at the kitchen table. Adie and Bessie were chatting about the puppies and Gus, but Mary barely heard them. Her thoughts were on J.T. How could a woman's dreams come true and die in a single moment? When he'd prayed, she'd felt the sincerity and wept. Fancy had lived and Mary had been ready to tell him about the baby they'd lost… and then he'd spoken glibly about dogs being dogs. If she told J.T. about the baby and he mocked her, her fragile trust would be shattered. Yet if she didn't tell him, the trust would be incomplete.

She needed time to build her courage, but she had another problem. J.T. hadn't told her about the meeting with Roy, and this morning's confrontation with Gertie had filled her with guilt. Would her sister come home if she knew about Abilene? Confessing to Gertie could ruin the good life she'd made for herself and her siblings, but not confessing was risking Gertie's future.

Adie touched her arm. "You're a million miles away. What's wrong?"

"It's Gertie."

"Has there been any word from her?" Bessie asked.

Mary told them about this morning's visit. "I'm scared to death for her. I'm thinking about telling her more about why I left Abilene." Adie already knew about the miscarriage. Bessie didn't, so Mary told her about her affair with J.T., the miscarriage and how she'd killed Sam O'Day when he'd forced himself on her, calling her a loose woman and worse. "I lost my reputation, and I'm terrified of going down that road again, especially with Gus and Gertie. People would treat them badly because of me."

Bessie's silvery eyes took on a shine. "With Gertie in danger, it's a chance you have to take."

But the cost... She could lose customers and go out of business. How would she support her brother and sister? She'd be called ugly names, and Gus would hear them. The thought disgusted her, but she'd gladly sacrifice her good name to save Gertie. Even if her sister failed to understand, Mary loved the girl too much to do nothing.

"You're right." She didn't want to wait another minute. "I'll talk to Gertie first thing in the morning."

The women commiserated until the men came inside. Josh escorted Adie and Bessie to the carriage, leaving J.T. and Mary alone. They both sat on the divan, but not too close. His declaration of love was dangling between them, but she ignored it. "Tell me what happened with Roy."

He looked annoyed. "I'd rather talk about us."

"I know," she said. "But I'm not ready."

"Ready for what?"

"For anything." *Or everything.* She pleaded with her eyes. "Can we please talk about Gertie?"

He gave her a long look and then took pity on her.

"Sure," he said, reaching for her hand. "The meeting with Roy had some surprises."

He told her about Griff Lassen, Roy's offer and the man's threats to Gertie. Mary wanted her sister home tonight, not tomorrow. If it meant pounding on Katrina's door, she'd do it. If Gertie refused to listen, she'd ask J.T. to make good on his promise to carry her home like a sack of flour. She stood and snatched her shawl from a hook by the door. "Let's go."

J.T. stood more slowly. "It's late. Are you sure?"

"Positive."

"If people see us, they'll talk."

Bless him, he was thinking about her reputation. "It won't matter after I speak to Gertie. I'm going to tell her everything about Abilene. If I do, maybe she'll believe me about Roy." And after she spoke to Gertie, she'd tell J.T. about the baby.

He looked worried. "I'll tell Gus we're leaving for a while."

He strode down the hall and opened the door to her brother's room. When he spoke in a hush, the comfort of it rocked Mary to the core. This could be her life—a home with J.T. and her siblings and Fancy Girl. Everything depended on his reaction to her revelation. If Gertie's situation hadn't turned dire, she'd have told him now. Instead, she followed him out the door, setting a fast pace as they walked to the women's hotel where Katrina lived.

"I hope we can get in." She doubted a clerk worked this late.

"I'll break down the door if I have to."

Mary felt the same urgency, but embarrassing Gertie would make the situation worse. She needed to convince her sister, quietly but with a full accounting, to come home right now. The hotel loomed in the distance. A three-story building made of brick and mortar, it had the look of a fortress. When a carriage halted in front of the hotel, J.T. tugged her into the shadows. "We'll wait here."

Tucked behind him, she watched a driver climb down from the seat and open the door. A man emerged. As he turned to offer his hand to a fellow passenger, she recognized Roy. Next she saw the hem of a shimmering gold gown, then the elegant reach of a woman's arm. Katrina emerged and glided to the boardwalk.

Roy turned back to the carriage and again offered his hand. Gertie followed in Katrina's steps, except she wobbled instead of moving gracefully, and instead of wearing the pink dress befitting her age, she was draped in a purple evening gown with a low-cut diamond neckline. Giggling, she lost her balance and swayed against Roy. As he steadied her, the three of them laughed far more than the situation justified.

"She's drunk," J.T. observed.

Furious, Mary fought the urge to run to her sister. Instead, she watched Roy position himself between the two females. With his elbows bent, he escorted them to the hotel entrance. He said something that made Katrina smile, then he turned to Gertie. Mary couldn't see her sister's face, but she recognized the lift of her chin. The foolish girl was inviting a kiss. When Roy obliged, Mary tried to push past J.T.

He caught her by the waist. "Not yet."

"But—"

"Be patient," he advised. "Roy's leaving."

The girls stayed on the porch, waving as if Roy were a departing king. As soon as the carriage took off, J.T. stepped out of the shadows and she followed. When they were within earshot of the girls, he called out in a full voice. "Good evening, ladies. It looks like you've been to the theater."

Katrina, having never seen him before, wisely didn't reply. She put an arm around Gertie and turned the doorknob.

"Katrina, wait," Mary called. "It's me."

Off balance and wobbly, Gertie struggled to focus her eyes. "Mary?" She slurred the word to mush.

"Yes, sweetie. It's me." She felt no anger toward Gertie, only pity. The girl had never touched alcohol in her life. Judging by the fruity smell, Roy had given her heavy red wine. Naive and determined to hide it, Gertie had consumed far too much.

Mary approached with J.T. behind her. Katrina glared at him. "Who are you?"

"A friend of Miss Larue's," he replied. "If you'll excuse us, we'd like a word with her sister."

"It's late." Katrina looked a bit unsteady herself. "Come back tomorrow."

"That's not acceptable," Mary countered.

J.T. broke in. "We'll speak to Mary's sister *now*." He shifted his gaze to Gertie. "Is that all right with you, Miss Larue?"

"I—I don't know." She looked positively green. "I think I'm going to be—" She heaved into the bushes.

"Sick," J.T. finished for her.

Katrina stepped back in disgust. Mary ran to Gertie's side and held her head as she lost the contents of her stomach. When she finished, Mary wiped her sister's mouth with her hankie. Groaning, Gertie tumbled into a heap and passed out. They wouldn't be having that talk about Roy tonight. Mary called to J.T. "Will you carry her home?"

"Sure." He climbed up the steps, giving Katrina a sharp look as he passed her, then he dropped to a crouch. Katrina gave Mary a look of her own. "Gertie lives here now. I'll help her upstairs."

"No, you won't." J.T. scooped her into his arms, straightened and gave Katrina a look full of pity. "Good night, miss. If you're smart, you'll keep away from Mr. Desmond."

He turned and strode down the street with Gertie hanging from his arms like a rag doll. Mary gave Katrina a pitying look of her own, picked up Gertie's reticule and followed him.

"You can't do this!" Katrina cried.

Mary turned on her heels, speaking as she backpedaled away from the younger woman. "Yes, I *can* do this, Katrina. And I'm doing it. Roy isn't who you think he is."

The girl smirked. "You're just jealous."

"Hardly."

"Gertie won't listen," she shouted back. "She's going to be a great actress, and I'm going to design all her costumes. You can't stop us."

"Maybe not," Mary countered. "But I can try."

Facing forward, she lengthened her stride to catch up with J.T. Tomorrow she'd have that talk with Gertie. She needed to have a similar conversation with J.T., but she wouldn't do it tonight. Her sister would need her full attention.

J.T. had a lot of sympathy for Gertie. He knew all about the dry heaves and headaches. He'd gone down that road alone, and he'd done it often. Gertie had Mary at her side, and she'd done it just once. He hoped she'd learned a lesson. She was home and safe, so he didn't have to give Roy an answer about Lassen right away. Stalling to give Lassen a chance to work offered the best shot at protecting the future J.T. wanted with Mary and her siblings.

While Mary put Gertie to bed, he waited in the front room with Fancy Girl, watching the puppies as they nuzzled and slept. He'd never seen anything so beautiful and so remote from his own experience.

"J.T.?"

He turned and saw Mary in the hall entry. Bluish circles fanned beneath her eyes. "You look done in," he said.

"I am."

He indicated the divan. "Sit with me." She could rest her head on his shoulder.

Mary stayed in the hall. "It's late. You should go."

He didn't like the idea at all. He wanted to know why she hadn't told him she loved him, and why she'd stopped a perfect kiss, but he wouldn't make demands. "All right," he agreed. "I'll head out. We can talk tomorrow."

Looking reluctant, she nodded.

J.T. wanted to kiss her good-night, but she didn't budge. He settled for patting Fancy Girl. The new mother raised her head and gave him a doggy smile. "You did good," he murmured.

Closing her eyes, Fancy lowered her head and slept. J.T. pushed to his feet and headed for the door. Mary finally crossed the room, and he hoped for an explanation, but she stopped two feet away. "Thank you for helping Gertie tonight."

He wished she'd appreciated his love as much. "She's a handful, but she's still a good kid."

Mary didn't move.

Neither did he.

What's wrong, Mary? Tell me. He pleaded silently until she let out a breath. "Will I see you tomorrow?"

"First thing," he said.

She smiled, but her mouth looked pinched. "Good night, J.T. Thank you again."

After a nod that should have been a kiss, he walked alone to the boardinghouse. When he reached his room, he unbuckled his gun belt and draped it over a chair. Usually he missed the weight of it. Tonight he experienced a lightness he didn't understand. Without his dog or a living soul to distract him, he sat on the bed and pulled off his boots. Pictures of the day played through his mind—Roy's threats…kissing Mary…the moment he thought Fancy would die.

Unable to sleep, he picked up the chapbook and read slowly, taking in the words a few at a time and seeing himself among the thieves and the lost. When his eyelids drooped, he blew out the lamp. Darkness filled the room, but tonight it had no power, and he slept like baby.

J.T.'s contentment lasted until six o'clock the next morning. After rising from the narrow bed, he washed and put on dungarees in preparation for dishwashing duty. As always, he strapped on his guns. Griff Lassen could come through the door. Roy could go on the attack. Trusting God to heal his dog was one thing. Trusting Him to watch out for Mary and Gertie struck J.T. as crazy.

He also had to figure out how to earn a living. He'd come to Denver to rescue Mary, not to be tied to her apron strings. Everything seemed wrong as he headed for the café. He'd cut himself shaving, and he missed Fancy Girl trotting at his side. By the time J.T. walked through the back door to the café, he felt more prickly than a cactus. The irritation increased when Mary saw him and didn't smile.

"Good morning," she said formally.

He grumbled a greeting and went to the cupboard to get an apron. Tying it around the gun belt, he felt like a wolf with feathers. He half filled the wash basin at the pump, lifted a kettle from the back of the stove and poured the boiling water into the cold. Mary was busy cracking eggs in a bowl. Trying to be civil, he spoke over the crunch of the shells. "How's Gertie?"

"She's sleeping." She tossed a shell in the scrap bucket. "I haven't spoken to her yet."

Gertie could argue with Mary, but she'd have a hard time putting *him* in his place. "Maybe we should do it together."

"I'll do it," she said too quickly.

Feeling useless, he whittled soap into the basin. Enid entered the kitchen with the first load of dirty plates. She didn't know what to make of J.T., so she ignored him. He didn't blame her. He didn't know what to make of himself. The man who sold his gun for hundreds of dollars was scrubbing egg slime. Working on the church had more dignity—he planned to finish the bell tower shingles today—and he could hold his own as a gunsmith, but neither occupation appealed to him.

"H-h-hi"

He looked over his shoulder and saw Gus. "Hey, kid."

The boy fetched a towel from a shelf and started drying the clean plates. As they worked, he told J.T. about Fancy and the puppies. They were doing well, and Fancy had consumed two bowls of water and eaten ham for breakfast. For the next hour they joked about names for the puppies, finally agreeing on Eeny, Meeny,

Miny, Moe and Isabel, just because Gus liked the name and thought that was the puppy he'd keep.

Mary interrupted. "Gus? Would you empty the garbage pail?"

"Sure."

It was Gus's regular chore, but there were still dishes to put away. The boy knew better than J.T. where they went, so J.T. indicated the plates. "Finish up here. I'll handle the garbage."

Gus grinned. "Lucky you! It stinks."

J.T. lifted the pail with one hand and opened the door with the other.

Whomp!

Something hard bounced off his chest. He set down the bucket and stared down the alley. This time he saw the rock coming. Only it wasn't aimed at him. The kid who'd thrown it—one of the boys who'd attacked Gus— had targeted Mary's window. The rock missed the glass but hit the siding.

Gus raced through the door, saw the boys and stopped in his tracks. "Th-that's them!"

A second boy threw a rock at Gus. Gus ducked, but the rock ricocheted off the wall and hit J.T. in the neck.

No one messed with J.T. or the people he loved. He'd sunk to washing dishes, but he could still scare the daylights out of a group of punk kids. That's what he intended to do. Gus was shouting and scrambling to find a rock to throw back. J.T. knew how he felt, but then he recalled Josh's advice to turn the other cheek. J.T.'s insides were boiling, but he saw a chance to turn a page in his life.

"Let's try a different strategy," he said to Gus.

"Wh-wh-what?"

"We're going give these boys breakfast."

"B-b-breakfast?"

"I know. It's peculiar." The old J.T. would have already put the rock throwers in their place.

Gus finally nodded, so J.T. called out to them. "Hey, are you guys hungry? The meal's on me."

Gus looked wary, but J.T. had the upper hand. The boys would either run away or they'd stay because they were hungry and surprised by the offer. He saw them gather across the alley behind a wood pile. "We've confused them," he said to Gus.

"G-g-good."

One of the boys who'd held Gus against the wall showed himself. "Do you mean it about breakfast?"

"Sure."

A second one came out from behind the stack of wood. He murmured to his friend. He couldn't look J.T. in the eye, but they both came forward.

"There were three of you," J.T. called. "Bring your friend." The third kid had been the meanest, the one who'd pummeled Gus.

The boys looked at each other, then indicated the opposite side of the alley. J.T. spotted the older boy under a stairwell. He looked scrawny, dirty and mean. J.T. didn't know who these boys were or why they'd turned into alley rats, but he'd once been like them. He also knew they'd brutalized Gus. Justice had to be served, or else Gus would be mad the way J.T. had stayed mad his entire life. He and Gus had turned the other cheek by offering a meal, but something had to be said about what these boys had done, and J.T. planned to say it. By speaking up, he hoped to teach Gus a lesson that worked better than hitting before you got hit.

"Come on," he called. "I'm serious about breakfast."

The oldest kid finally stepped into the alley. "It's a trick, isn't it?"

"No, it's not," J.T. answered. "I want you to apologize to Gus. If that's a trick, there it is."

The three boys looked at Gus. Gus glared at them, then looked at J.T. "I—I—I hate them."

He touched Gus's shoulder. "I know, kid. You've got every right to stay mad, but take it from me—you won't feel any better if you do. Let's try this Josh's way." If it didn't work, he and Gus would deal with the brats later.

"All right," Gus managed.

The third boy approached slowly. The two youngest looked sheepish, while the oldest wore a scowl that put crevices in his youthful face. J.T. stopped them all at the back door. "You," he said, pointing at the oldest one. "You beat up my friend. We're willing to put that aside, but you owe him."

The boy-man stared at J.T. "What do you want?"

J.T. turned to Gus. "It's your call."

When Gus's eyes widened, J.T. remembered the stammering and wished he'd been more careful. He couldn't backtrack without embarrassing Gus, so he silently hoped—prayed—the boy would speak clearly.

Gus looked the bigger kid in the eye and stared the way J.T. did when he wanted to look mean. The boy took a slow breath and then said, "I want an apology."

The words came out just fine. J.T. wanted to clap him on the back, but he settled for adding a hard look to Gus's request.

"Sorry," the two boys muttered.

"And—" Gus took another breath. Rather than seeming hesitant, it made him foreboding. "I want a promise. *Leave me alone.*"

J.T. looked at the three boys. "You owe him that much, even more."

The oldest kid narrowed his eyes. "Who are you, anyway?"

"J. T. Quinn."

The kid went pale. "*You're* J. T. Quinn?"

"The same." He offered his hand.

The boy stared at him for a good five seconds. In that silent moment, the two of them shared a sad truth. J.T. knew what he was talking about, and the boy knew it. The boy shook J.T.'s hand, then turned to Gus. "I'm sorry for what we did."

Gus said nothing. He didn't want to risk stuttering, but neither did forgiveness come easily. He was still scowling when Mary opened the back door.

"There you are!" she said. "I thought you'd— Oh. You're Todd Roman. I've heard about you."

The boy looked sheepish. What he saw in Mary, J.T. didn't know. But something had knocked a bit of the cockiness out of him. The boy's cheeks turned as pink as a girl's. "I'm sorry about what happened, Miss Larue. My mama would be ashamed of me."

Mary didn't soften. "You owe my brother an apology."

Todd didn't look pleased, but between Mary and his mother's memory, he was outnumbered. "It won't happen again," he said to Gus. "I'm sorry."

"Me, too," said one of the other boys.

"Same here," said the third.

J.T. thought of his own brothers hurting him in the alley. He'd once vowed to never forgive them, but some of the malice left as he watched Gus stand tall.

"J-just don't do it again," he said firmly.

Everyone ignored the slight stammer. Feeling proud,

J.T. traded a look with Mary. He wanted to trade more looks like this one, but she still had a formal air, and he still needed a job. Before he thought too much about the future, he had to settle matters with Roy, and he needed to find a job that didn't require an apron.

"What do you say?" He punched Gus's arm. "Shall we see who can eat the most hotcakes?"

"Sure."

"I'll get busy." Smiling, Mary went back in the kitchen. The boys followed her, with J.T. bringing up the rear. As he stepped over the threshold, he saw Mary waiting for him at the wash basin. She touched his arm. "That was wonderful."

"Gus did the hard part."

"Yes, but you're good with kids."

"Not really." He didn't know anything about babies and little girls, except that they terrified him. "I know boys and I know men, that's all."

He couldn't read her expression, so he took her hand and squeezed. "What is it, Mary? Talk to me."

"I have to get to the work." She sounded businesslike again. "We've got four boys who want hotcakes."

He let her go, but he followed her with his eyes to the stove. Whatever she was hiding, it posed a threat he didn't understand. Movement in the doorway caught his eye, and he saw Gertie in the purple dress she'd worn last night. With her head high, she walked straight to Mary. "How dare you drag me home like that!"

J.T. saw red. "Now wait just a minute—"

"J.T., no!" Mary's voice came out in a shriek. "This is between Gertie and me."

The girl gave him a look more superior than the one she'd used on Mary. "You have a lot of nerve to criticize Roy."

"He's dangerous, Miss Larue."

"And you're not?"

"Not like Roy." He had to convince her of Roy's true character. "He's not good to women."

She laughed, but it had an ugly sound. "You abandoned my sister when she was *with child,* and you think Roy is bad?"

Gertie's accusation hit him like the first drops of rain from a coming storm. *Mary with child...his child.* The drops turned into a torrent. A baby...his baby...their baby. Where was it? What had happened after he'd left Abilene? He thought Mary had come to trust him, but he was wrong. Could he have hurt her any more than he had? He didn't think so. Whatever Gertie had to say, she could say to both of them.

Chapter Nineteen

Forgetting the hotcakes, Mary whirled to face J.T. The anger he'd felt toward Gertie turned to stark confusion directed toward her. She felt the same churning, maybe more because she loved Gertie, and her sister had betrayed her. She wanted to scream at the foolish, bratty girl to shut up. She also wanted desperately to tell J.T. in private about the baby. Their future hung on his reaction, and she didn't want to blurt the story in front of Gertie.

She gave him a look that begged for patience, then she turned back to her sister. "How dare you!"

"Roy told me *everything*. You act all prim and proper. But you're not, are you? You're a trollop!"

Mary gasped.

J.T.'s voice boomed. *"That's enough!"*

Gertie spun in his direction. "Oh, no, it's not! You're a worthless piece of trash, Mr. Quinn. Get out of here."

Mary couldn't argue with J.T. and Gertie at the same time, so she concentrated on Gertie.

The girl had turned back to her and was screeching like a wet cat. "I want to act and you won't let me because you're selfish! It's not my fault you ruined your life. Do you know what I think? I think you're a hypocrite, and so does Katrina."

The hotcakes started to smoke. Flipping them frantically, Mary heard the thud of J.T.'s boots on the wood floor. She turned and saw that he'd whipped off the apron and was approaching Gertie with a steely look in his eyes. Mary couldn't stand the thought of the two of them tangling. She wanted to deal with Gertie on her terms, not his.

"Not now," she said as he reached the stove. "This is between Gertie and me."

He stopped in his tracks and stared at her. "Do you mean that?"

"Yes." She couldn't cook and deal with Gertie at the same time. The bacon was about to catch fire, and the biscuits had to come out of the oven *now*.

Enid came through the door. "Those boys want their hotcakes." She left an order and went back to the dining room.

"Please," Mary begged J.T. "Just go. We'll talk later."

"When?" he insisted.

The bacon spattered and she shrieked. Gertie headed for the door. "I'm leaving."

He blocked her path. "No, you're not. You're going to have a talk with you sister, and if you're smart you'll listen to her." He indicated the spatula in Mary's hand. "Give me that. I'll finish the cooking."

Mary held it away from him. "It would be best if you left."

"You need help."

"Please," she said again. "Leave this to me." In Abilene she'd wanted him to stay. Today she wanted him to go.

He studied her with sad, angry eyes. "Is that what you want?"

"Yes."

She hurriedly turned a strip of bacon and motioned to Enid in the dining room. The waitress hurried back through the door. "What is it, miss?"

"Finish up." Mary handed her the spatula. "I have to speak to Gertie."

The waitress shook her finger at the girl. "You're nothing but trouble, young lady. If you were my daughter, I'd—"

"Enid, no." Berating Gertie would only make her more rebellious. Mary gripped her sister's arm and dragged her to the back door. J.T. watched with a cool expression and then left through the door to the dining room. She had no idea where he'd go or what he'd do. She only knew the past had been opened like a grave.

She steered Gertie out the door and into the alley. It stank of garbage, and the morning heat promised a scorcher of a day. With no place to sit, she faced her sister standing up. They were equals in height but not experience, though Gertie wouldn't agree.

"It's true about J.T. and me," Mary told her. "We were more than friends, and I conceived. I lost the baby before I came to Denver." She told Gertie about the scandal, the miscarriage and the murder trial. "That time of my life was ugly and awful. I don't want you to make the same mistakes."

"Of course I wouldn't," she said, more naive than ever. "Besides, I'm old enough to know what I want. You're holding me back."

"I'm protecting you."

"No, you're not. I'm paying for *your* mistakes."

"That's not true." Her throat ached with the effort to be calm. "Theater life is more challenging than you know."

"It's *wonderful*."

"Yes, it is." Mary had loved being onstage. "But if you love it too much, you'll forget what's really important."

"That's ridiculous."

Losing hope, Mary pulled out her last weapon against Roy. "I know you don't trust J.T., but he knows Roy better than you or I do." She told Gertie about the dead saloon girl and Roy's debts. "He's using you to manipulate me. He threatened you."

"I don't believe you."

Gertie hadn't even asked how he'd threatened her, a sure sign that she'd been taken in by Roy and her own ambition. Roy hadn't seduced her yet, but Mary feared he'd try and succeed. Even more frightening, he'd use Gertie to get what he wanted from J.T.

Gertie shrugged. "I don't care what Roy supposedly said to J.T. I know Roy, and I trust him."

"But he's *using* you," Mary insisted.

"I don't care." Looking all of seventeen, Gertie lifted her chin. "Some people would say *I'm* using *him*."

Mary gave up. Stepping back, she spoke to her sister as if she were the adult she wanted to be. "No matter what happens, Gertie. I love you. You can come home anytime."

"I love you, too."

They'd be sisters forever, so Mary hugged Gertie tight. She didn't want to let go, but the girl broke away with a slight push. Looking foolish and brave, Gertie walked past the stinking garbage cans to the edge of the café. Without glancing back, she cut between two buildings and went to the street.

Alone in the growing heat, Mary thought about J.T. She'd told him to leave and he had. She needed to speak with him, but Gertie's betrayal posed an immediate threat. The gossip about her would start the minute someone set foot in Katrina's dress shop. Needing to pick up the pieces of her life, Mary headed to Swan's Nest without bothering to change clothes or even remove her apron. Enid would close the café for her.

As for J.T., she wondered where he'd gone and what he'd do. It was just like Abilene, except this time she'd ordered him to leave, and it was up to her to do the explaining.

J.T. had gone to the dining room, but he had no intention of leaving the café. He couldn't get the picture of a child—*his* child—out of his head. Had Mary given the baby away? Was she paying someone to raise it? He counted the months and years in his head. A baby would be over a year old. Did they have a son or a daughter? Could it walk yet?

He couldn't imagine Mary giving up a baby, but what choice had he given her? At the thought of an orphanage, he wanted to put his fist through the wall. His own child abandoned just as he'd been abandoned. The thought shamed him. So did the misery he'd inflicted on Mary. Other thoughts came unbidden. Not all babies were born. He'd been in enough brothels to know that desperate women did desperate things. Other times nature took its course. Babies came too soon and died, or they didn't come at all. Whatever had happened to Mary and their child, he had to know the truth.

He wanted to go after her now, but she needed time with Gertie. He settled for sitting down with Gus and the boys from the alley. Judging by Gus's hard look, he'd heard Gertie's accusation. J.T. didn't want the kid to have him on a pedestal, but neither did he want to lose

Gus's respect. He spoke in a tone just for them. "We'll talk later."

Glowering, the boy stabbed a hotcake. J.T. made small talk with the other boys, but he couldn't stop wondering about Mary and Gertie. His gut told him to go to her, but he had to honor her request to deal with Gertie alone. The boys polished their plates, thanked him for the food and left with friendly words for Gus. J.T. felt good about the meal, but the trouble with Mary put him on edge. He wanted to go after her, but Gus needed an explanation, and J.T. didn't want Enid to hear it.

"Wait here," he said to the boy.

He went into the kitchen, where Enid was scrubbing the stove. "Go on home. I'll finish up."

She looked at J.T. as if he were vermin. "If what I heard is true, Mr. Quinn, you need to do right by Miss Larue. She's a fine woman."

"Yes, she is."

Enid put her hands on her hips. "If you ask me, men are nothing but trouble."

J.T. had to agree. Mary had lost everything—a baby, her reputation, her career—while he'd run off like the father of Fancy's puppies.

Enid gave him another hard look, then wadded up her apron and walked out the door with her words echoing in J.T.'s mind. He wanted to do right by Mary, but he had nothing to offer except his bad name. He had no way to support her, and he cared about such things. Even if he asked, would Mary have him? Not telling him about the baby meant she didn't trust him after all. J.T. didn't know much about forgiveness, but he knew he had to ask for it again with full knowledge that he'd left her with child.

He went to the back window, parted the curtain and searched for Mary and Gertie in the alley. When he didn't see them, he figured they'd stepped out of sight or gone to the apartment. Frustrated, he went back to the dining hall. The boys had left, but Gus was standing by the kitchen door with his arms crossed, looking closer to a man than a boy and ready to hold J.T. accountable. If the situation hadn't been so serious, J.T. would have enjoyed the boy's audacity.

Gus stared at him. "W-w-we need to t-talk."

"Yes, we do." Wanting to give the boy the respect he deserved, J.T. sat so that Gus had the advantage of height. Knowing the stammer would be out of control, he spoke for them both. "You heard what Gertie said."

"I-i-is it true?"

"Yes, it is." The admission shamed him. "I didn't know about a baby until now, but that's no excuse. I need to square things with your sister."

Gus's blue eyes burned into him. "Are y-you going to m-m-marry her?"

"It's up to her."

"B-b-but you're going to ask." It was an order, not a question.

J.T. recalled the conversation they'd had while camping. "I love your sister, Gus. She's the reason I came to Denver. But it's not that simple. Do you remember asking me about loving a woman?"

The boy nodded.

"I made a mess of your sister's life. I'm doing my best to clean it up, but exactly how I do that is up to her."

Gus uncrossed his arms, but he still had the look of a riled brother protecting his sister. If he'd had a shotgun, J.T. might have been worried…or grateful. He wanted to make Mary his wife, but it felt wrong to ask her when he had nothing to give. He'd eat all the crow Gus or Mary could serve, but he needed a way to pay for the crow.

Still scowling, Gus started stacking the dirty plates. "Y-y-you need to f-fix things with her."

"You're right." Their child hadn't been conceived in the best way, but he wanted to give the baby and Mary a good life. He just didn't know how to do it. "I'm not leaving until she comes back."

"G-g-good."

The boy scowled again. Even with the stutter, he'd learned how to be menacing. Unable to hold back a proud grin, J.T. held out his hand. "Congratulations, Gus. You stood up for your sister like a grown man. I'm proud of you."

Stoic, the boy shook back hard. J.T. couldn't help but be amazed. A stammering twelve-year-old had gotten the best of him. Surprisingly happy about it, he indicated the dishes. "I better get busy. I don't want your sister walking into a messy kitchen."

For the next two hours, he and Gus washed dishes, scrubbed pots and swept the floor. With no sign of Mary, J.T. wondered where she'd gone. Maybe she'd convinced Gertie to come home and they'd gone for the girl's things. He thought about going to Katrina's hotel, but his presence would make matters worse. He also had to consider the impact of last night on Roy and his threats. J.T. had promised the man an answer about Griff Lassen. With Gertie back in harm's way, J.T. couldn't stall. As soon as he finished his business with Mary, he'd take Roy's offer, but just to buy time. First, though, he had to find out about the baby.

He needed to stay busy, so he found some vinegar and washed the windows. He wiped down the tables again and even dusted the pictures on the wall, but there was still no sign of Mary.

When the café couldn't be any cleaner, Gus had an idea. "Want to play checkers?"

"Sure."

He wanted to see Mary the instant she showed up, so he told Gus to bring the game to the dining room. Ten games of checkers later, J.T. couldn't stand the waiting, but neither could he leave.

"Hey, Gus," he said as they put away the pieces. "I need a favor. Will you see if your sister's at Swan's Nest?"

"Sure."

The boy ran off, leaving J.T. to sweep the boardwalk and the stairs. When Gus came back, he had news J.T. didn't understand. "She was there, but she left with Adie."

Knowing she was safe, he settled in to wait some more. He'd wait all day if he had to. He'd wait all night… all week…all month. He'd wait forever if that's what it took for Mary to come to him. He went outside to the stairs to the apartment and sat on the third one. As soon as Mary came home, they'd be searching together for the child he'd never known but wanted to love.

"I can't do it," Mary said to Adie.

"Yes, you can."

After hearing Mary's story, the minister's wife had looped her arm around Mary's waist and dragged her upstairs to change her clothes. "Like I said, we're going calling this afternoon."

Mary stopped in the hall. "That's the *last* thing I want to do!"

"Which is why we're going to do it," Adie said simply. "Right now Gertie is telling Katrina everything, and they're making up what they don't know or understand.

Every woman who steps into that dress shop is going to hear a half-made-up story. You can do nothing and let the rumors catch fire, or you can do what a fire chief would do."

Mary saw a glimmer of hope. "I can light a back fire."

"Exactly," Adie replied. "We're going to tell every woman we know the truth before she hears the gossip. It's the only way."

"Are you sure?"

"Yes."

Mary's pride balked. "But it's so private." Wasn't it enough that she'd made peace with God in her prayers?

"I wish Gertie would keep quiet, but she won't. Sharing what happened is embarrassing for you, but it might help someone else." Adie's hazel eyes turned misty. "You're not the first woman to give herself to a man too soon. Josh's sister crossed the same line. He'd give anything to change what he said to her."

Mary knew the story. Josh had said terrible things to his sister, and she'd fled Boston in disgrace. When she'd died giving birth, Adie had adopted the child as her own. She and Josh had found happiness, but Mary had her doubts about J.T.'s reaction to the miscarriage. If he said "good riddance," she'd feel rejected all over again. And if she didn't address the gossip, she'd again be a victim of the scandal. The thought disgusted her. She'd worked hard to start a new life. If she had to fight to protect it, she'd do it. And if J.T. had the gall to disrespect her feelings about the baby, she'd fight him, too.

Mary looked at the massive wardrobe against the wall. Adie used it for storage now, but it once held the dresses

Mary brought from Abilene. "I can't go in this greasy apron. Do you have something that will fit me?"

"I think so."

Adie flung open the double doors, fanning the air and stirring the yellow curtains. The scent of cedar filled the room and mixed with light coming through the window. Breathing in the familiar smells, Mary thought back to the first days she spent in this room. It was here she'd mourned the loss of the baby and grieved her career. It was here she'd uttered her first desperate prayers. The room had been a place of healing, a place of hope.

She hadn't left any clothing at Swan's Nest, but she and Adie were close to the same size. Approaching the wardrobe, she saw a gown that *had* been hers. It was the dress she'd been wearing when she'd left Abilene. She'd hadn't taken it to the apartment, because she couldn't bear to wear it. Today the stylish gown matched her mood. Jade green with satin trim and pagoda sleeves, it had a round lace collar and a pleated overskirt. The dress was bold, brave and just plain pretty.

"This is perfect," she said to Adie.

Together they dressed and did their hair. Wearing fancy hats and even fancier gloves, they climbed into the buggy and Adie drove to the impressive home of Rosalie Cates. A widow, Mrs. Cates attended church at Brick's because she liked Josh's Boston accent, not because she enjoyed the humble surroundings. She also frequented Katrina's dress shop.

A butler ushered Mary and Adie into a parlor and offered refreshments. Rosalie entered the room a moment later. Obviously curious, she looked from Adie to Mary, then back to Adie. "It's a pleasure to see you. And a surprise. I'm guessing the church is having a fundraiser?"

"No," Adie answered. "We're here to talk about gossip."

Rosalie masked her expression. "Am I the subject of it?"

Mary saw herself in the woman's sudden wariness, the lift of her chin and the donning of a mask that hid her feelings.

"It's not about you," Adie replied quickly.

Mary met the woman's gaze. "It's about me. I'd like to tell you the truth before you hear rumors."

"Of course." Rosalie indicated a brocade sofa littered with satin pillows. "Please sit down."

Mary saw sympathy in the woman's eyes…and sadness. The glimpse into Rosalie's heart gave her courage, and she told the story with an ease she hadn't expected. Somehow the details were less dramatic than they'd been in the alley with Gertie. "That's it," Mary finished. "I made a mistake and I regret it. I've also made a fresh start. I hope to continue to give my brother and sister a good home."

"Of course you do." Rosalie looked Mary square in the eye. "I admire you."

"You do?"

"Yes." The older woman pulled a hankie from her sleeve and twisted it. "My sister didn't have your courage. She was twenty-three and unmarried when she told me she was expecting. To this day, I don't know who fathered the child, if she'd been attacked or had gone to the man willingly. I only know she hanged herself."

Adie gasped.

So did Mary.

Rosalie shoved the hankie back up her sleeve. "Tell your story to everyone who'll listen. If Katrina insists on spreading rumors, I'll make sure she loses customers."

And so began a day full of surprises.... Rosalie insisted on accompanying them on the rest of their calls. As a trio, they visited eight women and heard eight different stories. No one shunned Mary, and four of them offered to join Rosalie in finding a new dressmaker. By the end of the day, Mary felt both humbled and awed. Her deepest fear had turned into a blessing that stretched beyond herself.

With dusk settling, she relaxed in the buggy with Adie. "That was easier than I thought."

Adie kept her eyes on the street. "It seems to me there's one more person you need to call on."

"I know." The time had come to face J.T. "He's staying at a boardinghouse off of Market. Would you take me?"

Adie immediately turned the buggy. "What are you going to tell him?"

"Everything."

"Can I give you some advice?" she said softly.

"Of course."

"J.T.'s a hard man. Don't be surprised if he says all the wrong things."

Mary heart sped up. "That's what I'm expecting." And that's what she couldn't bear. Saving her reputation had given her a measure of peace, but Gertie's betrayal had opened all her old wounds, especially the one from losing the baby. Adie chatted mildly about men, likening them to mules and mustangs. Some were hardworking. Others were wild and unpredictable. J.T. fit the latter description, though he'd worked like a mule washing dishes. She loved all sides of him, but his toughness could hurt her.

When they reached the boardinghouse, Mary turned to Adie. "He might not be here. Would you wait?"

"Sure."

Mary went to the door, spoke to the landlady and learned that J.T. had been gone all day. Discouraged and a little miffed, she went back to the buggy. "He's not here," she told Adie.

"Do you want to look for him?"

"I wouldn't know where to start." He could have gone to Brick's for supper. He could have been dealing with Roy or Griff Lassen. If he'd lost his moorings, he could have gone to a saloon or a gaming hall. Discouraged, Mary looked straight ahead. "Would you take me home?"

"Of course."

The streets were empty now, and the sunset had faded to dusky blue. Adie didn't speak, and neither did Mary. Her throat hurt from the day's conversations, and her chest felt heavy with dread. Gus had heard Gertie's accusations. She'd have to speak with him. She'd also left the café without doing the cleaning, and she doubted Enid's goodwill extended to sweeping floors.

As they approached the restaurant, Mary looked at the windows. This morning they'd needed washing, but now they sparkled. The boardwalk had been swept, too. Wondering if Gus had stepped up to help her, she turned her attention to the stairs to her apartment. Instead of Gus, she saw J.T. sitting on the third step and watching her with a glint in his eyes. As the buggy halted, he approached without a word and offered his hand, palm up and expectant.

Mary hugged Adie and whispered, "Pray for me."

"I will."

Turning, she accepted J.T.'s hand and stepped down from the buggy. Adie drove off, leaving them alone with hard questions that had to be answered. Gripping her hands in both of his, J.T. asked the hardest question of all. "What happened to the baby?"

Chapter Twenty

Mary tried to gauge his reaction, but his eyes were as hooded as hers. She pulled out of his grasp. "I don't want to have this talk on the street."

"Fine. We'll go upstairs."

"But Gus—"

"He'll understand." When he looked up at the window, she followed his gaze and saw Gus watching them. J.T. jerked his chin and the boy stepped away, presumably to go to his room to give them privacy. J.T. had obviously spoken with her brother, but he didn't seem to be have much patience with *her*.

"How long have you been waiting?" she asked as they climbed the stairs.

"Since morning."

"That's all day."

"I know," he grumbled. "I'd have waited all night if you hadn't come home."

She looked at him from the corner of her eye, remembering the windows and the clean boardwalk. Not only had he waited for her, but he'd done what he could to help her. Her blood thrummed with hope. In another minute she'd know if she could trust him with her deepest feelings. At the top of the landing, he reached around her waist and opened the door. She crossed the threshold, and he closed it behind her with a soft click. Standing in the light from a single lamp, he took off his gun belt and hung it on chair. In a dark corner, Fancy Girl greeted them by wagging her tail. The puppies lay at her side, their eyes still sealed as they suckled.

Turning abruptly, Mary faced him. "I lost the baby."

"*Lost* it?" He sounded like he was talking about a missing pocketknife.

Was he callous or confused? Mary's insides trembled. "I had a miscarriage. The baby was never born."

He let out a slow, even breath. "That's a relief."

Just like in Abilene, he'd hurt her. This time she wanted the satisfaction of telling him to leave for good. "Get out of here!"

"What?"

"I said *leave!*"

"No way." His voice came out in a growl.

"I will *not* let you disrespect that child!" For two years Mary had stifled her anger and hidden her grief. Tonight she had nothing to hide. "That baby was part of me. It was part of *us.* I was scared at first, but I wanted it. I loved it." She turned her back on him and stared out the window. "If you can't understand how I felt, I don't want you in my life."

"Oh, I understand," he said with deadly calm. "You're the one who's misinformed."

"I doubt that."

He walked up behind her, stirring the air with his long stride. "I'm not relieved you lost the baby. I'm relieved it's not living in an orphanage somewhere."

Turning slowly, she looked into his eyes. They were full of violence and bitterness and a possessiveness that gave her chills. She wanted to believe he cared, but she could only see the anger.

Glaring at her, he put his hands on his hips. "Do you know how I spent the day?"

"You cleaned the café." The answer struck her as inane, but it showed that he cared.

"That's right," he said. "I mopped and scrubbed and *worried* that *our* child was alone in this world. I thought *all day* about a child growing up like I did, eating garbage and stealing and getting punched and cut and—" He sealed his lips. Turning abruptly, he hid his face from her. "I can't stand the thought of it."

She put her hand on his shoulder, steadying him and absorbing the soft trembling that ran up her arm. "Neither could I. I was so scared—"

He turned and pulled her against him. "I should have been there. I should have—" He stopped short, but she imagined the declaration she'd once dreamed of hearing. *I should have married you.* He hadn't said the words, and she was glad. She didn't want him to speak out of guilt or obligation. They were new people, and she wanted a new beginning. The silence turned into a wall. Needing air, she turned to the window, where she saw the reflection of his face. He rested his hand on her shoulder, curling his fingers against the satiny fabric of her dress. His eyes dipped down the glass, taking in the gown he was likely to remember.

"When did it happen?" he asked.

"A month after you left." She spoke to his reflection. "I'd had pain all day, but I ignored it. I was about to go onstage when the bleeding started. I'd made the mistake of confiding in Ana." She'd been Mary's best friend at the time, and J.T. knew her. "She let it slip, so the rumors were already flying. When I couldn't go on stage, everyone knew for certain I'd been carrying your child."

"I'm sorry," he said ever so gently. "I'm sorry for the scandal, and I'm sorry you lost the baby."

She turned at last. "I am, too."

The air thickened with their mingled warmth. He cupped her face but didn't kiss her. Neither did he speak. The future beaconed like a baby's first smile. He'd made peace with God, and he'd told her he loved her. Earlier he'd almost made a declaration, but now he looked remote. Mary wanted to tell him she loved him and trusted him fully, but as she parted her lips to speak, he lowered his hand.

As if he'd come to his senses, he headed to the divan and sat with hands dangling between his knees, tapping his fingers in an annoying rhythm.

He wanted to ask Mary to be his wife, but a man had his pride. He couldn't propose marriage without a way to support her. He wanted her hands to turn soft again, not be callused from cooking and pushing a broom. He also figured babies would come, and he refused to bring a child into the world if he couldn't provide a good home. Unwilling to let Mary go completely, he looked at her standing by the window in a gown he recognized from Abilene.

"I remember that dress," he said. "You were wearing it the night I left."

"That's right."

"And you weren't wearing it this morning." He'd waited for her all day. "Where'd you go?"

"Adie and I went calling." She showed off the skirt with both hands. "I'd left this at Swan's Nest."

Her eyes were dancing and he loved the boldness. "Who'd you call on?"

"Eight women who will support me in this town." She told him about the visits and how she'd been received with dignity. "Even if the gossip starts, I'll be fine."

"That's good."

Her boldness had paid off, but J.T. wanted to give her even more assurance. Once he had the means to support her, he'd marry her. First, though, he had to find a way to make a living…a way that didn't involve guns or cards. His gaze drifted to Fancy Girl, and he thought of the ways God had shown Himself. Did the Almighty know how badly he needed a job? He had a little bit of work to do on the roof, but the church would be finished in a few weeks. He knew a lot about guns, but being a gunsmith would keep his reputation alive.

Mary was looking at him expectantly. They'd covered a lot of ground tonight, but more trouble lay ahead. He couldn't ask her to be his wife, but she needed protection, and so did Gertie. "I'm going to see Roy tonight. I have to give him an answer about Lassen."

Her eyes filled with worry. "Are you going after him?"

"No. I'm just buying time. I'll give Roy what he wants, and we'll wait for Lassen to make a move."

Footsteps pounded up the stairs. He heard a woman—no, a girl—sobbing uncontrollably. It was the sound a child made when it was hurt and had no pride, the sound *he'd* made when his brother cut him. He strode to the door and flung it wide. Gertie stumbled blindly into the room. He caught her shoulders and saw blood on her face and gown. Her nose was swollen, and a torn sleeve hung like a broken arm.

"Who did this?" J.T. demanded, though he already knew.

Mary flung her arms around her sister. Gertie fell against her, sobbing out the details of Roy inviting her into his office, offering her whiskey and touching her and—J.T. stopped listening. Roy Desmond needed to die.

Why, God?

Yesterday he'd trusted the Almighty and Fancy had lived. Tonight Gertie had been attacked. It made no sense at all. What a fool he'd been to trust Mary's God. No way would he turn the other cheek to a man like Roy Desmond. On the church roof he'd dreamed of taking off his guns. Looking at Gertie in her bloody dress, he vowed to wear them until the day he died.

"I'll be back," he said to Mary.

"No!" she cried. "Stay here."

Ignoring her, he snatched his gun belt off the chair. *No one* messed with J. T. Quinn. Not his own brother. Not Roy Desmond. Not even God.

Mary grabbed his arm. "You're too angry to go out there."

Telling him he was too angry made him even angrier. "I'm going, Mary. You can't stop me."

"We need to pray," she said desperately.

"I'm done praying." No way would he sit around like a little girl. He pointed to Gertie, bloody and weeping. "Are you willing to let this go?"

"No, but—"

"I'm going after Roy, and I'm going to kill him."

Shrieking, Gertie buried her face in her hands and wept

even harder. J.T. wondered if Roy had done worse than hit her, but he didn't want to embarrass her by asking. He knew how it felt to be humiliated, so he looked to Mary for an answer. Glaring at him, she murmured in her sister's ear.

"No," Gertie murmured. "But he tried. I should have listened to you. I should have—"

"It's over now." Mary rocked her sister in her arms, patting her back as if she were small. "Let's get some ice on your face."

With one eye on Mary, J.T. pulled the Colt and checked the cylinder, watching as Mary wrapped a hunk of ice in a towel. As he holstered the pistol, she held the ice to Gertie's swollen nose. Her tenderness met a need; his toughness would meet a different one. Healing and vengeance sometimes did a macabre dance.

Mary looked him in the eye. "I'm going to help Gertie clean up, then we'll decide, together, what to do. Do *not* leave until I get back. Do you hear me, Jonah?"

The old J.T. would have walked out and taken care of business. The new one had a vague sense of Someone watching and waiting to see what he'd do. That same presence had *watched* him get cut as a kid. That Some-one had *watched* Gus take a beating and Gertie being punched in the face by Roy. Every time she looked in the mirror, she'd remember tonight. That same Someone had also spared Fancy Girl's life, but J.T. counted the score as 1-3. He narrowed his eyes until they twitched. "I can't stay here and do nothing."

"Yes, you can."

She'd used the bossy tone she used on Gus. He didn't like it all. He glanced at Gertie and saw himself in her bloody, broken face. Being attacked made a person think they somehow deserved it. She didn't. No matter what stupid things she'd done, no woman deserved a beating, and neither did a child. Wanting to help her, he softened his voice. "I'm sorry this happened to you, Miss Larue."

Her lips quivered. "I feel so stupid."

Mary held her tighter. "You made a mistake. We'll go to the law in the morning."

J.T. huffed. "A lot of good *that* will do."

Gertie wiped at the tears and the blood. "You were right, both of you. The other actors mocked me, but I believed Roy. He told me things—"

"He tickled your ears," J.T. said. "That's how he works."

"I know that now." Gertie's eyes had the flatness of stones. Looking older than her seventeen years, she shuffled down the hall.

Mary challenged him with a look. "I have to go to her. *Do not leave.*"

In his heart he'd left five minutes ago. "I can't do it, Mary. I can't turn the other cheek."

"Maybe not," she acknowledged. "But you can wait ten minutes before you walk out. I know what you're thinking, Jonah. You think God doesn't care."

"You don't know *half* of what I'm thinking." She was too good inside, too full of kindness. He wanted to lash out at someone, but not at Mary. He'd never hurt her intentionally, not even her feelings. On the other hand, he had no sympathy for her God.

"I'm going after Roy," he said calmly. "Since I'm a reasonable man, I'll give him a choice." It wouldn't be a real choice. Roy would die for hurting Gertie, but Mary didn't need to know.

"What's the choice?" she asked.

"He can pay for Gertie's trip to New York, or he and I can square off outside of town."

The old coldness settled into his bones, a sign he'd gotten his sharpness back. Mary stared so long he wondered if he'd become a stranger to her. He felt colder with every beat of his heart, sharper and more clearheaded, until the chill went so deep he felt nothing.

Mary broke the silence. "It's not your place to kill Roy. Vengeance belongs to God. We have laws—"

"I'd say vengeance belongs to Gertie."

"It doesn't," she insisted. "If you kill Roy in cold blood, you'll be a murderer."

"So what?" He'd already killed fourteen men.

"Just one night," she pleaded. "Maybe Lassen will take care of Roy."

Or maybe Lassen would come after *him*. J.T. was tired of twiddling his thumbs. "I'm leaving."

"I'm begging you—"

"No!" He'd enough of her foolishness. "I'm doing what I should have done two days ago."

He looked at Mary a long time, taking in her tears and her determination, the pretty green dress and the way she stood her ground. They'd come a long way from Abilene, but somehow they were back at the beginning. He was going to leave her, and she wouldn't like it. This time, though, he wanted to come back. "I'll find you when I'm done with Roy."

Slowly, as if her body had turned to clay, she shook her head no. "If you leave now, we have no future. Every time you walk out a door, I'll wonder if you're coming back."

He held out his arms to show off his guns. "This is who I am."

"It's who you *were*. Give God a chance—"

"I'm done with God," he said without feeling. "If you're done with me because of it, I understand."

Breath by breath, her silence built a wall. It thickened with the tick of the clock. J.T. felt the weight of his guns. The belt rode high on his hips, embracing him and pulling him into the dark where he'd find Roy and kill him. He didn't have to go. He could take off his guns and do nothing, but he'd never be the man Mary deserved, or the God-fearing man she wanted. He glanced at Fancy Girl and the puppies. If he killed Roy, he'd have to leave Denver without her. He'd never see his dog again. And Gus…he'd have to leave without saying goodbye. Was killing Roy worth the cost? His heart said no, but if he didn't protect Mary and her family, who would?

Just like in the alley in New York, God had blinked and a child had been hurt. Justice had to be served, and J.T. intended to do it. He looked at Mary a long time, etching her face in his memory the way he'd done on that first day in Denver, then he walked out the door.

She watched through the window as J.T. paced down the street. She touched the glass with a silent plea, but he didn't turn around. A door opened in the hallway. Turning, she saw her brother.

"Wh-what happened?" he asked.

"Gertie got hurt." She stepped away from the window. "I'm going to get Bessie."

"Will she be okay?"

"I think so." She told Gus about Gertie's nose and Roy's threats. A week ago he'd have reacted like a frightened child. Tonight his eyes blazed with a man's instinct to protect the women in his home. He looked around the room. "Where's J.T.?"

"He's gone."

"I heard you b-both shouting. Is he c-coming back?"

Gus had hardly stammered a single word. He'd grown up this week. If J.T. didn't return, the boy would learn another hard lesson. Surely she and Gus meant more to him than killing Roy, though she understood the desire for vengeance. If Gertie's nose didn't heal right, she'd be marked for life. If J.T. had stayed, she could have sent them both to get Bessie. Instead she had to rely on her brother.

"He's not coming back tonight." *Maybe not ever.* "Would you get Bessie?"

The boy put on his shoes and hurried out the door. "I'll be fast."

Mary went to the bedroom, where she saw Gertie at the vanity, dressed in a pink wrapper and examining her nose in the oval mirror. "It's broken. It'll be crooked forever."

"Maybe not." She told Gertie that Gus was getting Bessie, then she pulled a pin from the girl's disheveled hair. "Do you want to tell me what happened?"

Tears filled her eyes. "I can't bear to think about it."

"It'll help to talk."

Mary pulled a second pin, then another. Gertie's hair came loose, and the story tumbled out of her. As Mary brushed away the elaborate curls, she listened to a story that could have ended with far worse than a broken nose. Roy could have raped her and then murdered her to ensure her silence. Trembling for her sister, Mary combed out the last tangle. "This doesn't have to ruin your life. You can still go to New York when you're eighteen."

Gertie shook her head. "I don't want to go."

Dreams didn't die that easily. Mary gripped her sister's shoulders. "Why not?"

"I don't have talent."

"Who says?"

"Everyone." Tears filled the girl's eyes. "I made a fool of myself. The other actresses laughed at me. I heard them. And now my nose is a mess."

"You've had a terrible experience." Mary spoke to Gertie's reflection and her own. "There's no shame in quitting if that's what you really want, but how about waiting until you're older before you decide?"

A sheepish smile curved on Gertie's lips. "That's probably smart. Maybe my nose will heal straight."

"Let's see what Bessie says."

Being careful of Gertie's bruises, Mary laced her hair into a braid. As she tied the ribbon, Bessie stepped through the door with Caroline at her side. The nurse set her medical bag on the bed, then pulled up a chair next to Gertie. "How badly did he hurt you?"

"My nose is broken."

"Anything else?" She touched the girl's arm.

Gertie understood the question. The fear that filled her eyes broke Mary's heart. "He tried, but I got away."

"Good girl." Bessie studied her nose with a clinical air. "It's broken, but I don't think it's displaced."

"Are you sure?" Gertie sounded hopeful

"As sure as I can be with all that swelling." Bessie pinched the bridge of her nose. "I don't feel a bump."

Caroline nudged Mary. "Where's J.T.?"

"He left."

Before Mary realized what her friend intended, Caroline steered her into the parlor and guided her down on the divan. "Is he going after Roy?"

"I'm afraid so."

Caroline gripped her hand. "Maybe he'll calm down before he does something stupid."

"I hope so." Mary slipped away and went to the window. She looked for J.T., though she didn't expect to see him. "If he comes back, there's a good chance he'll have blood on his hands."

"Oh, Mary."

"I've never seen him so angry."

Caroline came to stand next to her. "Keep praying. That's all you can do."

"I know. It's just—" She started to cry. An hour ago, J.T. had earned her complete trust. The last barrier to loving him had been shattered tonight. She hadn't said the words, but she'd given him her heart and he'd already broken it again. Forgiveness had come easily for what he'd done in Abilene, but tonight she felt bitter. "He left. How can I trust him?"

"Maybe that's not the right question," Caroline said.

"Then what is it?"

"Can you forgive him? And I don't mean just more time." The brunette looked past the street to the sliver of moon. "You know I was married once. I loved Charles with everything in me, but not a day passed that I didn't have to forgive him for something. The day he died was the worst. I begged him not to go that night. I knew something awful would happen, and it did. In the end, I had to forgive him for dying."

Mary's chest tightened. "How did you do it?"

"Just like you'll forgive J.T. I did it one hurt at a time."

"I don't know." Her voice quavered. "If he goes after Roy, he'll be guilty of murder. He might not come back."

"Give him time," Caroline advised.

"How long?"

"As long as it takes."

Mary smiled at her friend. "Thank you."

She couldn't always count on J.T., but she could depend on the women of Swan's Nest. Through the dim glass she saw a thousand stars. She didn't know how long J.T. would be gone, but she'd be waiting when he returned.

Chapter Twenty-One

Without Fancy Girl at his side, J.T. felt as if he'd stepped back in time. The night air cooled his face but not his blood as he headed for the Newcastle. Tonight he had a job to do.

The stars followed him without blinking, and not a cloud could be seen for miles. Refusing to look at the unfinished church, he went to the side door of the theater, kicked it down and strode to Roy's office. Wall sconces lit his way, flickering as he passed them. When he reached Roy's door, he kicked it down and found more darkness. He didn't know where Roy lived, but he had a good idea where to find him. Attacking Gertie would have fired his blood. Market Street offered women, liquor and cards, just what Roy would want to satisfy his lust.

J.T. headed back down the hall. Stepping over the splintered door, he saw the scaffolding against the church wall. He'd never climb it again. Someone else would have to finish the bell tower.

With only vengeance in mind, he turned down Market Street. Peering into saloons and dance halls, he searched for Roy while intending to avoid Griff Lassen. He spotted Lassen in a busy saloon, ducked out of sight and crossed

the street to a place called the Alhambra. At the counter
he saw Roy sipping whiskey. A smear of blood showed on
his cuff, and he had a scratch on his jaw. J.T. approached
him without a hint of anger. "Hello, Roy."

"Quinn."

J.T. signaled the barkeep. "Whatever my friend's
drinking for him. Whiskey for me." He wouldn't drink
it. The liquor was a sign to Roy that he meant business.
He kept his eyes straight ahead. "You jumped the gun
with Gertie Larue."

"You were dragging your feet." He meant J.T.'s promise to stop Lassen.

"I told you I'd get back to you today. Here I am."

"You were stalling."

"I was being careful."

"I don't believe you, Quinn."

The barkeep set down the glasses and poured. J.T.
ran his finger along the rim, distracting Roy as he slid
his other hand inside the duster, resting it on his gun.
"You've upped the price. I want two thousand dollars."

Roy laughed. "For that little brat?"

"Don't test me." He dug the Colt into Roy's side.
"Bring the money to the Slewfoot Mine tomorrow at
noon. You pay me off, and I'll finish with Lassen. If you
don't—" he cocked the hammer "—I'll kill you for what
you did to Gertie."

Slowly Roy turned his head. "The little trollop's just
like her sister."

If they'd been in a lawless cow town, J.T. might have
shot Roy on the spot. The only thing stopping him was
the likelihood of getting caught. He needed his horse
for a fast getaway, so he settled for twisting the gun
hard enough to leave a bruise. "Do you want to die right
here?"

Roy let out a breath. "Tomorrow it is."

J.T. eased the hammer back in place. "The Slewfoot at noon," he repeated. "Don't be late."

He holstered his weapon and stood. Tomorrow Roy would die. When he showed up with the money, J.T. would challenge him to a duel. He'd win, of course. But Roy had enough skill to call it a fair fight.

He paid for the drinks, left the saloon and headed to Swan's Nest to get his horses, taking a longer route to avoid Mary's apartment. When he reached the mansion he went around the back to the carriage house. Working in the dark, he saddled the buckskin. Rather than take the pack horse, he decided to leave it for Gus. When he got back to the boardinghouse, he'd write a note to the boy. It wasn't much of a goodbye, but it would have to do.

He led the horse into the yard, climbed on and rode down the street. A block later he passed a buggy coming in the opposite direction. He recognized Caroline and Bessie and hunkered down. Suspicious of a lone rider, Caroline nudged the horse into a faster walk and passed without looking at him. He'd become nothing to them, a stranger. Soon he'd be nothing to Mary. She'd be wise to forget he'd ever come to Denver. Gus wouldn't forget him, but now the memories would hurt. He couldn't bear to think about his dog. Fancy Girl wouldn't understand at all.

He could still change his mind. Instead of killing Roy himself, he could go to the law. He could apologize to Mary and trust God for justice. The thought sent bile up his throat. Tonight the Almighty had shown His true colors. He didn't care, and He couldn't be trusted.

At the boardinghouse, J.T. tied his horse out back and went to his room. As always he left the door open until he lit the lamp. Light flooded the tiny space, revealing both the contents and the emptiness as he shut the door and locked it. He missed his dog. He missed Mary. His gaze fell on the chapbook he'd left on the nightstand. Ignoring it, he took gun oil and a rag out of his saddlebag. It had been a long time since he'd prepared his weapons for battle, but he did it now the way a man greeted an old friend.

When he finished, he wrote the note to Gus on paper the landlady provided along with bedding and a washbowl. Tomorrow, when he finished with Roy, he'd deliver the note and the money to Swan's Nest and then leave town. He hoped Mary would keep the two thousand dollars. Not only was it Gertie's due, but he had nothing else to give her. He considered writing down his wishes, but talking about money seemed cold when he wanted to tell her he loved her.

Resigned to losing her, he put the note for Gus in his saddlebag, packed his things and then stretched on the bed and slept.

Morning came hard and bright.

So did hunger.

So did the knowledge he wouldn't be washing dishes for Mary ever again. He swung his feet off the bed, looked for Fancy Girl out of habit and felt melancholy. He tried not to think about Mary.

He shaved and washed, put on dark clothes and went to the kitchen for breakfast. He ate quickly and in silence, then returned to his room, where he put on his guns and duster. He'd told Roy twelve noon, but he wanted to arrive first. J.T. knew the road to the Slewfoot Mine well. He'd ridden it a week ago with Gus, and two weeks ago when he'd arrived in Denver with foolish dreams. The ride to the mine glistened with memories of the camping trip. It was by the dying fire that he'd come to understand love. It was in the same spot he'd won back Mary's trust and dared to hope for a future with her.

His hope was dead, and the old J.T. was back in business. Riding slowly, he approached the played-out mine. Someone had boarded up the rectangular entrance, but time had eroded the planks and a man could get inside. Overhead the sky burned with a blue heat broken only by billowing white clouds. Today he felt no wonder at their distant beauty, only an awareness that clouds came and went. He rode past a hillside covered with gravel-like rock, then looked to the right where scattered boulders offered cover. The mine loomed in front of him. Knowing it led to a maze of dark tunnels, he turned away from it.

"Quinn!"

The raspy voice didn't belong to Roy. It belonged to Griff Lassen, and he sounded as mean as ever. J.T. was high on his horse in open space. He needed cover and he needed it now, so he backpedaled the buckskin to a lone boulder. Sliding out of the saddle, he gripped his Colt and sized up the terrain. He didn't like what he saw at all. The apron of rock above him would give neither cover nor purchase, and the road he'd just ridden stretched for a quarter mile before it turned. A couple of cottonwoods offered protection, but not much. Aside from the mine, he had nowhere to go.

He'd picked this place so he could see someone coming. Instead he'd ridden into a trap. He felt like a fool. Instead of Lassen doing in Roy, Roy had tricked J.T. into facing off with Lassen. There was bad blood between J.T. and Griff, but today they had a common foe in Roy. Before J.T. did anything, he needed to know where he stood with his former partner. "Is that you, Griff?"

"Yeah, it's me," he called back. "I can't say I was expecting you. Desmond's supposed to show up with the money he owes some friends of mine."

Griff sounded downright pleasant. Maybe he'd forgotten about Fancy Girl and the squatters. "Funny you'd mention Desmond," J.T. called with equal friendliness. "He's got business with me, too."

"Maybe we should come out from behind these rocks and talk."

"I don't know, Griff." If J.T. moved, Griff would have a clear shot. "You weren't too happy with me about that dog incident."

"I know."

"I left you in a lurch." He wouldn't apologize, but Griff would get the drift.

"Forget it, Quinn. I say we let bygones be bygones. Come on out."

As a precaution, J.T. took off his hat and put it on a stick. "Here I come," he called, waving the hat.

A bullet went through the brim. Pivoting around the boulder, J.T. jammed the hat on his head and fired back.

In the volley of gunfire, Griff cursed. "You're a traitor, Quinn! That squatter in Wyoming put out my eye. You're going to pay for that."

J.T. had no intention of dying, but he'd gotten himself in a bind. The entrance to the mine offered cover, but he'd be trapped in the maze of tunnels—dark tunnels that went nowhere. He turned and looked down the road he'd just taken. It offered no protection at all. His best chance lay in making a deal with Lassen.

"Let's talk," J.T. shouted. "You want Desmond. So do I."

"I don't need your help."

"Sure you do."

Lassen answered with a low laugh. "Face it, Quinn. You're about to die." He fired to prove his point.

J.T. counted to three, twisted around the boulder and fired back. He caught a glimpse of Lassen and fired again, but not before Lassen got off a shot of his own. The bullet ricocheted off the rock an inch from J.T.'s face. He'd die if he didn't make a move, so he broke for the mine, firing as he ran at full speed until his foot landed in a hole and he stumbled.

He heard a crumbling like dead wood, and then he was falling…falling…falling into a black hole without a bottom. Cool air rushed by him. His shoulder banged on the side of the shaft and he lost his grip on his gun. Rocks and dirt tumbled with him until he landed on his back thirty feet below the surface. Pain shot through his chest and shoulders. He couldn't breathe, not even a gasp. Vaguely he realized he'd fallen down an air shaft and landed in the belly of the mine. His thoughts formed an unwilling prayer.

Dear God, what have I done?

He'd gone off today like a stupid kid. He'd left Mary and Gertie at Roy's mercy, and now he was going to die. Silently, he endured the pain in his body, not crying out because he couldn't make a sound.

He managed a small, painful breath. Then another. Finally he could breathe a little and he realized he wouldn't be dying in the next ten seconds. Lying flat on his back, he took stock of his injuries. He'd had the wind knocked out of him, and he couldn't move his right shoulder without knife-like pain. He checked it with his good hand and decided it was dislocated and not broken. His head hurt so bad he couldn't focus his eyes. He tried to sit up, but the pain forced him down.

Staring at the circle of blue sky, he thought of his horse. Lassen would steal it and take the money in the saddlebag. He'd also look for J.T.'s dead body and maybe fire down the shaft to finish the job. No matter how much it hurt, and how much he hated the dark, J.T. had to take cover. Swallowing bile, he dragged himself six feet into the pitch-black. Twice he nearly passed out, but he made it to the chiseled rock wall. Cradling his arm, he sat up and vomited. Whether the nausea came from the knock to his head, the pain or fear, he didn't know. He could only hope the mine had another way out.

Looking up, he saw a waterfall of light but not the mouth of the shaft. As a shadow erased the glow, a small landslide of dirt and rock tumbled over the edge. "You down there, Quinn?"

J.T. held in a curse. He couldn't let Lassen know he'd survived the fall.

"I saw you go down." Lassen's chuckle echoed down the shaft. So did the click of a gun being cocked. "The mine caved in a year ago. There's no way out."

Sweat poured down J.T.'s back. He wanted to scream, but he couldn't let the man know he'd survived. If he did, Lassen would shoot into the shaft. He didn't have a clear shot, but bullets could ricochet. Instead of leaving, Lassen pulled the trigger of his gun. The bullet hit two feet from J.T.'s thigh. By a sheer act of will, he didn't shout. Lassen fired again and again. The bullets flew and ricocheted until he'd emptied his pistol. Roaring with laughter, he holstered the weapon and walked away.

J.T. didn't have lead in his belly or his head, but sweat was pouring out of him in rivers. He could breathe almost normally, but his bones felt as if they'd been crushed. Sitting up, he spotted his Colt six feet away in the circle of light. A lot of good it would do him. No one except Roy knew where he'd gone, and Roy wanted him dead. He'd never been more alone in his life. He stared at the gun a long time, then crawled to it and put it in the holster still tied to his thigh.

The walls closed in on him. So did the dark. He had to get out. There had to be a way.... Panting with pain, he leveraged to his feet and hobbled into what seemed to be a tunnel. He moved forward cautiously, dragging his good hand along the wall. Dirt collected under his nails. With each step, the mine grew colder. He sniffed for fresh air but smelled only dust and sweat. Ten paces later he reached a dead end. He backtracked and stumbled on a downed timber. He circled the area again, then a third time, and still there was no way out.

Cold and bleeding, he limped to the light. With his pulse thundering, he looked up at the sky and screamed for help at the top of his lungs.

Chapter Twenty-Two

Mary didn't expect J.T. to show up to wash dishes, and he didn't. She served breakfast as usual and then went upstairs to check on her sister. When Adie arrived with a box of chocolates for Gertie, she told Mary that J.T.'s buckskin was missing from the carriage house, but that he'd left his pack horse.

"Maybe he just went for a ride," Mary said hopefully.

"I don't think so." Adie's eyes filled with sympathy. "Someone kicked down the side door to the Newcastle."

It had to be J.T. Mary imagined Roy dead at his desk with a bullet between his eyes. She hated the man, but she couldn't tolerate murder. She braced herself for bad news. "Has anyone seen Roy?"

"Josh saw him this morning."

Relief flooded through her, but it disappeared in a wave of fresh worry. Had Roy bested J.T.? It was possible but unlikely. She'd been about to bring Gertie a lunch tray, but she set it down and headed for the door. "I have to find J.T."

Adie gripped her arm. "You can't go after him."

"Why not?"

"Roy might try to hurt you the way he hurt Gertie. Josh is talking to Deputy Morgan right now, then he'll go to J.T.'s boardinghouse. Brick offered to check Market Street, and some of the other workers are looking, too."

J.T. had friends, and he didn't even know it. Mary felt a bit calmer, but nothing could ease the burden of having parted with angry words. She'd thought a lot about Caroline's story. She could forgive J.T. for anything, and she loved him enough to wait for him to come to his senses. She might not always trust J.T.'s judgment, but she could trust God. She just had to be patient.

Adie broke into her thoughts. "Do you have any idea where J.T. might be?"

She thought for a minute. If Roy was walking around Denver, J.T. would have stayed in town to watch him. Was he lying low until Lassen made a move? Perhaps he was setting up a ruse of his own for Roy and Griff Lassen. The other possibility, that he was dead or dying, scared her to death.

"He could be anywhere," she admitted to Adie.

Her friend squeezed her hand. "When J.T.'s ready, he'll come to you."

"I hope so."

"He loves you," Adie said with confidence. "He'll be back."

Mary wanted to believe her, but she knew life could be unkind. She didn't always understand God's ways, but she could pray for J.T. with every breath. It was the best and only thing she could do.

The remainder of the first day passed with J.T. trying to climb out of the air shaft. He found a rope, but it crumbled in his fingers. Even if it had been strong, what could he have done with it? His shoulder was hanging like a broken wing, and he'd fallen too far.

He took off his gun belt and set it on the ground. Of all the useless things to have…he needed water and food, a blanket and clothes that weren't soaked in sweat. He needed someone with a rope and a horse to pull him out, but no one knew where he'd gone. He controlled his fear by looking up at the circle of sky, but dusk brought total darkness. He preferred physical pain to the panic, so he decided to try and fix his shoulder.

Lying flat, he maneuvered the arm forward and back. His groans echoed in the shaft, but he worked the joint until it popped into place. Relief from the pain was instant, but the panic made him sweat again, and sweating reminded him of how badly he needed water. He tried to moisten his lips, but his tongue felt sticky and dry. A man couldn't go long without water, and J.T. had consumed just one cup of coffee at breakfast. The day before he'd been so worried about Mary that he hadn't eaten anything, and he didn't recall drinking more than a few sips of water while cleaning the café. The coolness of the mine worked to his advantage, but he didn't have more than three days, maybe four, before he'd be a corpse.

Fighting to stay calm, he searched the patch of sky for even a single star. A white dot emerged from the gloom, growing brighter as he stared. He wanted to pray, but he'd pushed God away. Mary had pleaded with him to wait before going after Roy, and he'd pushed her away, too. Now he was buried alive and Roy was walking around Denver, a threat to Mary and her family. He wanted to shout and break things, but no one would hear him and he had nothing to hit. Instead, he closed his eyes and recalled the nights Fancy Girl had warmed his toes. He remembered his talk with Gus about babies and love, and mostly he thought about Mary. For a short time, she'd carried his child. He couldn't think of a more generous gift, and what had he given her in return? Nothing but heartache.

His leg cramped, a sign of needing water. Straightening it to kill the pain, he opened his eyes and looked again at the star. It hadn't moved, and he drew comfort from the point of light. He'd have given anything to climb out of the hole, but he could only lie in the dark, dreaming of Mary and wishing he'd done things differently.

On the second day, Mary woke up early and dressed for church. She'd never seen Gus so glum, and Gertie's mood matched the plum-colored bruises on her face. The girl didn't feel ready to answer questions, so she asked to stay home from the Sunday service. Gertie needed time to heal, so Mary hugged her sister and left with Gus.

They arrived at Brick's place early. Instead of an empty saloon, she found Josh in a circle of men, quizzing them for news about J.T. Brick had made another tour of Market Street, and he'd learned J.T. had met with Roy at the Alhambra. The meeting had seemed amiable to the barkeep, and the men had left separately and an hour apart. Mary didn't know what to think. Had J.T. set up a future confrontation with Roy? And what had happened to Griff Lassen? No one knew what he looked like, which made finding him impossible.

Just as disheartening, Josh had made a second visit to J.T.'s boardinghouse. This time he'd asked the landlady to unlock the door and he'd inspected the room. Wherever J.T. had gone, he'd taken his things.

When people started arriving for the service, the

meeting broke up. Mary took her place in the front row, but she couldn't stop turning to the door with the hope she'd see J.T. She sang the usual hymns, but today they brought no comfort. She could believe J.T. would do something stupid to Roy, but she couldn't believe he'd leave without a final goodbye. He loved her. He loved Fancy Girl, and he cared about Gus. Nor would he have left Denver with Roy still a threat.

At the end of the service, Josh led a prayer for J.T.'s safety, ending it with a hushed "Amen." He gave the usual invitation to supper at Swan's Nest, but Mary made excuses and left. Alone and scared, she walked the streets, looking in every crevice and corner for the man she loved, until her feet were sore and her knees were throbbing. At the end of the day, she dragged herself up the steps to her apartment.

Gus came out of his room. "Is he coming back?" he asked.

"I hope so."

But with every minute, she grew more convinced he was dying or dead. Aching inside, she went to the window and stared at the horizon. Clouds towered in the west, boiling and churning as thunder announced the coming of a storm. Mary bowed her head. "Please, Lord," she said out loud. "Keep J.T. safe. Show Yourself to him, and remind him that You love him."

Choking on tears, she whispered, "I love him, too." She'd have given anything to have said the words before he left. Instead she'd let him leave in bitter silence. Tomorrow she'd look for him again. She'd search until she found him, just as he'd been looking for her when he'd come to Denver.

J.T.'s second day in the mine began with a shift in the light from black to gray. His belly ached with hunger, and his throat felt as dry as sand. Predictably, his head hurt worse than yesterday. He could move his shoulder but not easily. As the hours passed, the pain sharpened his thoughts to the simplest of facts.

He was going to die here.

He'd left Gus without saying goodbye.

He'd never see his dog again.

Worst of all, he'd left Mary twisting in the wind. Not only had he left her in danger from Roy, but she'd never know what had happened to him. They'd quarreled, but J.T. didn't doubt she cared for him. By dying in this hole, he'd done the unthinkable to the woman he loved. He'd left her to worry and wonder forever.

"Mary, forgive me," he whispered.

He closed his eyes and pictured her face. Two days ago he'd earned back her trust. He'd had hopes for marriage and had wanted to find a decent way to make a living. He'd dared to believe that God cared. Then Gertie had been attacked, and again he'd lost confidence in anyone but himself. Prideful and sure, he'd dug this grave with his arrogance.

For hours he stared at the circle of sky. As the sun rose to high noon, the pale glow turned into hot gold. It warmed his face and blinded him with the same light. He couldn't see, couldn't blink. He felt the goodness of the light and almost wept. He wanted to be a man, not a squalling child, so he took a breath to steady himself. It worked, but just barely.

More hours passed. His mouth turned to cotton and he felt feverish from lack of water. He thought of Fancy Girl and the puppies and how she'd licked them into life. He relived the camping trip with Gus and the water fight, the way he'd fallen back in the stream and how the water had rushed over him. He imagined Mary singing songs he'd heard in Abilene, then the hymn she'd been singing when he'd found her in church. Two weeks had passed, but it seemed like a lifetime.

He tried to moisten his lips, but he didn't have enough spit. He wished he'd stayed with Mary. He wished he'd done things her way instead of his own. His belly hurt with hunger, but the thirst plagued him far more. He had the shakes and his legs wouldn't stop cramping. He didn't have much time, maybe a day or two. The end would come soon. He'd go crazy and soil himself like a baby. He'd die alone and without dignity.

His gaze slid to his gun belt. He looked at the Colt for several minutes, then he stretched his arm and curled his fingers around the ivory handle. He slid the pistol from the holster, pulled it to his side and closed his eyes. He imagined the gun barrel in his mouth. It would taste like metal and gun oil, smoke and traces of sulfur. He knew exactly how far to cock the hammer, how gently to pull the trigger for a clean, quick shot.

He opened his eyes wide and stared at the patch of sky, refusing to blink as the blue vanished behind a cloud. Instead of blocking the sun, the cloud made it brighter. He recalled standing on the roof of the church and how he'd longed to take off his guns. He remembered Fancy giving birth, how he'd cried out and how God had answered. And he remembered praying with Josh and calling God by name.

"I don't know how you can stand me, Lord Jesus," J.T. said to the cloud. "You know how weak I am, how stubborn and stupid. You saved Fancy Girl, and I turned my back on You. You gave Mary to me, and I walked out on her. And Gus—" He thought of the boy standing up to him. "I walked out on him, too."

J.T. tried to swallow but couldn't. There was nothing

left in him, not even a drop of spit. He licked his lips, felt the dryness and spoke again to the unreachable sky.

"I don't deserve another chance, Lord. But I'm begging You to be good to Mary. I love her and I let her down. Keep her safe. And Gus—" he could barely speak. "Help him grow into a good man, a better man than me. And for Gertie, heal her nose and help her to grow up." He thought next of Fancy Girl. "Fancy's just a dog, but I love her. Make sure she has lots of bones and someone to scratch her."

He took comfort in knowing Mary would give his dog a good home. She'd always had a heart for strays. He thought of the way she loved him when he didn't deserve it and how she saw the good in him when there wasn't any. He took a final breath. "Spare Mary the pain of missing me, Lord. I have so many regrets—" He choked on his dry tongue. "I wish—I wish I'd trusted You."

Trust Him now.

The thought was in his head, but it seemed as loud as thunder. He thought of the hot bench, vengeance, darkness and turning the other cheek. He thought of Gus, boys eating hotcakes, puppies being born and Gertie running home to her family. Mostly he thought of Mary and the baby they'd lost, how much he loved her and how she'd forgiven him.

J.T. had asked God to show Himself, and He had. He was showing Himself now in a shaft of light that pierced the dark of this living grave. J.T. had taken fourteen lives. He'd hurt the people he loved. He'd done terrible things, yet the light had found him in the darkness, and he knew the light to be love. It pinned him to the ground and on his back. He couldn't fight and he didn't want to try. The light warmed him to the bones. It comforted him and promised hope. He felt the mercy of it on his face and knew he'd lost this final battle. He had no right to take another life, not even his own. Defeated by love, he shoved the gun out of reach.

He closed his eyes and murmured a prayer. He felt a tear on his cheek, except it wasn't warm. Another one trickled toward his ear. His eyelids flew open and he looked at the sky. Instead of a burning white mist, he saw the gray bottom of a thunderhead. A drop of water hit his cheek, then another…and another. Rain…blessed rain was falling from the sky.

Bolting upright, he stared at the sheen of water mixing with silvery light. Thunder rolled down the shaft. He blinked and the mist turned into a torrent of rain. Laughing crazily, he tipped his face upward and opened his mouth. He tasted the water on his tongue, felt the moisture on his lips and cheeks. The water was coming in buckets, running down the sides of the shaft and making puddles the size of wagon wheels. When he'd drunk his fill, he grabbed his hat and held it to catch a supply for later. He wouldn't die today and probably not tomorrow. He didn't know when he'd die, but he wouldn't die alone. God had shown Himself yet again, and J.T. wouldn't ever forget.

He pushed to his knees and lifted his face to the sky, feeling the rain on his skin as it washed him clean. With the storm raging and night approaching, he raised his arms and rejoiced.

Chapter Twenty-Three

On the morning of the third day, Mary closed the café after breakfast, borrowed a buggy from Adie and Josh and drove to J.T.'s boardinghouse. Desperate for a clue, she wanted to see the empty room for herself. No matter what she found, today she'd resume her search.

At the boardinghouse she asked the landlady to show her J.T.'s room. As the woman led her down the hall, Mary realized that not once had she seen where J.T. lived. In Abilene, he'd come to her. He'd had a room in the same hotel, but he'd never invited her inside.

"This is it," the landlady said.

Stepping into the room, Mary saw a wool blanket on the narrow bed, a mirror that had been wiped clean and a little book on the nightstand. She picked it up and recognized one of the chapbooks Josh sometimes gave to visitors. He'd given it to J.T., but J.T. had left it behind. It held no clues to his whereabouts, but its presence signaled he'd gone back to his old ways.

With her heart breaking, she surveyed the room and saw nothing except a few sheets of paper on a desk. On top of the stack sat a pencil. It was thick and round... and dull. Someone had used it. She crossed the room in four steps, lifted the top sheet of paper to the window and saw indentations. Most of the marks were faint, but she could make out a *D* and *Gus*. The rest of the words were fragments, but she recognized *horse, sister, man* and *Fancy*.

J.T. had written the note, but it hadn't been delivered. Something terrible had happened to him, she felt sure of it. Only one man could answer her questions, and that was Roy Desmond. She wanted to race to the theater and make him talk, but what threat did she pose? She needed help, and she needed it now. She thanked the landlady, climbed into the buggy and snapped the reins. The church was closer than the sheriff's office, so she went to find Josh. She reached the building in minutes. When she didn't see the minister, she called to one of the workers. "I need help. Where's Josh?"

"He went to buy paint."

Mary needed him now. She could almost hear J.T. calling her name. Surely she wouldn't feel such hope if he were dead. Her gaze shifted to the Newcastle Theater. She didn't dare go inside alone. She'd be putting herself in danger, and the risk would dishonor J.T. and his promise to protect her. She considered going for Deputy Morgan, but Josh would be back any minute.

Nervously she studied the theater. The new side door was ajar, as if someone had entered but not closed it for fear of being heard. She turned to the street, saw J.T.'s buckskin and gasped. She'd found him, but he was finally going after Roy. She had to stop him before he committed murder.

She leapt out of the buggy and ran through the door. The carpet muffled her steps, but a single gunshot shattered the silence. Terrified, she pressed herself against the wall. Had J.T. shot Roy? Or had Roy killed J.T.? She knew better than to go alone into Roy's office, but how could she wait? The man she loved could be dying this very minute.

With her heart pounding, she edged down the hall to the office. Trembling, she peeked around the corner and saw Roy facedown on his desk, blood pooling around his thinning hair and soaking into the blotter. She hated Roy for what he'd done to Gertie, but she couldn't abide shooting an unarmed man. Behind the desk she saw a wall safe left open and empty, an indication that J.T. had taken all the money. It seemed he'd returned fully to his old ways. She couldn't overlook the violence or the thievery. He'd have to pay for what he'd done, but she still loved him. He needed her more than ever, so she raced into the hall. She hadn't seen him leave through the side door, so she headed for the belly of theater.

"J.T.!" she shouted. "Talk to me."

As she rounded a corner, she glimpsed the shadow of a man turning down a hall. She charged after him, but he'd vanished down another corridor. Approaching slowly, she spoke in the low tones she'd use with a child. "I love you, Jonah. We'll go to the law together."

Snide laughter filled the hallway. J.T. never laughed like that. Confused, she stopped in midstep. She'd seen his horse in front of the theater. Who else could be in the hall? Before she could turn and run, a one-eyed man came around the corner with his gun aimed at her chest.

He cocked the hammer. "Take another step and I'll shoot you, too."

"You're not J.T.!"

"He's dead."

"He can't be." She could barely breathe.

"He's dead, all right." The man grinned. "If a bullet didn't kill him, the fall did."

"What are you talking about?" She had to know. Where was he? What had happened?

Lassen looked her up and down. "I got what I wanted. Quinn's dead and Desmond paid his debt. You're a pretty woman. If you want Quinn's body, you can have it."

No! No! No! She couldn't stand the thought of J.T. being gone. She hadn't told him she loved him. Gus needed him, and so did Fancy Girl. "Where is he?"

"At the bottom of the Slewfoot Mine." With a sly grin, he started to raise his gun. Knowing she'd become a witness who could identify this man, she turned and fled back into the theater.

She ran out the front door and hurried to the buggy, scanning the church for Josh. She didn't see him, but she spotted Deputy Morgan talking to Brick. She ran up to him, told him about Lassen and where she was going. Unwilling to wait another minute, she jumped into the buggy and drove as fast as she dared to the Slewfoot Mine.

J.T.'s third day in the mine dawned just like the second. When fear nipped at him, he looked at the sky and thought of Mary. He didn't know the words to the hymn she'd sung in church, but he remembered the tune and he hummed it now. If this hole in the ground turned into his grave, he'd die with the promise of loving her for eternity.

He dozed until the sun shined directly over the air shaft. In the silence he imagined Mary singing. He could hear her voice in his head, softly calling his name. Maybe God had sent an angel to fetch him up to the clouds. The cry grew louder, then louder still. His eyes flew open and he bolted to his feet. God hadn't sent an angel to take him to Heaven. He'd sent the woman he loved to take him home.

"J.T.!" she shouted again. The rig rattled to a stop.

"I'm down here," he shouted. "Stay back! The ground's not stable."

"You're alive!"

He could hardly wait to hold her in his arms. If she'd come in the buggy, there'd be a few tools under the seat. "Do you have a rope?"

"I'll get it."

With rescue just minutes away, J.T. took a last look around the mine. He saw his gun belt in the shadows and the Colt Navy lying next to it. The old J.T. had died in this place. The new one didn't want that gun to ever fill his hand again. It seemed a fitting end to a life he no longer wanted. He could only hope Mary would be a part of the new one. He had nothing to offer—no job, no money—but he loved her. He wanted to give her another child. To Gus he'd be a big brother, and for Gertie he'd be a pain in the neck to every man who came calling. Fancy would get an extra bone tonight, and he'd give her the longest scratch she'd ever had. He could hardly wait to see them all.

Mary finally called from the surface. "I've got the rope."

"Tie it off to the buggy and throw it down. But whatever you do, don't get too close."

"I won't."

He waited with his eyes on the sky, watching until she shouted, "Here it comes."

A coil of rope spiraled into the mine. He made a loop, hooked it under his arms and held on tight with his good hand. "My shoulder's hurt," he called to her. "The horse is going to have to do the work."

"We'll go slow," she answered.

The rope tightened around his chest, then lifted him to his toes and finally into the air. He used his legs to walk up the wall, being careful not to bang his bad side against the shaft. As the light intensified, the pain faded and he squinted in the brightness. He had ten feet to go, then five. He smelled dust and hot air and finally grass as the horse dragged him over the rim of the hole. The ground crumbled but only slightly. With the horse still pulling, J.T. waited until he was ten feet from danger before rolling to his back. Squinting because of the brightness, he took pleasure in the sunshine on his face. He heard footsteps and smelled cotton and rose-scented soap. When he opened his eyes, he saw Mary on her knees with tears streaming down her cheeks.

"You're alive," she murmured. "I thought you were dead."

"Me, too." He cupped her face. "How'd you find me?"

She told him about Lassen and Roy. The two scorpions had stung each other as J.T. had hoped, but he recoiled at the thought of Mary in harm's way and Lassen being on the loose. It troubled him until she told she'd seen Deputy Morgan at the church. "I told him Lassen was in the theater."

J.T. thought about his horse and the money. Maybe he'd get them back. "Morgan'll go after him."

Mary took a hankie from her pocket and wiped his brow. "You're a mess," she said, scolding him. "What happened?"

"Lassen left me to die." He sat up and told her about Roy tricking him, the gunfight, the fall and the rain that had made him a new man. He didn't mention the Colt and how he'd nearly used it, only that he'd left it behind. "Lassen got what he wanted." He cradled Mary's hand in his. "J. T. Quinn is dead and gone. From now on, I'm Jonah Taylor."

Tears filled her eyes. "I love you, Jonah."

"I love you, too."

She deserved far more than he had to give, but he'd already wasted too much time. He held Mary's hand in his, lifting it as he looked into her eyes. "I spent three days thinking I'd never see you again. I don't have much to offer, but whatever I have and whoever I am, I'd be honored if you'd be my wife."

She didn't say yes.

And she didn't say no.

Instead she kissed him full on the lips. It lasted so long that he started to laugh. "So you like that idea?"

"I do," she said. "But I have a condition of my own."

She could have anything she wanted. If she needed a dishwasher, he was the man for the job. If she needed a friend, he'd be there. He'd be her protector, her lover, the father of her children and the man who sometimes annoyed her, because he'd always be a bit of a scoundrel. He hardened his expression but just a little. "What's the condition?"

"I need a partner to help run the café." Her cheeks turned rosy. "What do you think of hiring someone else to wash dishes? Maybe one of the boys you impressed for Gus?"

"I like that idea."

"You can learn to cook." She looked pleased. "And someone has to fix things and paint the walls now and then. The chairs take a terrible beating. They get wobbly and—"

He stopped her with a kiss. "You know what else I want to do?"

She must have seen the shine in his eyes, because she blushed pinker than a rose. "What?"

"I want to have a baby with you." It wouldn't replace the child she'd lost, but he'd be glad to do what he could.

Mary blushed again. "I'd like that."

With the sun bright and the sky full of clouds, Jonah Taylor took his wife-to-be in his arms. His shoulder hurt, but that didn't stop him from kissing her the way he wanted. In that shining moment, he thought of his challenge to God to show Himself. J. T. Quinn had finally seen the light, and it was bright indeed.

Epilogue

August 1876
Swan's Nest

Mary and Jonah spoke their marriage vows on Sunday morning at Brick's saloon. Gertie stood up with Mary, swollen nose and all, and Gus stood with Jonah. Because she was part of their family, Fancy Girl joined them at the front of the church. In place of the bandanna she usually wore, Adie tied a pink ribbon around the dog's neck. Josh did the honors and then invited everyone to Swan's Nest to celebrate.

That's where they were now, surrounded by friends and family as Mary climbed the steps to toss the bouquet. A year ago Adie had done the honors, and Pearl had caught the flowers. She was here today with her husband and their two children, and earlier she'd told Mary she was expecting a baby in time for Christmas.

When Pearl's turn had come to throw the flowers at her own wedding nine months ago, she'd aimed them straight at Mary. Mary had nearly thrown them back, but today she felt only joy as she looked at her husband. Dressed in a new black suit and crisp white shirt, he was waiting not-so-patiently for the festivities to end. As soon as she tossed the flowers, they'd leave for the elegant hotel where he'd booked the bridal suite. Thanks to Deputy Morgan, Griff Lassen was in jail and Jonah had gotten his horse and money back. Yesterday he'd put the finishing touches on the bell tower, and he and Gus had tested the bell.

Mary was ready to leave the celebration, but she had to make sure Caroline caught the bouquet. She spotted Bessie, but she didn't see Caroline anywhere. She refused to throw the flowers to anyone else. Mary looked again at J.T. He mostly went by Jonah now, but she'd always love the scoundrel who'd first made her blush. He lifted his eyebrows as if to say, "What's taking so long?"

"I need Caroline," she called to him.

He nodded once, went to the kitchen and guided an unwilling Caroline into the crowd of women. Before she could protest, Mary walked up to her and put the flowers in her arms. The women applauded and hugged her, but Caroline barely smiled. "You shouldn't have done that."

"Why not?" Mary asked.

"It's time I faced facts. I'll never marry again."

"Caroline!"

"It's true." She took a breath. "I've accepted a position as a nanny for a rancher in Wyoming. He's a widower and he's ill. Bessie is going with me."

Mary nearly burst with curiosity. Just how ill was this man? Did his children need a nanny, or did they need a mother? And did the rancher need a nurse or a wife? She pushed the flowers into Caroline's arms. "I want you to have them."

"They *are* pretty." She sniffed a late-blooming rose and then forced a smile. "I'll write to you."

With the bouquet safely in Caroline's arms, Mary looked for Jonah. He'd slipped through the crowd and was two steps away. "Let's go," he said, offering his arm.

She grasped his elbow and smiled. "You sound like a man in hurry."

"I am." He gave her the look they'd first shared in Abilene, the one that had sent shivers down her spine and always would.

"Me, too," she whispered.

Arm in arm, they left Swan's Nest to the roar of thunderous applause. Mary thought of her days on the stage. She'd enjoyed that life, but it paled against the future waiting for her as Jonah Taylor's wife. She wanted to have children with him. She wanted to grow old together. He had returned to her, and she intended to cherish every moment of the starring role God had written just for her.

* * * * *

Dear Reader,

Thank you for reading *The Outlaw's Return*. J.T. and Mary have quite a story, but the character who charmed me the most is Fancy Girl. She's smart, loyal and just plain good for him.

Every book is written in the context of the author's life, and I'd be remiss not to mention the family dogs that inspired Fancy Girl's character. Our first family dog was Chico, a Chihuahua-Welsh corgi mix who had no idea he weighed just thirteen pounds. Like Fancy Girl, he'd have taken on the world to protect his family. This dog could bark! Imagine the Chihuahua yap with the corgi volume. Sometimes I think he embarrassed himself with how loud it could be.

My sons loved Chico to pieces, and he loved them. He passed away after sixteen years of a happy life. We mourned him, but we also treasure many wonderful memories. Chico was the best dog ever.

With Chico gone and our sons grown, my husband and I adopted a Jack Russell-beagle mix. His name is Hartley and he's just plain crazy. Anyone who knows Jack Russells will understand. For no reason at all, this dog will take off barking and running like a rocket. We call it "turbo time," because he's going full speed. He also eats apples, which strikes me as totally strange for a dog.

Hartley doesn't have Chico's courage and intelligence, but he's got his own special gift. Just like Fancy Girl, Hartley knows how to make us smile. My husband says that Hartley got an extra dose of "happy." So did Fancy Girl. This story belongs to her just as much as it belongs to Mary and J.T.

Best wishes,

Victoria Byb

QUESTIONS FOR DISCUSSION

1. When the story opens, J. T. Quinn has made a decision to walk away from his life as a gunslinger. What motivated his decision? Have you ever faced a similar choice?

2. Mary Larue, a former actress, is raising her two siblings. What are her greatest concerns? How do Gus and Gertie benefit from her past experience?

3. J.T. faces temptation every day. What motivates him to resist the urge to drink and gamble? What temptations have you faced in your life? What are the most effective ways to fight temptation?

4. Mary is determined to protect her reputation by keeping a secret. Do you agree or disagree with how she handled her past? Are there secrets that should be kept? Are there others that should never be kept? Where do we draw that line?

5. Fancy Girl has a tremendous impact on J.T. Do you have pets? How have they enriched your life? What does J.T. get from his dog that he's never received from people?

6. Gus has a problem with stuttering. Modern research shows that there's far more to this affliction than nervousness, but J.T. still had a strong influence on the boy. How does he help Gus? How does Gus help J.T.?

7. Gertie is young, stubborn and rebellious. Do you think Mary was right to be supportive of her sister's dream, or was she too easy on her? What do you do when a son or daughter is determined to take a difficult road?

8. Mary and J.T. have a past, and he hurt her terribly when he left her. What does he do to earn back her trust? What are the major turning points?

9. The scandal in Abilene makes Mary's life extremely difficult. What does the scandal cost her? Which losses hurt the most? How does the scandal influence her faith?

10. Throughout the story, J.T. grapples with the concept of turning the other cheek. When is it appropriate to make that choice? When is it time to respond with "an eye for an eye"? How does this question apply to the situation with Gus and the bullies?

11. When J.T. realizes that Mary's faith is important to her, he challenges God to show Himself. What does J.T. see in Gus? What does the white bench represent? What other symbols do you see?

12. Mary doesn't want to tell J.T. about the miscarriage because she thinks he'll be disrespectful. Did his reaction to the news surprise you? Did it surprise Mary?

13. Several characters have an impact on J.T.'s decision to become a Christian. How does Gus influence

him? What role does Josh play? Including Mary and Fancy Girl, who do you think has the strongest impact?

14. In a very literal way, J.T. hits bottom when he falls down the mine shaft. He comes out a changed man. What symbolism do you see in the mine, the clouds and the light?

15. How are trust and forgiveness related? Is it possible to forgive someone but still not trust them? What ultimately allows Mary to fully love J.T.?

Love Inspired.
HISTORICAL

TITLES AVAILABLE NEXT MONTH

Available March 8, 2011

REQUEST YOUR FREE BOOKS!

2 FREE INSPIRATIONAL NOVELS
PLUS 2
FREE
MYSTERY GIFTS

Love Inspired
HISTORICAL
INSPIRATIONAL HISTORICAL ROMANCE

YES! Please send me 2 FREE Love Inspired® Historical novels and my 2 FREE mystery gifts (gifts are worth about $10). After receiving them, if I don't wish to receive any more books, I can return the shipping statement marked "cancel". If I don't cancel, I will receive 4 brand-new novels every month and be billed just $4.24 per book in the U.S. or $4.74 per book in Canada. That's a saving of at least 23% off the cover price. It's quite a bargain! Shipping and handling is just 50¢ per book in the U.S. and 75¢ per book in Canada.* I understand that accepting the 2 free books and gifts places me under no obligation to buy anything. I can always return a shipment and cancel at any time. Even if I never buy another book, the two free books and gifts are mine to keep forever.

102/302 IDN FDCH

Name _____ (PLEASE PRINT) _____

Address _____ Apt. # _____

City _____ State/Prov. _____ Zip/Postal Code _____

Signature (if under 18, a parent or guardian must sign) _____

Mail to the **Reader Service:**
IN U.S.A.: P.O. Box 1867, Buffalo, NY 14240-1867
IN CANADA: P.O. Box 609, Fort Erie, Ontario L2A 5X3

Not valid for current subscribers to Love Inspired Historical books.

Want to try two free books from another series?
Call 1-800-873-8635 or visit www.ReaderService.com.

* Terms and prices subject to change without notice. Prices do not include applicable taxes. Sales tax applicable in N.Y. Canadian residents will be charged applicable taxes. Offer not valid in Quebec. This offer is limited to one order per household. All orders subject to credit approval. Credit or debit balances in a customer's account(s) may be offset by any other outstanding balance owed by or to the customer. Please allow 4 to 6 weeks for delivery. Offer available while quantities last.

Your Privacy—The Reader Service is committed to protecting your privacy. Our Privacy Policy is available online at www.ReaderService.com or upon request from the Reader Service.

We make a portion of our mailing list available to reputable third parties that offer products we believe may interest you. If you prefer that we not exchange your name with third parties, or if you wish to clarify or modify your communication preferences, please visit us at www.ReaderService.com/consumerschoice or write to us at Reader Service Preference Service, P.O. Box 9062, Buffalo, NY 14269. Include your complete name and address.

LIHII